Doing Life in Paradise

a novel

Gary N. Lines

Clink Street

London | New York

Published by Clink Street Publishing 2015

Copyright © 2015

First edition.

ISBN: PB: 978-1-910782-53-8
EB: 978-1-910782-54-5

To Maggi

He who despairs of the human condition is a coward, but he who has hope for it is a fool.

...Albert Camus

We don't see things as they are, we see them as we are.

...Anaïs Nin

Prologue

It is my modest hope that within these pages you will come to know a little of the lives of some of the inhabitants of the City of Paradise. They are, I believe, friends of mine. I hope you will find it, if in a somewhat peculiar way I'll admit, enlightening.

As might be the case for all of us in our own particular way, these inhabitants are unhappily harmed, and thus flawed, even absurdly in some cases, but, nonetheless, these are their true stories. I trust you will find room in your heart to think well of them. And in the spirit of that generosity, I hope you will find it possible to extend your sympathy to myself also, or if not sympathy, at least a modicum of understanding, for I suspect we are not so unalike in thought and deed when push comes to shove. But it is too early for you to make that judgement. You might be better placed to judge these matters when you discover who I am and what I have done, and after you have witnessed the true stories to be found in these pages.

It came to pass that the city changed its name, although I will leave it to you to decide the relevance and significance, or otherwise, of this event. The City of Paradise, formerly known as Adelaide, is a pretty enough city. This city has many parklands, many birds, many churches and a vibrant, sunny botanical garden. From every perspective it is a very liveable city and not one that you would believe would have any harshness to it. It is not a city that you would expect to let you down or where anything out of the ordinary would happen to you. That is what you would expect. But there is a plague in Paradise. Some say that this insidious 'plague' is the dependence on hope: it is true that people in Paradise hope.

The events and lives described in this tale occurred during recent times. Many agreed that considering their somewhat extraordinary nature, these events were out of place in a city that would call itself Paradise, but I disagree. Paradise offers no extraordinary solution to the turmoils of human life. It might even add to them by plaguing its inhabitants with misguided and unrealistic hope within their city, which is a midsize Australian city on a gulf leading out into the Great Southern Ocean. It is ordinariness that strikes one first about the City of Paradise, where the ubiquitous Minister of the Interior works tirelessly for the betterment of the citizens.

But perhaps the time has come to drop preliminaries and cautionary remarks, and to launch into the narrative proper. In the following pages, I hope to demonstrate to you just how interconnected certain events are; how one small prosaic moment, perhaps tragic, certainly trivial on any human scale, ignites many other events and, as a consequence, affects innocent lives, conceivably, my astute Reader, even your own; but that depends on your angle of vision, or as the French writers prefer, *le point de vue*.

It was sometime in the future when she found him hanging in silence from a rope tied to the staircase railing. She found him circling and warm.

PART ONE

1

RUBY

'Tea?' Ruby asked of no one while standing alone god-naked in her tiny white kitchen. Ruby was in the middle of making teacakes. She was twenty-two years old, nearly twenty-three, and shy with strangers. She had no selling experience, lived alone and had a large menacing spider in her stomach.

Ruby lived in a near-constant state of nausea, barely able to maintain any control over the spider. Of course she knew this wasn't good enough. She knew she had to fight back. She knew she had to try harder in life. Ruby felt she had lost years. She couldn't remember what she did when she was eighteen, or even what she was doing or thinking last year. She had trouble discerning what her view of the world was and her place in it. Time was indifferent to her; it seemed to ignore her, rolling on around her without taking her along. She hoped she would find love one day and that this would be the trigger to rid herself of the spider. She hoped for happiness. She wiped her brow with the back of her hand and in so doing, smeared some flour across her skin. She picked up the phone and pressed the speed dial for her mum.

'Hi Mum.'

'Ruby?' Ruby found it odd that her mother always had to confirm it was her only child on the phone. Who else would start a conversation with the words 'Hi Mum'? But this was only one of the oddities displayed by her mother which maintained an inexplicable distance between herself and her only daughter; a distance Ruby was always trying to reach across.

'Darling, is everything all right? It's just that I must fly, I'm sorry, I always seem to be in a rush whenever you call.'

'Oh sorry, no that's okay, I wasn't ringing for any particular reason, just, you know, to see how you are. I'm making a batch of teacakes, so I thought...'

'That's nice darling, I'm fine, and so is your father darling. He sends his love. He's watching the telly. Thanks for calling but I really must fly, we'll speak soon, I promise.' She hung up.

Ruby put the phone down and remained still. She saw her reflection in the toaster and looked into her blank eyes. A bird flew into the kitchen window and made a loud bang. Ruby jumped at the noise and then watched the bird as it sat on the sill. It remained motionless. It looked worried. It had no idea what it had just hit. It wobbled some but then it flew away.

Ruby was proud of the single fact that she made delicious teacakes. It's at least one thing I do well, she thought to herself as she started to sift the flour. She had been the recipient of her grandmother's recipe when she was young, but she had refined it and introduced her own take and this resulted in her teacakes being especially succulent. Not that making teacakes was that mystical, but others did agree that her teacakes were special. She would be pleased to give anybody who might be interested, her teacake recipe. She would love to make them for her mother one day. In fact, she'd be delighted to show her mother how she made them, and reveal to her mother all her little secrets. When she made her teacakes, she felt exposed. She felt like an artist creating a story, then corrupting it, changing it, and most importantly, building it — she never knew how it might turn out.

Notwithstanding her teacake prowess, there were other things about Ruby of particular interest. She insisted on keeping her toes meticulously pedicured, and her nails always painted pale pink. Her skin was as soft as clotted cream and displayed a patina reminiscent of mother-of-pearl from the dazzling light which poured in through the window, splashing over her body. Her smile, whilst rarely evident, was easily described as beautiful. She had a nervous way of unconsciously swishing her long blonde hair that made people feel like they wanted to hug her, or protect her. What else? Ruby kept her tiny flat immaculately clean and, importantly, and this *is* important, she was hopeful about her future.

Ruby tried very hard to be hopeful; it was difficult though, especially as she lived alone, except for her unwanted spider. She wished she knew for sure if it was truly important to be hopeful, given the effort that being hopeful required. 'Everlasting vigilance, Ruby.' She reminded herself of her father's favourite saying as often as she could remember to do so, which itself took everlasting vigilance. Ruby found paradox unsettling and preferred to try to live her life without it, but then, she did live in a city called Paradise.

As a general rule, Ruby kept herself calm. Silent. She tried not to dream too much. Not to wish. Not to hope excessively, as to do so seemed greedy to her. On the other hand, she had to hope. It was best, she thought, to keep her life still.

Today was a new day and it was to be a special day for Ruby, but this was unknown to her as she dragged herself back from her nightly terrors. She had woken with her usual gasp, as though re-establishing her conscious self every morning was a shock. From her bed she squinted through the crack in the curtain and saw it was a bright Paradise morning. She realised there was a curious and surprising thought forming in her mind. She thought about the thought. This thought was a big thought, even a grand thought, a thought that could change a person's life. In that moment, she felt the flush of tickling tentacles of optimism flutter across her skin. She kept her body perfectly still and held her breath. She was adept at stillness and breath-holding. She had put a lot of practice into both. The act of living, she occasionally mentioned to the girls at the supermarket where she worked, was more a matter of 'practice' than people realise. Ruby practised everything, especially her stillness and breath-holding. In fact these two habits were the only things she did which could be said to match her culinary mastery over teacakes.

Lying in bed, her blonde hair cascading across her pillow, she tried to savour this new feeling. The thought was not grand by Paradise standards, but it was grand for Ruby and it scared her. But then most things did – which was one of her disappointments in herself, and something she had every intention of changing. 'I must not be scared'; she had taken to uttering these words the moment she woke each day. She dared to think she might be able to start a new life as a Paradise car salesperson. She had a moment's hope. She waited to see if it, the bubble of hope, would be pricked by the spider's fangs.

Ruby felt she was always waiting. She waited for light after dark. She waited for protection and love – especially love. She waited for her life to start and the white noise to end. She waited and dreaded the day when she would have to confront the spider. She lived with the anxious feeling that people had to die in order for her to progress up the waiting queue. This made her feel guilty every time she felt she was waiting for something good to happen. Guilt and anxiety were like two older sisters to Ruby –

they were horrid to her but she served them as best she could. They were family. Alas, Ruby had few friends to speak of, which was a direct result of her melancholy. She was aware of the concrete-like aura of melancholy which encased her. If she had more friends, she would have less reason to be melancholy. She had been an *only* child and now she was an *only* adult. She could only hope that waiting would pay off.

Just in that second, as she lay in her bed, unusual though it seemed to her, the thought of selling cars for a living started to take shape, and gave her spirits a little kick; a kick not dissimilar to the electricity from an exquisite kiss, she thought. She dreamed often about the elusive exquisite kiss.

'Could I sell cars?' She said this out loud, a little louder than she intended, her voice startling her. No one answered, of course. As comforting as Teddy First and Teddy Last were, they were not quite up to conversation, and, at any rate, they were sound asleep under their bunny rug on their chair next to the other side of her bed. She pushed her breath out with a thwack. When you lived alone there were two things that were important as reminders you existed: the first was the incidental noises you made when you moved about and did things, and the second was your reflection. She reached over and picked up a mirror sitting on her bedside table and checked her reflection as she did every day. 'I must not be scared,' she said.

This morning, like every morning, she looked up at her beige ceiling. She scanned the familiar dark patches in the corners. They looked like big armpit sweat marks. The building was stressed, she thought, or maybe she whispered it. She couldn't help but feel kindness for her building – she had a lot in common with it. She found the feeling of having something in common with something, even if it was only an inanimate object such as her building, comforting on some level. Being alone, you have to make do. She opened her eyes fully and her daily anxiety and panic caused her to gasp for Paradise air. She closed her eyes again and reached for her teddies. 'I must not be scared,' she said again softly. Her spirits sank into a black tsunami.

Of course, she was only too aware of the cause of her anxiety – it was the large spider creeping inside her stomach. As always, the spider stole her optimism and made it splutter away. She gasped again, and felt the spider's long hairy legs twitching. She shuddered and felt nauseous. A single spontaneous perfectly-formed tear trickled down her cheek as she faced yet another day. She caught the tear with her finger and waited to see if there would be another. There was. The spider made her cry; it made the teddies cry. She couldn't see how she would ever be rid of it. She hummed softly. She hummed the words 'I want to be a car salesman' to some Broadway tune, the name of which escaped her this morning. She hummed for herself. She hummed to distract, or soothe, the spider. She felt it move. It stalked malevolently deep in her stomach as a constant reminder of the day when she witnessed a nine-year-old girl die on the Great Southern Road in front of her. She could still remember the smack the girl's head made when it slammed into the bitumen. She smelt the warm blood splash over her; she was only nine herself.

She was dressed in her red cotton pyjamas and at that moment, for reasons she couldn't identify, she became aware of two things: her armpits were damp and her nipples were tingling. It was a beautiful sunny morning in the city of churches. That didn't help her understand her life, or her tingling nipples, but she knew all too well why her armpits were damp. She was already stressed and her day had not yet started, but then, if she was to be honest, neither had her life – and, she knew, she and she alone must do something about that and maybe, just maybe, it would be today.

2

MADELINE

Madeline's story does not start here, but her life, the one she now lives with all her nerve endings firing in a kaleidoscope of ebullient ecstasy every day, does.

Tell me what you want, he urged the first time they made love. She couldn't really call it 'making love'; it was too urgent for that description. His voice seemed pale and spare but, still, it was full of pure tenderness for her, and it was this that caused her to fall madly, stupidly and deliciously in love with him. The combination of brute strength and tenderness would destroy the inner fabric of any woman, she thought. He was so young and so beautiful and so definite, in a muscular way, that he seemed to cause himself actual James Dean-like physical pain in his determination to satisfy her, but not just sexually, although that certainly, but in his care and tenderness for her.

'Fuck me,' Madeline said, shocking herself. She had never said such a thing before in her life. For a start it seemed, well, just so banal. But it just came out. She ventured further, like a biting reflex, she urged him on by empowering herself. She recalled the word cunt, and released it. She said it out loud to him in her bed and issued him with her instructions. It was an indisputable fact that the focus for both of them right at that moment was her cunt. This had never been the case for Madeline and she luxuriated in it. It scared her. She had never been so scared.

She mouthed it now to herself in the David Jones department store's toilet cubicle with utter disbelief. She felt her engorged capillaries and the cubicle pulsing. She felt the c word was hers and in a way she couldn't completely understand, it made her feel exquisitely sexy. She recalled the weight of his body and his intoxicating male scent covering her. She flushed red in stark contrast to her white surrounds. All her life she had never even thought this word, not as a teenager, not as an adult, not as a wife. Now she was using it for her own purposes, saying it out loud, over and over, like a mantra – a

David Jones toilet cubicle, forty-two-year-old-widow, sex-mantra. 'Cunt, cunt, cunt.'

Listening with wonder to her shallow breaths while sitting in the David Jones toilet cubicle, Madeline felt 'the Great Sadness' as she liked to describe it. This was her observation.

Madeline held herself to be an optimist, in fact an optimistic romantic, although she thought this a redundancy, as a romantic had to be by definition an optimist, she rationalised. She often experienced a surge of life appreciation, which contradicted the Great Sadness. Life's balance, you could say. Equilibrium was both compelling and her default setting. The Yin and the Yang principle, not that she could really claim to understand all that these things stood for. But what was it about life she found so remarkable? In her own case, she marvelled at the vast numerics of life, the contradictions and imponderable coincidences, the incredible near-misses, the 'what if's, the 'what for's and the 'how come's, and the great nemeses, the dreaded 'if only's. In short, the sheer audacity of human complexity in Paradise. Take coincidence for a start. How many times had she turned one way, instead of another, and then saw someone she knew, or noticed a woman in David Jones buying makeup only to see the exact same woman hours later window shopping in Glenelg and oblivious to Madeline? These were the coincidences. Breathtaking coincidences. But how many similar occurrences did she not experience simply because she may have looked left instead of right, or stopped for a second looking in a window and missed another coincidence? The phenomenon of coincidence seemed anything but coincidence and if all coincidences were known, there would be no such thing; instead it would be just a given of life, which, coincidentally, it is.

Madeline was a philosopher. She thought things, then she thought about them. More often than not her philosophical thinking was courtesy of the emotional storm let loose by the onset of her period. Madeline had given over considerable time to her periods, and to thinking about thinking. It seemed in her case the two were linked ever since her puberty. Periods and philosophical thought – they were twins. Mr Cause and Ms Effect.

'The older you get the more you think about life, well, your own life,' she said recently to Sheila in the *Paradise Found* beauty salon, prominently positioned on the busy main shopping street at the seaside village of Glenelg. Madeline squirmed replaying this sentence to herself. It sounded better in her head, but spoken, it failed to represent all of her thoughts and fell flat on the hairy floor. Like Glenelg, she thought, life is a palindrome; it is the same forward as it was backwards. The future is history and history is the future, but this was too serious for the salon banter.

'Huh, tell me about it,' Sheila responded.

'The older you get the more you think about getting older.' Madeline felt obligated to continue now that Sheila had joined in, but still felt she hadn't said what she wanted, and she wished she could stop the conversation – Sheila's salon was not the place to draw attention to yourself, even though its sole purpose was just that.

'You are only as old as the man you feel, darling.' This was one of Sheila's catch cries – one of many. Sheila never allowed herself to be hampered by a lack of originality. Sheila's penchant for a cliché was legendary. Some of the other women in the salon faked a laugh, others kept their heads buried in their respective magazines or crossword puzzles, one or two slept under the driers. Outside, a tram rattled by, drowning out the salon chatter, even the hum of the driers. It was like a big anodyne masculine monster on its course to the beach, its slow moving shadow penetrating every cavity in the salon. Sheila flicked her hair with her usual dramatic purpose. She was most proud of her long blonde and pink streaks. In full bloom, they snapped and whipped about with intent like punctuation on top of her short and ample cone-shaped body. Sheila's truncated centre-of-gravity-defying figure, poised precariously above her stiletto heels. Sheila could totter like no other.

'Bit by bit, you find yourself in the things you find,' Madeline said to her son Peter, some time ago. They were sitting in her kitchen eating cashews and drinking tea. Peter was trying to get over Belinda at the time; it was taking quite a while. Madeline wanted to help him, but she had to admit he was beyond the kind of help she could provide. Madeline had been in therapy herself and as a result didn't feel she could interfere in her son's life with any confidence or authority. It ripped at her heart to see him so desolate. Even Ryan, her son's best friend and eternal enthusiast, had gotten exasperated with him and had suggested to him, on more than one occasion, that he should get some help. But her son was a victim of his own great capacity to love, and he had loved Belinda. Or so he thought. The problem was, as Madeline saw it, Belinda left at the height of Peter's infatuation. This left him in a frozen state of unreality. He never did find out if he also loved her, or if he would always love her. 'Infatuation is like a big cake of soap, you don't know until it wears away if love is hiding underneath,' Sheila was once heard to say this; everyone in the salon winced but not so Sheila noticed.

'Don't you find when you are young, forever young, there is nothing to think about except having fun – and whilst having fun is fine for the young, it is not a natural platform for philosophical thought?' Madeline continued with Sheila after the tram had passed, dragging its rattle along with it. She took a sip from her lukewarm coffee; its surface rippled in an act of *homage* to the passing tram.

'That's the spirit luv,' Sheila added somewhat absently, which indicated Madeline might have crossed the line of the usual superficial banter allowed in the salon, which consisted of celebrity gossip: who has stacked on weight, or who has an eating disorder. Anything more substantial was discouraged.

'And after a while, fun is not enough – fun fades.' She thought she should say this to Peter but then she realised it couldn't help him. Peter was the exception to this theory. Fun wasn't something he was having, and hadn't since Belinda left, although if Madeline was to be really honest, she would have to admit her son had never been an overtly happy boy. He seemed to be always in a constant state of concern, at least from age sixteen, when something he has never spoken about happened to him. She had spent years longing to help him in some way – but then she was still trying to make sense of her own life.

'Live each day as though it is your last. That is my philosophy, you just have to make the best of every damn second,' Sheila said with her usual consistent unoriginality and with a sense of finality, signalling that this discussion was now closed. The thing about Sheila, though, was if it was her last day in Paradise, she would choose to spend it in her salon. The salon was Sheila's life, her Paradise, her self-imposed prison, her boxed Eden. She is her salon. Jetty Road, Glenelg, formed her boundaries. Sheila clung to her Paradise and did her life sentence there. We all have our territories, Madeline thought; Paradise within Paradise, like an enigma wrapped inside a Chinese puzzle held inside a Chinese puzzle. We are only ever ourselves, when you boil it all down, no matter what exterior we effect. As one of the city's many billboards opined, 'Wherever you go, there you are. So you might as well stay put and save the bus fare.' Wise words from the ever-smiling Minister of the Interior; his ubiquitous billboards around the city were testament to the fact that he had plenty to say and couldn't be stopped from saying it. The billboards appeared before and after the city's name change and all featured the Minister's smiling face and advanced his many homilies and urgings. People are their clichés and sayings, it is a coping mechanism for everyone and the Minister capitalised on this aspect of the human condition.

Madeline had to accept that she had not always made the best of her life. No one does. This then was what Madeline saw as 'the Great Sadness', the universal disappointment in one's attempt at living one's life. You never fully believed you were making the best of it but always thought you had time to change it. But you don't – thus the Great Sadness. Changing the city's name had exacerbated this, rather than, as promised by the Minister of the Interior, assisted with it. He argued that the citizens would wake up every day feeling more hopeful. However, contrary to this, sadness seemed even more profound, disappointment seemed more intense with universal disappointment at the failure of the hope inherently promised in the name *Paradise*. Madeline instinctively knew this when the name change was first proposed. Madeline understood that you cannot live your life subject to external influences. Such influences often turned out to be confinements or boxes of a sort. Much to her regret, and until recently, this is how she had lived most of her life. But now she had Steve, at least for the moment.

3

RUBY

Ruby had one main hope, other than finding a job she might enjoy. She hoped that there was going to be someone special for her in Paradise. But so far no one had been provided. She worried how creepy having a spider in your stomach would be to others and she knew that until she could find a way to get rid of it, she was doomed. She knew no one would want her. So she remained alone. However, and Ruby found this very strange, the strange thing about *Being Alone* was that *Being Alone* framed her life. She once tried to explain this to her mother, then once to one of the girls at work, but to no avail; it wasn't that easy to explain. She didn't understand it herself. But it was a peculiar fact that the feeling of *Being Alone* was such a large component of her life that she felt it had its own presence and lived with her in her flat. So much so that it sat on the sofa in the living room, and left an indentation in the cushion. It ate at her small kitchen table. It slept next to her in her bed and held opinions about her life. This feeling of *Being Alone* was so tangible, so prominent, such a living manifestation, that it kept her company. She even felt affection for it. She even capitalised it as though it was a proper noun.

She kissed the teddies and got out of bed. She slipped out of her pyjamas, folded them, placed them under her pillow, then made her bed. She felt hungry and thirsty.

'Tea?' Ruby whispered again in her kitchen that morning, like every morning. She had a light voice and blue, watery eyes.

Ruby's mother promised her that she would be a great catch for someone someday; all she had to do was 'be bold'. Her mother's favourite saying about everyone's life, which she had read in a *Reader's Digest* once, was that, all life's problems were solvable, all you had to do was 'be bold and great powers will come to your aid'. Ruby wanted to believe this. She tried to believe it. Each day she thought to impose it on the spider. She might, one day. But she also knew when that day came, it would be a gargantuan struggle and that there would only be one winner – Ruby or the spider. Only one would walk away. Only one would survive. This thought caused movement of black legs starting deep in her stomach and ending in the back of her throat tasting like vomit. She swallowed and braced herself against the sink. A small bubble of saliva popped out the side of her mouth, which she wiped with the back of her hand before steadying herself again.

Of course it wasn't only the spider she had to contend with. Ruby, like everyone in Paradise, had her share of ordinary everyday demons too. She was philosophical about her demons. She admonished herself if they got the better of her, which they often did. Demons specific to life, her personality, and where she had come from, that is to say her past and of course, well, just the everyday demons of life in a City called Paradise. For Ruby, so far, Paradise was no paradise.

'A for anxiety,' she sang softly, dropping a single slice of wholegrain bread into the toaster. 'U for unsure about unimportant matters' (since life was mostly made up of unimportant matters, she was very often unsure), 'and T for timid with strangers.' She reprimanded herself, although more harshly than seemed strictly necessary for a young woman who lived alone in a small Clovelly Park building with ceiling sweat marks, in a city that had changed its name to Paradise, promising more hope than it had any expectation of delivering, and with a spider in her stomach and indentations in her cushions. 'People have much worse handicaps and disabilities and manage worthwhile lives,' she said to her rooster tea cosy. 'You can cope with a silly old spider in your stomach. You are young with your life in front of you,' she continued bravely to her reflection in the toaster, sounding a bit like her mother on any Sunday morning, 'and you have full lips,' she said repeating her mother and daring one of her rare but gorgeous smiles. 'Some sugar?' she practised, but then flicked her hair from side to side as her voice quavered, losing its way.

Ruby absent-mindedly stirred her tea. She longed for someone on whom to lavish her endless capacity for love. Well, at least she thought she had an endless capacity for love. She didn't really know. How can you? She so wanted to experience the breathtaking free-fall of true love. But, alas, there was no one. There hadn't been anyone for a long time now. Not since Todd. The things that Todd had done to her teenage heart by doing nothing more than walking past her in the school-yard at lunch, or swimming up to her in the school pool as he often did, couldn't be described by a thousand Shakespeares or a million Miltons in a trillion books dedicated to the description of love.

'I didn't love him,' she blurted one day in the supermarket tearoom during her lunch break. It just came out; she was daydreaming, not listening to the other girls, when the words were out and interrupting the usual chatter about boys, boys, boys. It brought the chatter to a standstill; the other girls stared at her. She felt hot and confused.

'Who didn't you love?' Cathy asked, trying to break the silence, but not sounding that interested.

'Oh, just a boy I knew from school, his name was Todd,' Ruby answered, embarrassed by her outburst and for interrupting the flow in the tearoom. She felt the spider stir. She could feel red blotches erupting on her throat.

'Huh! High school love, it doesn't count,' Cathy said. The seventeen-year-old checkout girls all laughed and fell back into in-depth discussion about their own more mature love lives.

Todd, whom Ruby thought at the time she had loved, was involved in a car accident when he was sixteen. As a hapless consequence of his accident, he broke his left patella, tibia and fibula, bruised his islets of Langerhans, momentarily interrupted his Krebs cycle in a number of isolated liver cells, and declared his homosexuality by swallowing a penis – not his own, needless to say. This declaration brought to an end Ruby's sixteen-year-old romantic life. In fact it put an end to a lot more than that, not the least of which, for example, was that she had no one to discuss the merits or otherwise of whether or not she was suited to selling cars. Decisions were doubled in difficulty for a single person. After his accident, she wanted to ask Todd why he didn't love her in return, but she was just sixteen and couldn't ask those kinds of questions. She still ached just thinking about it all. In fact she ached even when she wasn't thinking about it. But still and all, there was a tiny part of her, deep inside, that was hopeful she might find her Prince Charming one day and his exquisite kiss would melt all her fears away and she would awaken and live her life the way she had dreamed it would be. She worried sitting in the tearoom, she might have actually puckered her lips at the thought of the kiss.

'You okay Ruby? You look like you are in agony; your lips are all screwed up?' Cathy waited until the other girls left the room to start their shift on the supermarket's checkouts that day. 'My mum used to say that if the wind changes, you will be stuck with your expression forever,' Cathy said.

Ruby smiled at Cathy and tried to will her face to relax but instead felt a tic in her cheek. It unsettled Ruby that Cathy was four years younger but so much bolder than her and with no tic or blotching tendency or unconscious lip-puckering habits.

'Yes, my mum used to say that too.'

Ruby moved around her flat, back and forth through a shaft of white cold sunlight pouring in the kitchen window. She remained naked but didn't seem to notice the chill in the air. The goose bumps displayed a delicate texture across her skin. She felt faintly positive. The prospect of a new career buoyed her even though she had no idea if it was somehow possible, but the thought of making a change seemed both scary and exhilarating at the same time. I must not be scared, she thought to herself. She tried to imagine herself talking to men and sliding across the cool upholstery. She wondered about showing them through a car and taking them for a test drive and smelling their aftershave. She became aware of a tingle across her skin. Then in an instant, her positive spirits vanished as she realised she didn't know anything about cars. She ran a brush through her hair and, without thinking, set out two cups, two saucers, two teaspoons and two white perfectly ironed cotton napkins. She slipped on an apron, looping the ties around the small of her naked back and tying it at the front in a practised ritual. She set about making teacakes. Ruby always made her teacakes while wearing nothing more than an apron around her waist. She ended up with flour traces catching on her goose bumps like a light dusting of snow across a soft field. There were times in her life when Ruby wished the wind would change.

4

MADELINE

Madeline released a big sigh. She spread her legs and eased herself open with her fingers and inserted a tampon. She dropped the cellophane outer between her thighs. The empty cellophane floated carefree on the toilet water below. Madeline sat on the toilet staring into a blur of white. She was still in the stark white end-cubicle of the ground floor bathroom of Paradise's David Jones department store. The store itself faced onto Rundle Mall, where bits of rubbish danced around the architectural sculpture of silver balls, and whipped the legs of grey people leaning into nasty gusts of wind, like black-and-white cartoon characters defying the laws of physics. Madeline felt this Paradise cold air between her legs; it stiffened her muscles. She clenched her teeth.

She stared unblinking in silence; her eyes watered. She stared at the white shiny walls of the cubicle, deep in the belly of the building, and pondered over several things. The things she pondered were her freckles, her legs, her life, and in particular, her continuing need for tampons and her cunt of course. She was widowed and handsome, forty-two years old, and had a fixation on yellow hats. She was annoyed that her period had arrived because in just over an hour she was due to be making love. The thought of this caused her to feel giddy. Giddy at her age, who would have thought? She thought how all life starts in the cubicle – a box, a walled city.

Madeline examined her naked thighs and worried they might be just a little too pale. Right at that moment, she wished there was someone she could show them to, for confirmation, or otherwise, on the pale factor. She sighed again but she didn't know why – maybe it was to do with sitting in a public toilet thinking about life. She stroked at a largish freckle on her leg – one of many; blemishes, they were. She thought of them as imperfections, flaws but, even so, Steve had kissed every one of them.

She imagined each freckle as a tiny planet in a vast endless Milky Way galaxy, then as a tiny galaxy in a vast endless Universe, and finally, a tiny

Universe in the vast and endless nothing, perhaps a grand cubicle. She wouldn't have been at all surprised about the cubicle. The whole notion had a certain poetic resonance, she thought. Anyway, it was life in Paradise, everything was inside something, answers trapped inside questions, ideas were held captive in grander ideas. She didn't want to accept that at the end, there was nothing. This couldn't be; after Paradise there was what? Oblivion? She wanted to believe there had to be something after Paradise. Since Paradise was hardly perfect, there had to be something else, something better, a release, otherwise it seemed a lot of effort, a lot of wriggling and worrying work, a lot of pain, and much agony and its twin, ecstasy, for nothing? But what? Heaven? Then what, Utopia? Madeline didn't know, but she believed in something though. She had to. It was in her nature to harbour romantic notions. This was just one of them. It was one of the things she liked about herself and one of the things she disliked about herself.

She let the last two months of her life flash through her mind. She could barely hold the truth of it in her heart. She could barely stop her heart from racing away. The thought of those events shocked her and rendered her breathless and, ridiculous as it was for a forty-two-year-old mother and widow, she couldn't stop herself from thinking about these two months and how shockingly different this period had been compared with the way her life had been in the past. She luxuriated in the sexual feelings all this evoked. In truth, she had always suspected these feelings had resided deep inside her, but, for most of her life, went unanswered. But there was a downside; she also couldn't help but think that it all might not last. She hoped for the best, but knew the disinterested cruelty of life would never cease. She understood how hopeless hope could be. She sometimes thought that the only purpose of hope was to set you up for devastating disappointment, and yet hope was hardwired into the human condition. This suggested to Madeline that the human race could never escape disappointment, as though disappointment was blood and air for the psyche. However, this aside, and for the moment, she lived a fantastic life in Paradise, a life of fabulous sex, perhaps she didn't need Heaven or Utopia. She was in love – beautiful, head-over-heels breathtaking clichés of love. She worried at the thought. Her body salivated at the thought.

It was agonising that she couldn't tell anyone about her life. Especially that she couldn't tell her son, Peter. Not about the sex of course, she didn't want to tell him about that, but about how her life had changed, how it had been saved, that's what she wanted to tell him – it's never too late to live, she would say. She wanted to tell him that even if there was no Heaven or Utopia, it didn't matter, because it was here and now that counted and there is nothing more here and now than the rush of new love. She felt that if she could tell her son, it might give him some hope for his own life too. A life he walked around in, as though it was a big empty warehouse. But 'the complication of the relationship with her lover' prevented her from telling him and she dreaded the moment when it would have to be revealed to Peter, provided of course it lasted.

Outside her cubicle, in the sterilised *Space Odyssey* whiteness of David Jones's bathroom, she heard a tap dripping. It dripped with clichéd relentlessness and echoed black and white film noir, she decided. She rocked in rhythm with the drip – her thighs flattening against the toilet seat with each forward motion in her semi-trancelike state. Drip, drip, like sands through an hour-glass. She squinted through her black lashes at the white walls giving her the impression she was looking through a grid of a spider's legs. Sometimes it felt safer to squint at life this way. It blunted the searing pain of lost love doing the rounds in her mind.

She felt the tampon now snug inside her, and wondered at that moment, that very second in her life, how the invention of internal tampons ever came about. Who would have thought of such a thing? Who would have thought of pushing a tampon inside a vagina? Madeline closed her eyes. She had strong bones and white straight teeth and excellent definition, and two disarming dimples whenever she smiled. And while her legs were pale (freckles notwithstanding) they were nonetheless firm and shapely, unless flattened against a toilet seat, like now. She lifted each thigh in turn to unstick her skin from the plastic. She squeezed out a sigh and tried not to think of the Great Sadness in Paradise.

Madeline considered the 'bright young things' on the other side of the door, manning the cosmetic counters. She thought of their lipstick sliding over their puckered lips. She thought of all those viable fresh carnivorous cunts below the counters. She thought of them accommodating penises or tongues or tampons, and that the white noise coming from the background hum was disguising their yearning orgasms. She considered how they would receive their periods with inevitability, as she did at their age. Nothing more than perhaps a minor nuisance interrupting their busy sex lives, or enhancing their sex, for all Madeline knew. But young women would not think of their periods as a vicious countdown. Not at their age. Not until they were Madeline's age. But as poignant and sobering as all this was, it wasn't in fact the crux of Madeline's one big regret in life.

5

RUBY

Later that day, trying to feel confident and overcome her nerves, Ruby sat straight-backed and posture-perfect in front of the pock-faced Sales Manager of Easy Motors, 'the pre-owned cars for all the family' specialists on the Great Southern Road, not far from her flat. She waited. She waited while his black seal-eyes roved over her breasts and then up her shiny legs. She waited while he leered at her in a way that men had always done. Ruby had learnt to be patient with Paradise men, especially when it came to her body, which could be described as gorgeous and lovely, but not perfect. For perfection, she thought, her hair could be more pure blonde, her eyes might be a shade darker, her teeth a little straighter, her complexion more sun-exposed and less pale, and for some tastes, she might be a centimetre or two shorter or taller, but it was these small imperfections that combined to make her gorgeous. Ruby recalled her father saying, 'perfection comes in many guises and can only be appreciated and understood by few and then ironically, only through the prism of imperfection' (he loved the word ironically, Ruby remembered). He would look over his newspaper at breakfast as though he was just reading something of interest and exclaim, 'Only flaws can highlight beauty, it's one of life's ironies. That is why Paradise is perfect, it is tragically flawed and as such, not perfect.' This was one of her father's favourite sayings. He laughed his big father laugh whenever he said it. Ruby loved to sit with him at breakfast even though she didn't understand most the things he said. She loved to watch him eat his toast. He'd take big father bites and a mouthful of tea, and operatically gulp it all down with fascinating noise – it made her think of cartoon characters chomping through a picnic ham. He had little time for the ambitious Minister of the Interior whose brainchild the Paradise name change had been. And he held a particular view on the ritual slayings of young single women. Well, just about everyone in Paradise did; there were more theories than government promises.

'I haven't any selling experience,' Ruby offered to the Sales Manager of Easy Motors, her voice reluctantly filling the small, cluttered office. Her delicate scent introduced a faint sense of feminine hope to the resident male squalor.

'Perfect,' the Sales Manager responded with an alarming expansion of his nostrils, like an animal sensing prey across the savannah.

With her hands clasped in her lap holding a white linen handkerchief and her legs crossed tightly, her skirt rode up her naked thighs. This caused the Sales Manager to loosen his tie and collar to accommodate the swelling. He swallowed hard several times between his words, and splashes of red blotches exploded across his lunar face like a fireworks display. He adjusted in his seat as though he could not find comfort.

'I will try very hard,' she said in an attempt to get his eyes from her legs. She felt a tic flickering in her hot cheek and she hoped that he hadn't seen it. Thank goodness for my legs, she thought as she uncrossed them. She couldn't let him see her tic. A tic would be a disaster for someone wanting to become a salesperson, she thought.

Even so, it might not have been the best decision to wear her short white leather mini after all, or maybe it was, she just couldn't say and it was too much to worry about all at once. She moved her handkerchief back a little on her lap to expose more of her legs and tried to control the tic in her cheek and felt a heatwave rush over her face. She began.

'I know I don't have any qualifications for this position, but I hope that being helpful will count a little. I am good at being helpful, I like people, er…' Her sentence trailed off and she flicked at her hair. He squirmed in front of her. It didn't quite come out the way she wanted. She wanted to say something positive, make a statement of importance, disarm him. She was desperate to impress in her interview but she didn't know how. She felt his eyes scanning her.

'Don't worry darlin', I think you are the kind of girl our customers are going to like.' He stuffed his mouth with a large bite of one of the teacakes Ruby had thought to bring to her interview. 'Yeth thir little darling, you are the goodth, for sure, nith teacakth.' Several bits of cake splattered across his desk as he spoke and chewed at the same time. He gulped it all down and then stuffed another whole teacake in his mouth. 'I think the cuthtomers are going to like you fery muth.' He took a long slurp from his tea. She watched his animated tongue swipe over his lips like a big slug sliding out of his mouth and symbiotically licking his face. She thought it capable of independent behaviour.

Ruby felt relieved, sort of. She thought, yes, there was some truth in what he had just said. By and large, people did seem to like her. She thought selling, if it was about anything, must be about being liked. So perhaps she had a chance, but then, apart from her somewhat pleasing appearance, which surely wasn't something a person could be blamed for, there was one big problem she had, and that was her melancholy, which she was aware of but could do nothing about. She could only hope the Sales Manager hadn't noticed it. It was like this: strangers found themselves drawn to her at first, connected to her, as though her melancholy was a reflection of some kind of universal melancholy which everyone experienced, but was something they only felt in themselves when they looked into Ruby's eyes. But when that happened, they often recoiled from her. This left her feeling responsible and rejected. She had learnt to limit the time people could look into her eyes.

'Would there be any training? I'm a quick learner.' She looked down. Teacakes could often divert people from her melancholy.

'Yeth. Yeth, definitely training, for thore.' He swallowed, his wet words batted out by his tongue and slapping around the office, careering onto the dusty walls and hitting framed photos of sports cars and a chipped, cheap trophy sitting on the floor next to a rusting metallic Christmas tree, all in their search for her ears. 'But I wouldn't worry, you are a natural.'

She wasn't sure how he could know that, but she was hopeful. There wasn't much else she could think of to do, nothing at all. She knew she couldn't continue at the supermarket any longer. It was just too demeaning at her age, not to mention boring. She thought her life must come to more than knowing the price of spray-on starch or the kilo cost of aubergine. All the other girls were just seventeen and looked at her as though she was ancient. Without adolescent pimples boiling red across her face, to them she stood out like an imperfect subspecies. They all seemed to have an endless supply of boyfriends – pimply, gangly and frightened, but boyfriends nonetheless with whom they had quick sex behind the stacks in the back of the warehouse whenever the manager was occupied with his own carnal life. She was sure it was her melancholy that stopped the love she craved from finding her. And the existence of her spider, of course. She wondered sometimes if there was someone else in Paradise who might also have a spider in his stomach.

At the end of her interview at Easy Motors, the Sales Manager came around his desk. He put his arm around her, and gave her a squeeze and a kiss on the cheek to welcome her, as he said, to the 'team'.

'Welcome to the team at Easy Motors, Ruby lass.' He smiled at her and she smiled back.

He smelt like wet dog hair. His sharp, acrid breath struck her in the face. She had to swallow hard to stop herself from gagging. She didn't know what to do at that moment but she had a feeling she needed to be an adult, a grown-up woman. I must not be scared, she recited under her breath.

'Thank you, thank you very much,' she said feeling gratitude toward this man who barely came up to her eyes and who wore a colourful tie with food stains. Not only his own food stains, of which there appeared to be numerous – now including teacake crumbs – but food stains embroidered on the tie by the tie designer. She had to fight back the nausea, which jumped into her throat.

'I will try very hard,' she assured him. She was also assuring herself that this was the right job for her, even the right place for her to start her career in car sales. Her words spluttered out of her, carried with the air in her lungs as he kept jolting her body against himself, with his claw-like arm around her shoulders. At that moment, she missed her mum. Ruby imagined the little girl lying dead on the bitumen, the screech of the tyres still filling her ears. Ruby wanted to swap places with the dead girl.

Ruby, so relieved and trying to be pleased with herself, took herself to the little cafe on the Great Southern Road next to the hardware store just down from the Tonsley Park Hotel and ordered her favourite drink, a pineapple crush.

Sitting in the low glaring sun at one of the outside metal tables, she felt the chilly whoosh of the traffic rush over her skin. She closed her eyes and sucked up the sweet icy-cold pineapple pulp into her mouth. She sat still and silent. In the wind, and the moment, she felt the exquisite shock of a fleeting kiss on her cheek. She knew not to move. To do so, or to look around, would cause her stranger to disappear.

Some early mornings in her bed, between sleeping and waking, Ruby imagined the erotic caress of a kiss across her lips. Her lips, she had been told, were 'the guardians of her salacious, sirenesque smile'. Her mother's voice echoed from Ruby's past. Ruby touched her lips with her fingers. She parted her lips, and longed to have them kissed. Sometimes she imagined a dashing dark stranger; she gave him a black eye-patch to add to his mystery. Other times she dreamt about a boy from high school, and remembered that as intimate as he had been with her, he never kissed her. She longed for that kiss. She had felt from that day on that she was owed a kiss. When she closed her eyes, she could imagine that exquisite freshly shaven smell that men have and their mysterious honey-breath, but this was only possible with her eyes closed. She bit down hard on the straw and let herself succumb to the roar of traffic and the rocking burst of air as each car and truck battered her when they passed only metres away, threatening to seduce her into their vacuum. She closed her eyes more tightly, hurting her muscles around her eyes. For as long as she held her eyes closed and kept still, he would be next to her, brushing his lips over her, saving her from the traffic. Her skin tightened across her chest. She allowed for a moment her private sensation to build. She had just got a new job.

She wasn't aware there was a young man, a very skinny young man, across the road watching her; staring at her. She was preoccupied, enjoying the moment and hoping the spider would let her be. She felt the sudden chill of a cold front approaching, and she could smell the freshness in the air of imminent rain. Contrary to popular understanding and appearances, and the Minister of the Interior's insistence, things were not always perfect in Paradise – not by a long shot. But today was a good day. The very moment this thought germinated, she crashed into sadness. She knew nothing about cars; she didn't even have one herself. She had driven only as much as it took her father to teach her before she gained her licence. She knew nothing about selling. The fall into sadness was so swift and sudden that tears ran down her cheeks unchecked, as the spider arched up on its hind legs to its strike position and the mirage of her dark stranger's kiss disappeared.

6

MADELINE

In the warm safety of the toilet cubicle, Madeline focused on the white-tiled floor and the grey grouting and wondered how far off it would be before she would no longer need tampons. The realisation that she'd already had more periods in her life than she was going to have in the future had hit her savagely.

Madeline liked to calculate things.

'If you could just calculate the number of stars and planets in the Universe, or freckles on your legs, you could know yourself. You would know the answer. And there is an answer to everything, don't you think?' Madeline asked Peter this on a recent visit to his apartment, hoping to prod him into a conversation. Madeline found a certain satisfaction in calculations. She found solace in the detail. The big questions of life might well find their answers in the small questions if the truth was known. If only the truth could be known. Get the small questions right and the big ones will take care of themselves, she thought. Well it was one way to think about the world, not that Peter chose to agree or disagree. He continued to polish his football boots with Zen-like zeal, as though the zeal was the point, not the polishing. It wasn't only calculations Madeline found satisfaction in though; there were other things, personal things; things to do with her past. Weather in particular. Like bright winter days when the warm morning sun shone on her bare arms, reminding her of when she was a young woman in Adelaide walking through the speckled light. And the comfort she got from childhood memories such as the yellow blanket of soursob flowers across the glistening parklands in winter. Other things too. She liked over-sized wood-framed mirrors (bevelled) in entranceways, frosted anodised cups on picnics, and of course, yellow hats. Yellow hats were important to Madeline – she wore yellow hats for luck; if she couldn't wear one because she had just been to the salon or the outfit she was wearing would have clashed with it, she carried it in her handbag.

But calculations were her favourite. And she calculated she had maybe one hundred and fifty periods to go, give or take. Continuing with her reckoning, she would need around three thousand tampons to see out her periods. This thought of her periods ending came as a profound moment to Madeline, as it does to all women, she thought. This of course was the genesis of the Great Sadness – the inevitability of everything having to end, including and especially life, and the particular realisation that after all, she might be powerless to alter anything. A favourite Paradise saying was, 'everything happens in the end'. For Madeline, this had two meanings depending on where she placed the emphasis. '*Everything* happens in the end' or, 'everything happens in the *end*.' She believed in one, but not the other.

She remembered herself much younger.

Madeline's method of dealing with life's difficulties was to remind herself, and her son Peter, whenever she could, of the troubles of the known Universe, or how close anyone was to their fate at any given moment. She could, if she wanted to, if her personal feelings of sadness were proving difficult to shift, evoke the memory of the day she saw a young girl die; a profound moment. This memory brought her back to earth. She reached for her yellow hat.

The death occurred in front of her on a shimmering hot summer's day where she stood ready to cross the Great Southern Road, her nine-year-old son Peter beside her. But that was not the worst tragedy Madeline saw that day. Indeed not. It was also the day when she saw herself. Standing right next to Madeline, close enough for their arms to brush, was another young girl, a girl from Peter's class: an alarmingly pretty girl, a beautiful innocent angel. They shared the unfolding of the accident. Something compelled Madeline to turn her head from the girl's body on the road and look into the eyes of the young girl who stood next to her. In that frozen moment of all pasts and futures, Madeline saw, in those flawed eyes, her own tragic inescapable melancholy. Madeline knew instantly she was connected to all who had passed, and all who were still to come. She forced herself to turn away from the girl, leaving her to cope with the accident unaided, even though Madeline had to fight an overwhelming instinctive nurturing response to embrace the young perfect creature standing next to her. Madeline just couldn't look into the girl's eyes a second longer. To do so, she was sure, would have resulted in the disintegration of her own soul. She had to make a choice. She chose to look at the body lying on the bitumen. She watched its milky blood empty from the lifeless skull and saw one eye turned skywards. Madeline had to accept the guilty exhilaration of the fact that but for a hesitation, a breath, a pause, a single instinctive step forward, a coincidence of synchronicity, her life might have ended instead. The best she could do was to reach out to the girl next to her, without looking into her eyes, and fix her little hand to the bus shelter so she could hang on. Madeline remembered her name was Ruby.

From that day on, Madeline never left home without a yellow hat. And from that day on, Madeline knew death had acknowledged her, and that she would need her philosophical thinking to keep it at bay. And deep within Madeline, there was a part of her that could never forgive herself for making the choice she did on that awful day. Ever since, she had been trying to make amends. She often wondered about Ruby and what she might be doing in her life, even at this very moment as Madeline sat in silence in the David Jones toilet cubicle. She didn't even know if Ruby was still alive.

Madeline had visited that same spot of the accident many times since, looking at the bus shelter pole to see if she could see any trace of Ruby. From that terrible day, Madeline wanted to be something to Ruby, some comfort or help, she didn't know what or how, but something. She had never seen Ruby or heard anything about her again. Ruby was somewhere living her life and Madeline had developed a habit of looking at people everywhere to see if any of them might be Ruby.

'You can't argue with the inevitable,' Sheila once said apropos of nothing in particular, while wrapping bits of foil in Madeline's hair. Madeline had counted the bits of foil; there were twenty-one. Sheila was exactly halfway done.

'Strange how life is hundreds of little betrayals, missed opportunities if you like. The trick is to make the best of everything, and not expect perfection,' she had told Peter, her son, many times. 'Wake up calls. They are all opportunities. They are the signposts announcing decay,' Madeline would say, 'life is all about entropy.' She kicked herself for saying this to him though. She had sensed his adolescent eye roll at her banality. But banal or not, it was still a truism.

Sitting on the toilet, still rocking back and forth, Madeline had the feeling that someone was in the bathroom outside her cubicle. She couldn't recall hearing the door open and close, but there was a distinct stillness in the room, as though someone might be there, holding their breath and listening.

7

RUBY

'You do make a struggle of life, don't you, Ruby dear?' One of Ruby's final-year high-school teachers made this observation one lunchtime in the schoolyard. Ruby could smell pungent warm cucumber sandwiches from open Tupperware boxes and hot chips in brown paper bags. The teacher's words hit her hard. It was true though; even Ruby knew this about herself. She had difficulties with the expectation side of life, the part on the double helix where hope and optimism were located. And she didn't know what she could do about it. From the age of nine when 'death' abruptly introduced itself to her, she had in effect clicked into passive mode and been stuck there ever since. She couldn't bring herself to tell the teacher this, as much as she wanted to, and as much as she hoped it would make a difference if she did. Her fight to break out was her own. It wasn't easy, just surviving took 'everlasting vigilance', as her father often reminded her over his toast at breakfast.

'Sometimes I feel frozen in a silent kind of noise,' she explained to her mother. She would have liked to discuss this with her mother, as much for her mother's input as for her own possible discovery of its meaning, but her mother continued to iron in the family silence and Ruby was left to think about it in her own silence.

On the day of Ruby's ninth birthday, death arrived in her innocent life and it stayed. She was too young for it. Too young to have seen the blood issue from the girl's skull and creep toward her as she stood holding on to the bus shelter on the Great Southern Road. She saw this moment as her epiphany, but this realisation came later when she understood the word. Since that day, she found it hard to mount the energy to be hopeful, and yet hope was all she had to cling to, and then later on, Todd turning out to be gay, in a way, finished her off. Now in her twenties, she resolved her thinking to the fact that the hope that life offered was a false promise. She had hoped for that kiss, but it never came and left an aching hole in her life.

Ruby did well in school but not in the way her teachers, or indeed her father, had hoped. She got good grades but it somehow still disappointed everyone. Her report card would read, 'Ruby has done very well again'. When Ruby read these words, her emotions sank; she felt there was a disappointment attached to these words and that there were missing words implied, like, 'The truth is, Ruby has done very well again, but still not well enough', or, '…but we are still disappointed in her'. The words seemed to say to Ruby that 'we are weary and find it inexplicable that Ruby has only done very well again and nothing else'. When she handed her report card to her father, her heart muscle flip-flopped like a fish drowning out of water when she saw his sadness, although he always tried to hide it from her.

'Well done, baby,' he would say in his absent-minded way, followed with a kiss on her hair.

'Thank you, Daddy.'

'Everlasting vigilance, baby.'

'Yes of course, everlasting vigilance, Daddy.'

Ruby's flat was located in Clovelly Park, one of Paradise's southern lower-order suburbs. It was repeated on many of the city's billboards by the smiling Minister of the Interior that 'all suburbs in Paradise are to be equal'. Much had been promised with the name change. The Minister appeared on television every night, before the name change, urging that life in Paradise would be much better for us, and tourists would come, we need to re-brand our product, we will feel better about ourselves, he insisted. He spoke in homilies, clichés and adages. The slayings began soon after the name change. Ruby secretly preferred the old name of Adelaide; it conjured up a carefree younger version of herself, in a pretty white cotton dress, skipping through a field of tall grass on a sunny spring day. Adelaide made no bold promises and it therefore never let anyone down. In Adelaide, everlasting vigilance was not as necessary as it was in Paradise.

Ruby kept her flat spotlessly clean. On every level surface available, apart from her small kitchen table, she displayed her collection of small, and she had to admit, silly childhood toys. She had them in order and lined up according to size and style. Forty-one tiny mechanical toys, some operated by wind-up mechanisms and powered by rubber-bands and others by battery. They were collected, by and large, throughout her childhood, some during her teens. It wasn't a collection that could be said to be complete by any description, or vast, or even an excellent representation of its like. It suffered notably from the absence of a dolphin, she thought. She meticulously and ritually dusted every one of her treasures each morning as soon as she woke. I must not be scared; she would tell each and every one of them. She only rented the flat, but she wanted it to feel homely. She had made some curtains for her bedroom window and two antimacassars for her small sofa. She had crocheted a cover for her toilet seat, in the shape of a toilet seat, but it didn't quite fit even though she had been so vigilant about getting the measurements correct. This confounded her.

One Saturday afternoon not long ago, in grey winter light and biting gusty wind, Ruby walked into a crash repairer's workshop on the Great Southern Road, which, as it turned out, was next door to Easy Motors, although this meant nothing to her at the time. With the football commentary from a radio rising and falling in the background, she approached a young man working alone, crouching with his back to her, rubbing the bumper bar of a car with such concentration and deliberation she hesitated to interrupt him.

'Excuse me sir,' she said after waiting for a few seconds.

The young man didn't turn around, he continued to rub and blow on the chrome bumper.

'I have to paint the ceiling of my flat which isn't far from here and I wondered if I could borrow a ladder for the afternoon? I promise...' Before she could finish her sentence, he moved, and Ruby saw her distorted reflection in the shiny chrome. The young man stood, turned and looked into her eyes. She recognised him. Her body flooded with embarrassment. He never spoke a word to her. He looked over in the corner of the workshop then walked over and lifted the ladder up off its hook and brought it to her. She couldn't tell if he had recognised her; after all, the last time he saw her, she had been naked. That was many years ago when they were both only sixteen. She remembered his nickname from school, it was Hawkey but she didn't use it, she had never used it. She didn't know his real name.

'Thank you,' she whispered.

He nodded. It seemed all he could manage, or it was all he thought was necessary; there was something efficient about his manner. He had mastered minimal movement and speech, editing out all extraneous actions, and reduced his life to only the necessary. This much of him hadn't changed; this was how she remembered him from school.

She noticed paint on his cheek. She wanted to wipe it away for him. She wanted to serve him tea and teacakes in her kitchen. She wanted to touch his blond hair. She wanted for them both to act like what had happened between them when she was sixteen never happened. But she couldn't do any of these things.

She heard the football commentary rise as she left the building with the ladder, and remembered another boy from high school who had been a very good footballer. His name was Peter. Peter and Hawkey had been friends. It was Peter's kiss she had wanted on her sixteenth birthday, but it never happened. At that moment, she realised she still wanted Peter's kiss.

She painted the dark spots on the ceiling of her bedroom, but the patches re-appeared almost before the paint had dried, so she let them be. She bought two acrylic Eastern-style rugs, one for each room. They helped to lift the rooms with some colour. That was her flat. She took the ladder back but Hawkey was nowhere to be found.

'Your flat is wonderful, darling,' her mother told her on the only occasion she visited, just after Ruby had moved in.

'Do you really think so?'

'Do you have any sugar, darling?' her mother asked.

Ruby felt disappointed in herself for forgetting the sugar. She served teacakes and English breakfast tea to her mother. She set the table with two napkins she had bought at David Jones. She was annoyed with herself; she had run out of fresh tea and had to use tea bags for her mother's visit. They sat opposite each other in the cramped flat and jiggled.

'Maybe some paint,' her mother said, her voice trailing off.

8

MADELINE

Madeline's one big regret, apart from her awkwardness with her son, for which there seemed no remedy and which wasn't so much a regret but more a frustration, was simple: RAPTURE! She hadn't had anywhere near enough of it. 'Rapture'. Surely rapture was life's ultimate reward. The subject of rapture came up in the salon one day when Sheila posed the topic for the day's discussion. 'What is your one big regret?' No one seemed to know, but Madeline knew hers.

'Rapture, or specifically, the lack of it, is my one big regret.' Madeline instantly regretted volunteering this to the rapacious Sheila.

'Good answer, girl.' Sheila laughed. 'And what are we going to do about that then?' Sheila swished her streaked hair about her head emphasising the rising end to her question.

Only twice in Madeline's life had she felt any rapture. The second time had happened recently when her handsome young man knelt in front of her inspecting the damage to her car. Her skin radiated heat and her limbs trembled and some strands of her hair turned white, which Sheila had fixed in no time. Of course there was no way she was ever going to release that information to Sheila.

Madeline's life was presently full of rapture, so overflowing with it, that she couldn't help but feel embarrassed, and hoped Sheila didn't notice the top of her head flooding red as she thought about it. This rapture was a direct result of Madeline being in love. The first and only other time she experienced rapture in her life was when she witnessed the young girl's death. That was a strange and uncomfortable rapture. She couldn't explain it and she felt guilty about it, and rather preferred not to speak of it, or think of it, even though Sheila wanted her to reveal all her secrets to the salon. Keeping secrets is unhealthy for women, Sheila would laughingly argue. It's against the natural order of things. 'It's a well-known fact. Like men die within a week from lover's balls due to a lack of sex, women suffer a similar fate if they are required to keep a secret. Isn't that right, Jane?' Sheila liked to drag everyone into the conversations. Jane moved her head but kept at her crossword puzzle, hoping that the Sheila spotlight would move on to one of the other women in the mirror. All were averting their eyes.

'Rapture is complex though, don't you think?' Madeline continued. Sheila's attention span lifted whenever she thought something juicy was about to be revealed. 'It's not necessarily just one thing. It can be good or bad. It can be pleasure or pain.'

'Now you're talkin', Maddy,' Sheila said.

'In fact it can be all these things at once. Anyway, whatever it is, it's not to be missed,' Madeline said.

'Amen to that.' The other women nodded in sync; some held their breath, all were reluctant.

Madeline recalled this salon subject of a couple of weeks ago and it threw up memories of her philandering ex- and now-dead husband. She didn't believe in blaming other people for her own life's disappointments. It took considerable will on Madeline's behalf not to blame her deceased husband for depriving her of important elements of her life.

Madeline decided she must make a move to leave the toilet cubicle soon. She knew she couldn't sit there all day lost in her memories and thoughts; besides, she had an appointment in an hour. She tore off a piece of toilet paper and blew her nose. This action produced more noise than she had intended. She marvelled at the capability of her body to produce a variety of noises all with their own specific genesis. And her body, especially lately, was capable of some extraordinary noises. This impressed Madeline. Rapture for Madeline had announced itself and for the most part quite noisily. The screaming of a banshee would not have been an inappropriate metaphor during her climactic rapturous orgasmic explosions with her young lover. But also she recalled the rapture during the sound of squealing brakes, tyres skidding, bones being crunched and life being extinguished. That too, was a compelling seductive rapture.

'Do you think of yourself as a seductress, Madeline?' Madeline's thoughts returned to the same conversation with Sheila in the salon, a few weeks back. The vision of Sheila scraping something from under one of her long painted false nails triggered Madeline's train of thought.

'I don't think so,' Madeline responded, remembering how shocked she had been at the question. But strangely, that might be the case when she thought about it. Madeline acknowledged that indeed she had always felt, well, sexual. There had been some intense sexual moments in her life but up until the last two months, and by way of a benchmark, she had never felt the kind of constant all-consuming, breathless heady rapture in the way heroines are portrayed in historical romance novels, for example. Fictional heroines never had to deal with tampons for a start, she thought. During her marriage, Madeline often escaped into the period-free fiction of heaving bosoms, high passion and scarlet flowing hair. There were always tall mysterious strangers. Sometimes with shadowy black eye-patches, which suggested a battle, the prize of which was to liberate a distressed damsel from continuous torrid sex in confinement, only to replace this with more torrid sex on the hero's stallion. More recently, she had ordered the racier books under the category title of *Black Lace* and with titles like *Sex Slave Susan*, or *Tiffany's Epiphany*. She coveted these books as much for instruction as for curious interest in the sex. A sigh came and went, but for no reason she could clearly identify – just another of her body's inexplicable noises. Sheila's question had unleashed a white storm.

Madeline had never resisted being a mother. She hadn't resisted being a wife either and always acquiesced to her husband's sexual imperatives. She did whatever was required even though not much had been. Still, it was no more than obligation without fulfilment for Madeline, and no rapture and no noise, if you didn't count the silly high-pitched squeaking her husband made upon the delivery of his climax. For most of her marriage she had secretly dreamed that someone tall and dangerous would whisk her away to a far off land, where she would be bathed, hand-fed, adored and worshipped. And she would wear a flowing white diaphanous gown, and nothing else.

She thought of Steve's tenderness, his caresses and gentle exquisite kissing. It was both everything she deserved and so much more than she deserved. During sex with Steve, she felt like a voyeur, watching him take her with the ferocity of farmyard frenzy, like he was an endowed cloven-hoofed beast. He snorted and grunted as he lined her up. She sighed again but the sigh was accompanied by an unannounced impact-induced moan; maybe several moans as she imagined his entry. This startled her even though the moan was hers. She opened her eyes and blinked to accommodate the white glare of the cubicle. She read the graffiti on the toilet door. 'Someone is watching you'. Were any other cubicles occupied? She blushed and strained to hear movement, did she just hear someone move? Yes, maybe. 'Cunt. Cunt. Cunt. Cunt.' She chanted this sacred word, luxuriating in the freedom she felt in her heart. She felt anonymous. For sure she knew it would bring the chatter in the salon to a standstill, if she was ever to use it there. It might even cause Sheila to gasp. She was sure she could hear the precise sound of fascinated silence in the public toilet, but she didn't care and she continued her chant. Cunt, cunt, cunt… She knew she was listening to the sound of someone holding their breath.

9

RUBY

On a bright and sunny day, Ruby found a second-hand book on epic Medieval English poetry lodged in her letterbox. Whoever put it there either preferred to remain anonymous or forgot to include a card. She tried not to think that the book had been given to her by mistake, and in a dreamy way, she hoped it was from someone she might meet one day. Perhaps it was from one of the tenants in her building, although this seemed unlikely. Perhaps it was from someone who was secretly and perhaps even desperately in love with her and would have no issue with her spider, or had one of his own, and would understand. She imagined him with a black eye-patch. She treasured the book and kept it on her bedside table and tried to read the poetry almost every night before she fell asleep. She had to teach herself the ancient English before she could understand its meaning, but strangely it lost some of the meaning as she mastered the language. Ruby had no argument with this oddity, in fact it being an oddity, she found comforting.

Ruby woke early and gasped. The day had come. She was due to start her new job at the car yard. She felt proud that she had achieved this in her life and that it represented a stand of defiance against the spider, although she should not dwell on this self-approval for fear the spider would rouse. She dusted the toys, showered and had a piece of toast with the new and improved (no butter needed) lemon-flavoured Elysium spread, and a mug of tea, black with honey and lime rind. She preferred lime to lemon in her tea. She was very particular about her tea. Before she dressed, she applied mascara to her eyes and *Angelips* lipstick to her lips and pressed them together. She forced a smile to check her teeth. She chose *Sacred Scarlet* – her preferred lipstick colour. In regard to makeup, she had no particular policy except that she used it sparingly. She applied some perfume on her wrists, pressed them together then dabbed her neck and between her breasts. She left her hair natural, and resting on her shoulders; it suited her that way. She felt the spider stir and she swallowed hard. She steadied herself and hummed to keep the spider satisfied. She recited a line or two from her poetry book and held on to the door.

Ruby stood in front of her wardrobe, and pondered her options. She wanted to look her best on her first day in her new job. It would have been good if she could have discussed it with somebody. She rang her mother but there was no answer. Ruby suspected her mother somehow knew it was her daughter calling and deliberately didn't answer the phone. On the rare occasions when she did pick up, she always sounded surprised as though she had misplaced her daughter, or had forgotten she even had one. Ruby waited for it to ring out, not because she thought her mother would pick up, but simply because it was mesmerising. It was like she imagined her mother's heartbeat would have been to her when she was still unborn and there was no spider to torment her; she couldn't see her mother, but she knew she was there.

Ruby's mother had encouraged Ruby to leave her cleavage visible when Ruby's breasts emerged and astonished everyone. Ruby was only twelve when this happened to her. When she was thirteen and already fully developed, her mother stood her in front of the bedroom mirror and undid Ruby's blouse and training bra. 'Ta Daa!' her mother fan-fared at Ruby's buoyant breasts.

'You are very lucky you are your mother's daughter. I gave you these.' Ruby's mother cupped Ruby's breasts as if to lay claim to them, and to suggest that something new had now started. Ruby felt a change between herself and her mother, even though she hadn't understood it. Ruby's mother cupped her own breasts and looked at herself in the mirror, first front on, then her profile.

'Don't worry darling, there is nothing to worry about.' Ruby's mother had produced a black lacy bra from a wrapped white tissue paper and presented it to Ruby. To be frank, Ruby didn't need a bra; her breasts were firm and more than capable of holding themselves up. But Ruby's mother had explained the bra was for visual effect more than it was for structural support. In Ruby's father's architectural parlance, had he been called on to make a comment, which he hadn't, he would have said it was, 'in this case, form over function.' Ruby remembered looking at herself semi-naked that day, with her mother beside her. She had an eerie feeling that the reflection in the mirror looking back at her didn't recognise her. Her father had not appeared to notice Ruby had turned into a young woman. The only desire she could ever remember him expressing to her was that she go to university and become an architect, like him. Ruby was an only child. She knew she was never going to be an architect, and she knew her father knew too. Eventually, she gave up on him, as he had on himself, and both of them had to accept that as far as this life in Paradise for Ruby was concerned, it would be for her a matter of 'function over form', while the habit of the way she dressed herself would be for both.

She chose her lucky white leather mini skirt again (no stockings), white bra and white cotton translucent blouse. She added a splash of colour by tying a blue silk scarf around her neck for any women she might encounter. She left the top two buttons of her blouse undone. This was how she dressed. She should have checked the weather because a cold front was on its way.

On her first day, she was to start three hours later than what would be her usual starting time of eight o'clock, as the Sales Manager had appointments most of the morning, and, as he had said, he wanted to give her his undivided attention. Ruby hopped on a bus into the city. She wanted to fill in the time doing something, rather than sitting in her flat, with the spider, waiting for the time to pass.

'Good morning,' she mouthed to the Sales Manager. He was on the phone when she arrived around fifteen minutes early. He waved and gestured for her to take a seat in the showroom. She sat on one of the visitor's chairs and waited while the Sales Manager continued his conversation. She wore a pair of open-toed white-strapped patent-leather high heels. While she waited, she sat forward and started counting her perfectly pink-painted toenails back and forth. She continued to do this until she fell into a kind of trance. The more she concentrated on them, counting them forward and then back, the more ridiculous her toes became and the more her eyes watered and blurred.

She recalled the Sales Manager's speech from the day she had her interview. He said how he liked to hand-pick his sales people and how he placed a great deal of importance on team participation. She thought it important to remember his words; they may be of constructive help in her new job. 'Ruby lass, I want you to know, I like to hand-pick my sales people, and I place a great deal of importance on team participation.' He had cleared his throat as though he was about to say something profound while his eyes feasted on her body. 'It's important that when I choose a new sales executive, that I am sure she will fit in with the team spirit here. You know what I mean, be co-operative?' He looked up at her and grinned. There was no forgetting his grin. His grin unnerved her.

'Yes, I want very much to fit in,' Ruby had responded but her throat went dry. She had tried to sound as positive as she could. This had been only her second job interview in her life and she wasn't confident about what to say. At her interview, listening to him, and watching him look at her body, she suspected the worst. She worried about the wet dog smell. But in the end he had told her she could start as soon as she wanted. The spider in her stomach danced light of step.

'You won't be the first girl we've had here, the girl before did very well,' the Sales Manager said with a glazed look. 'Very well indeed, she had been cooperative. She was a quick learner.'

This gave Ruby some encouragement that she might have a chance too. The Sales Manager didn't mention why the girl was not with the company any more and he didn't use her name, she was just 'the girl'. Ruby assumed that maybe she had moved up to the big Ford dealership higher up the Great Southern Road.

Ruby sat in the chair in front of the plate glass window, waiting to start her new career. The sunshine caught her toes. The cold front had come and gone. She repeated the Sales Manager's speech several times over while she waited. She found herself assigning every word from his speech to a toe until she ran out of toes and had to start again. Feeling the warmth in her bones from the sun shining through the glass, and the blurring in her head, she could have happily sat there for the rest of her life.

I am never going to be able to do this, she thought to herself. She felt overwhelmed and stressed. She felt so alone and scared and wondered for a moment if she just shouldn't slip out the door and go home and try to vomit up the spider, and, after, crawl into bed with the teddies.

10

MADELINE

Madeline had been sitting in the cubicle for most of the morning. She had lost track of time. She accepted it was an odd place to be thinking about her life, but, on the other hand, it was as good a place as any, maybe better than most. It provided the irony necessary to dissect her life. Apart from the 'silent presence' she felt sure she had detected in the bathroom, the toilet cubicle was the one place in the world where you could be truly alone and think.

Someone entered the bathroom. Madeline stopped breathing. She heard a tap being turned on and the water running, and the sound of someone splashing themselves. An intoxicating perfume filled the entire room again. She listened. Was this the same person, drawn back to her? It seemed unlikely but still she felt deep within her a strange stillness, a connection. The tap stopped running, paper towels used and thrown in the receptacle. Madeline could hear the silence of this stranger straining to listen; again she was sure she could detect her visitor was holding her breath.

Then Madeline heard the door open letting in the white noise from the sales counters before it clicked shut. Only the dripping tap now. The perfume remained strong and exotic. It triggered memories. She recalled the days when she sprayed some of her mother's perfume on herself so she would feel grown up, but mostly to entice the boy next door.

Rhonda, the head beautician at Sheila's *Paradise Found* beauty salon, told Madeline recently, 'Your eye muscles need wegular exercise to keep the winkles at bay, so bwink.' According to the enigmatic Rhonda, so too must one's sexual encounters be remembered or they will be lost forever. Madeline wondered for a moment if her name was Rhonda or Wanda? Madeline was never sure and too embarrassed to ask, Sheila only ever called her darling, so maybe Sheila didn't know either. Anyway, Madeline thought this notion of 'use it or wose it' was a ruse to get you talking about yourself. Rhonda took her job seriously; she considered she was not only there to provide physical salve but psychological as well. She saw herself as Sheila's deputy, 2IC, if self-appointed. Madeline felt Sheila was just a little uneasy with another 'personality' in her domain, and sometimes detected a slight impatience in Sheila's voice when she spoke to Rhonda. Madeline had conjured up mental pictures of herself and her teenage sexual awakening from time to time, to avoid the risk of losing them to the daily atrophy of memory, just in case Rhonda/Wanda was right with her 'use them or wose them' theory.

'Did you know you lose brain cells every day?' Madeline said to Peter on the phone. 'It was in an article I was reading in the salon today.'

'Yes, Mother,' Peter responded while brushing fluff off his slacks in his light and immaculately clean kitchen.

'Are you brushing yourself or cleaning your kitchen?'

'What are you talkin' about?'

'But how do you know this?' Madeline wondered aloud.

'How do you know what?' Peter finished getting the fluff off, then worked the sink with a cloth to remove a water stain.

'How can you detect it, I mean? The brain cell loss. How do you know what you no longer know?'

'I don't know,' Peter said.

'It begs the question, how many answers to questions have we already lost to brain cells already sacrificed to the ageing process?'

'At least you can still remember reading the article. Who are you again?' Peter asked.

Madeline laughed at her son's remark; she wished she could laugh with him more often. 'That's twisted logic, might be one to put to Sheila next time I'm in the salon, providing of course that I remember it.'

Madeline's sexual memories worked their way back into her head. Some very clear memories, others clouded and corrupted by time. She remembered the fabulous feelings though; she had often called upon the memories of those feelings of her late teens whenever she had needed them during her marriage. Madeline flicked her head a little, as though to shake loose a memory.

When she was fifteen, she had short hair, long pale legs, plenty of freckles, bright wet eyes and no concept of death. One day she drenched herself with her mother's perfume and lured the boy next door over to her backyard. She recalled them play-wrestling on the back lawn in the fading twilight of a hot night. It was a typical mid-summer stinker, a four-day forty-degree heatwave, like a virtual advertisement for Hell. All the adults in the street had slowed down, their vigilance ebbing. The boy had tickled Madeline between her legs in a sort of not-so-innocent wrestling match. It was her first time to feel *sexy*. It took her breath away. She remembered not stopping him. She made no attempt to stop her dress riding up or her panties being lifted. She remembered the delicious heaviness as the tickling continued and became less innocent – more tickling, less wrestling. She had longed for it to happen again. She barely saw him after that night, except occasionally while riding her bike to school. She never understood his distance. It all contributed to making her cry softly each night in the dark for the rest of her life, or so it seemed at the time. Whatever happened to that boy, she wondered, where is he now, how had his life turned out? What of life's coincidences and how have they framed his outcomes? He was, through that memory, still having an effect on her life, many years later, while she sat on a toilet in Paradise. But he may have escaped Paradise, for all she knew.

Many times after that night with the boy, she went out the back after dark, when she was supposed to be in her room doing her homework. Once she took off her panties and lying down on the cool tickly lawn, with her dress up over her tummy, she looked up at the vast and magical Milky Way and felt a part of it. This was when her only demand from life was fun.

But every life has a little sadness. Madeline's was to have to wait most of her adult life before she would feel that incredible sexual feeling again. At least now she was no longer constrained by her own innocence. And not just the loss of her sexual innocence, as profound as that was for every teenager growing up. She also lost innocence the day she saw the life fade from the little girl's eye, lying on the Great Southern Road. She realised from that day of the accident, the wrestling with the boy in the backyard had been fun, but fun was not rapture. Rapture was the result of the catalytic action of the awareness of mortality on fun. This is what converted fun into rapture.

Madeline had tried to explain to Sheila the difference, that fun felt like it would last forever, while rapture, you knew wouldn't. You knew it would end, which had the effect of intensifying it. Rapture was doomed to its own little death, separated from each individual's inevitable end. Sheila scoffed and ordered her pimply assistant to bring a new colour or tint or more aluminium foil; a scoff being Sheila's retort to all thoughts philosophical that she herself hadn't advanced or didn't quite understand. The salon was after all her sovereign territory. She was the High Priestess of hair devices and exotic unctions and various mysterious paraphernalia. She was also the purveyor of clichés and home grown homilies, however twee they may be, and they were never too twee for Sheila. Sheila needed them to continue on, she needed the structure and boundaries and familiarity they provided to live in Paradise. She needed the knowing nods from the other women in the salon.

11

RUBY

The 'team', according to the Sales Manager, consisted of himself and one other salesman who had a discouraging shiny smear across his chin. The 'orientation', as the Sales Manager liked to call it, consisted of introducing her to the other salesman and showing her where the toilet was. It was a chipped yellow-painted brick outhouse at the rear of the building under a giant fig, which had several of its larger limbs missing and the stumps painted white, although one was yellow, same as the toilet. The toilet smelt of stale urine and had its own population of bloated blowflies. Strewn on the floor were several faded sex magazines of females in various poses highlighting their breasts and everything else. Ruby thought she would have to give the toilet bowl a scrub before she could use it and some disinfectant, maybe a whole bottle of disinfectant. She didn't know if she should remove the magazines or not. She thought of her toilet seat cover at home, as though this toilet seat was perhaps its real destiny.

Easy Motors was about a hundred metres north of the Daw Park Road intersection on the East Side of the road at Edwardstown – a working class, semi-industrial suburb of Paradise. Huge billboards lined the road, advertising the Minister of the Interior's latest feel-good propaganda. The Great Southern Road continued on to empty itself, with carotid mayhem, into grids of triple-fronted brick-veneer suburbs south of Tapley's Hill. Ruby never understood the suburbs of Paradise – they were like a repetitive nightmare, rows of oversized old-fashioned biscuit tin houses. They were populated by manic men wearing singlets and shorts mowing front lawns in one long line every Sunday morning and then a shimmering vista of endless car washing, and bedroom windows with drawn blinds and a pre-menstrual silence which was deafening, and, to a child in the intense fire of summer holidays, impenetrable.

The car yard, with its 'pre-owned' and 'won't last' and 'one owner' and 'beaut second car' signs in white paint on the windshields, was only two hundred metres from Ruby's Clovelly Park flat. Not far away from her childhood home in English Avenue, near where she had gone to school at the Great Southern Road Primary and then on the other side of the Great Southern Road, to her high school. Marion High School, as it was called, had been demolished. It was as though the supply of children had mysteriously dried up behind the façade of the *Paradise Trust* red brick duplexes (formerly known as State Housing Trust). They sprawled over the quadrangle that had once contained children's innocent lunchtime laughter, the methodical beat of turning skipping ropes and the thump of the boys kicking their footballs, and pungent scents of warm tomato soup or chips and pies with tomato sauce, and squishy vanilla slices.

The car yard was a far cry from her girlhood dream of one day being an elegant catwalk model. When she was little, she had always wanted to grow up and be elegant. She got this idea from the time her grandma had taken her into town during school holidays, and they walked around the cosmetic counters of the city's premier department store, David Jones. Ruby had been captivated by the ladies who sprayed exotic perfumes on her wrists and neck. She thought that day how she would love to be one of those elegant ladies. She asked her grandma if she could, and her grandma answered, 'Darling, with your looks, I wouldn't bother.' This was disappointing news because Ruby had innocently embraced the store's slogan, 'There is no other store like David Jones'. She believed this and as such, this was the place she wanted to be. To this day, whenever she got the chance, she took herself into town and meandered around the cosmetic counters allowing the girls to spray perfume on her. She then retreated to the quiet white bathroom at the end of the counters to wash her wrists and neck, so she could go back out and be sprayed again.

Earlier that morning with a few hours to fill in before she was due to start her job at the car yard, she decided to go to the department store and walk around the cosmetic counters. She still entertained her dream to work for the store. She allowed herself to be sprayed as usual, then headed for the bathroom at the end of the counters to wash the excess perfume off, just like she had done many times before. This time something happened which shocked her. She heard gentle moaning and several sighs from the end cubicle. A soft female voice repeated a shocking word over and over. Ruby couldn't move; she stayed perfectly still in fascinated silence. She held her breath and listened. She had never used this word herself and had never heard another woman use it, but it was crystal clear, echoing around the stark chamber. She was mesmerised by the repetition. Hearing it caused her skin to tingle. Then the voice stopped and Ruby left the room without exhaling. She meant to leave the store but then she did a turn around an aisle of Lancôme and Clarins. She let an ebony beauty spray her wrists. She again returned to the bathroom, as though she was compelled by some strange connection with the stranger in the cubicle. She stepped into the white silence and listened. She turned the tap on and washed her wrists. Ruby was sure she could hear faint breathing but nothing else. She strained, listening for the barest sound from the closed cubicle. She left again and walked toward the store's front doors, humming to herself the store's advertising jingle which just popped into her head, 'There's no other toilet like David Jones.' The soft moan stayed in her head long after she left. She caught a bus to the Great Southern Road and to Easy Motors, next to the crash repair shop.

12

MADELINE

Madeline examined her hand, pinching her skin under the cubicle's garish fluorescent glare.

'Skin loses its elasticity with age,' Sheila had said, reasserting herself one day when the topic had strayed too far from Sheila's control.

Madeline's skin was still pliable according to Sheila. Madeline saw no reason to doubt Sheila on this subject; it *was* after all, Sheila's specialty. Madeline stood and pulled up her black lacy knickers, adjusted her dress, and stepped out of the cubicle. She took out her red lipstick and smoothed it over her lips, careful to use the maximum, without over-doing it. In Paradise, people agreed that 'less is more', or by contrast they might say 'more is never enough' parroting the Minister of the Interior, but, for Madeline, precision was the true goal.

Madeline checked her hair, face and eyes and adjusted her yellow hat. She looked vital, she had always looked *alive*, it was one of the best things about her. Sheila was always commenting on how *vital* she looked. Madeline felt a satisfaction in her reflection. Recently, she had in fact decided that a little more makeup was okay, within the tolerances. Even her lipstick was a brighter red than she had thought to wear during her married years and with its racy name, *Sacred Scarlet*, she felt younger too. Her face was open and smooth and she had a nice smile, or so she had been told often. Funny how she had never noticed these things during her marriage, in fact not until Sheila had pointed them out to her had she any idea at all that she had a bit of the 'siren' about her, or so Sheila exclaimed. But then she heard Sheila say that to another client as well.

Madeline's now-deceased husband had been unfaithful, not only once, she discovered, but many times. It had devastated her. She looked at her face to see if she could see the devastation. She had felt so betrayed, so powerless. She tried to see the evidence of this devastation in her eyes. She thought it might be there, like a ghostly remnant. She read the graffiti on the inside of the cubicle door, 'you don't die suddenly; you die all your life'. The betrayal she resented was her husband saving his lust for other women. His sex with her was just a ritual, a function of physiology. He had deprived her of her lust.

She walked out of the restroom, through the makeup department and out into the cold swirling air of the Paradise Mall. Wind-blown people hurried past her. The day had turned grey from the earlier sunshine, and the mall was all but empty. She heard the Town Hall clock strike while she waited for the lights at Beehive Corner before crossing King William Street. She walked down Hindley Street past the many fast-food outlets and discount furniture shops, down to the Paradise Hotel. Rubbish danced around the street and bounced off gutters and gathered in bus shelters.

She checked her watch, and took a seat in the hotel's lobby. He would walk through the automatic doors any second, dressed in his leather jacket and jeans and dark sunglasses. With the light from the street behind him, she imagined he would look menacing, like celebrity sometimes does. Given the unfortunate timing of the arrival of her period, she hoped he would be satisfied with her improvisation. She felt the heat surge across her skin at the thought. She wasn't sure if she hadn't moaned again. The concierge looked over at her. Maybe she had moaned.

Just when she was succumbing to feelings of glorious abandonment, a shard of guilt pierced her heart. Madeline knew she shouldn't be in the hotel, not today. She had obligations, responsibilities. She should be on her way to Paradise Hospital; she was not only a mother and a lover, she was also a daughter. But still, she couldn't resist Steve. She was powerless to resist her body's demand for rapture. Rapture over-rode guilt without extinguishing it. Rapture made you irresponsible.

Madeline the wife or Madeline the mother, or Madeline the daughter, could never have imagined that she could be Madeline the heroine with heaving breast, embraced by a hero with square jaw and deep penetrating eyes. She was truly in love. She loved everything about Steve, even the faint smell of paint and milk he carried with him. She loved him for the determination he had to escape his difficult past. She winced at the thought of her son ever finding out his mother was sleeping with one of his school friends and she regretted the strain it would put on their already difficult relationship. Her rapture came with its own betrayal, as rapture does; the greater the betrayal, the more intense the rapture, or the guilt, or both. She walked passed a billboard featuring the words 'Paradise is Heaven', except someone had spray painted the word 'Hell' over the word 'Heaven'.

13

RUBY

The car yard was just that: it was a yard, gravelled, not concreted like most of the better yards along the Great Southern Road. Salvation Jane and yellow soursobs were establishing themselves along the edges of the yard where the gravel thinned and the weeds thrived.

Before Ruby found herself at Easy Motors, she had tried to get a job at the Ford dealership further up near Blackwood Hills Road. The modern Ford dealership had an acre of concrete for their used-car division, no gravel, and an endless supply of helium-filled balloons attached to all the cars, like mutating lollipops reproducing themselves madly along the front row. There were no weeds anywhere on the lot.

'Darlin', you're a bit on the young side for us,' the Sales Director had said, 'we only retain experienced sales staff. Maybe track back along the Great Southern Road and get some experience at one of the smaller yards first. Cut your teeth, come back in a few years, when you have learnt your trade, then we can talk. There's a future for girls like you in the automotive business. Trust me on that.' Thus raising the question of whether people are the clichés of their profession, or become the cliché forever trapped in the language of their world. Ruby felt that this man had a quiet underlying disappointment in himself, like he might have wanted to be a doctor or a lawyer, or an architect, but life conspired to make him a Sales Director selling cars instead.

He had said 'automotive' automatically, as though avoiding the term 'car sales'. And when he said 'girls like you' Ruby had felt uneasy. He possessed a smile which Ruby was later to appreciate as something common amongst 'automotive' salesmen. She would spend several fruitless hours in front of her mirror trying to effect the smile in case it was an important plank of a car salesperson's armoury. But that smile, that particular smile, was inaccessible to her. She had to settle with trying to fake it.

As Ruby walked out of the Ford dealership lot, one of the balloons exploded near her. She noticed it caused a sudden panic and loss of bravado amongst the salesmen standing nearby, as though their fortunes were inexorably dependent on the balloons.

'Sorry,' she mouthed to them and hurried off. As she left the lot, a playful wind rushed about the cars and the salesmen's baggy pants.

That cloudy day, she had walked down the Great Southern Road in the hope that a car yard opportunity would present itself, but her energy dissipated. Her head was light and flushed as she scurried down to the suburb of St Mary's, past English Avenue towards the less salubrious car yards.

This part of the Great Southern Road was the area of her childhood and she recalled how her childhood had been about being alone, and really nothing much had changed. Ruby realised early in life that she had never felt truly connected to either of her parents, at least not at the same time. It was as though they took it in turns with her. Her father doted on her during her childhood. He played with her whenever he wasn't reading or at work. But he became awkward and distant with her as she left her childhood behind. Her mother then took over as she entered puberty and developed her figure. It was as though Ruby had been a baton passed between them as she grew up. She missed her childhood when her father had loved her and protected her. Those were innocent times. Those were safe times. Those were spiderless times.

When things ended with Todd, her parents were sympathetic, but as always there was something in them which bordered on disinterest. She wanted to resent them for it but it wasn't in her. She felt sorry for them and for herself. She wanted them to understand that it was not so much Todd's silly car accident that had upset her, but the memory it brought back. The memory of the day when as an innocent nine-year-old girl, she was splattered in blood.

That was the day when she felt she met the face of death. She gripped the pole, her hand covered in a spider's web. Death looked into her soul and had settled there, and had taken the form of the spider. Ruby felt that in Paradise, death was ever present in life, as if you were never meant to get comfortable. It amazed her how matter-of-factly people of Paradise accepted death. Perhaps it was because they had never seen it like she had. A popular saying emerged after the name change, 'there is only one way out of Paradise, Angel.' This was said with good cheer, as though it was a good thing.

After leaving the Ford dealership, she found herself standing at the exact spot where she had witnessed the girl's death. It was in front of the electrical appliance store, opposite the small supermarket where she had worked for the past four years. She paused and stood at the kerb. She would always remember how shocked she was by the weight of the blood. It felt like someone had thrown a hot wet overcoat on her and made her schoolgirl legs buckle. She gripped the pole of the bus shelter in exactly the same position Peter's mother had helped her to do, while they all watched the accident unfold and the life force leave the body on the road.

Across the road, through the glass pane of the bus shelter, Ruby was unaware that someone was watching her and that he had shadowed her down from the Ford dealership.

After she broke up with Todd, and probably because of it, and after the incident on her sixteenth birthday behind the chook shed with the dolphin and the two boys (one of whom was Hawkey from the crash repair place next to Easy Motors, where she had gone to borrow the ladder to paint her ceilings, and the other was Peter, who did not kiss her), she quit school. She got a job at the small independent supermarket and moved away from home. She found her little one bedroom flat in Clovelly Park in the street behind the supermarket, like it had been there all the time waiting for her. It was flat three. The building was an older style, red-bricked construction, comprising ten flats. The building gave off an air of being exhausted like it was disappointed with its tenants, or perhaps resigned to them. Ruby had little to do with the other tenants; they, like her, lived alone and, by unspoken protocol, agreed on no excessive interaction. Everyone kept themselves to themselves. She thought one of them was not well. She often heard someone labouring up the stairs with heavy stertorous breathing. Other than that, the only contact she had with any of the tenants was when she might occasionally see them on the stairs or at the letterboxes. On these occasions the most that might pass between them would be a nod, or maybe nothing, as though both parties agreed to acknowledge the presence of the other by no gesture at all, but even this she found exhausting. She noticed in the stairwell a pungent lemon odour. She assumed it was one of the tenants' after-shave. She ran the tenants through her thoughts and tried to figure out which one might have given her the book of poems; she wanted to offer her smile, but none of them seemed likely. There was also the odd cat, and an older woman who dressed rather eccentrically, Ruby thought.

She was a friendly woman though and always smiled at Ruby whenever they passed on the stairs. Also, there were some suspicious dark stains on one of the landings. The building had been designated for rejuvenation by the government. She couldn't help but sense the building, like its tenants, would have preferred to be left alone.

Inside her flat, the low beige ceiling forced her to breathe shallowly, as though the ceiling was squashing the air from the room. The best thing about the building was the grapevine hanging along the handrails; Ruby sat for hours on the cool concrete outside steps peeling and eating grapes all through the summer and flicking at the occasional fly. She counted the number of bricks with cracks in them and then counted the number of bricks without cracks in them, then counted the number of cracks around the bricks. And sometimes, using model aeroplane glue, she mended any of her toys that had become a little worse for wear. She lifted her skirt to tan her legs in the Paradise sun and with a plastic basin of warm water and soap, a towel and pink nail polish, she meticulously attended to her toes.

She couldn't afford the flat on her wages, as inexpensive as it was; she managed it because her father gave her the money.

'Where will you live?' he asked her.

'I have found a flat in Clovelly Park, will you come and see it?'

She cried the day she moved away from her home. She couldn't be sure but maybe there was a distant tear in her father's eyes too. She hoped as much.

She was lucky at sixteen to get a job only a five-minute walk from her flat at the local supermarket. She often stood in the bus shelter opposite the supermarket, and let the memories flood back; she only vaguely knew the girl who had died in the accident. They had paired once as lunch monitors but never spoke again. But to this day the smell of hot chips reminded her of the girl. They were in different houses. Ruby was in Celeste and the girl in Eyre. Ruby remembered the accident like a punctuation point in her life. It was a hot day, an inferno of searing Paradise heat. The kind of day, Ruby remembered, when the tar melted and stuck to the bottom of her school shoes and beads of sweat ran down the small of her back under her school dress, then dried in the burning sun. It was the kind of day when concentration was sucked away into the simmering glare. That day, Ruby had stood on the footpath waiting to cross the busy Great Southern Road. Something made her hesitate. She heard the screech, and felt the hot blood splatter over her. She recalled Peter's mother standing next to her wearing a yellow hat. Peter's mother stared at her, looking directly into her eyes. Ruby wanted to disappear into her adult arms but the woman turned away and wrapped her arms around her son on her right. Peter was in Ruby's class. His mother covered his face and comforted him. She only managed to reach out to Ruby, grasp her hand and guide it to the bus shelter pole, so Ruby could steady herself. The spider's web attached to the pole felt thick and sticky and held on to her hand. Ruby was so grateful for Peter's mother's help, without it she felt for sure, she would fall forward onto the girl. Ruby was covered in the blood – a nine-year-old girl covered in another nine-year-old girl's blood. She stood motionless and saw the life drain from the girl; the body looked warm and peaceful to her. She felt the tug on her own life. The dead girl's life was dragging Ruby's with it, as though all lives were joined in one long white line, in an unbroken chain, from Paradise to Heaven or maybe some other place. She felt desperate. She wanted her own mother to be there and hold on to her and stop her from sliding away. But this did not happen. Ruby had felt connected to Peter's mother in a way she had not felt connected to her own mother, and Ruby wished often after that day that somehow she might see Peter's mother again.

These days there was no trace of anything on the bitumen where the accident had happened, nothing to remind anyone that a life had ended there, except the faded yellow paint of the pedestrian crossing, which appeared soon after the accident. Ruby had always felt an overwhelming sense of sadness and loss for this girl she hardly knew. Ruby remembered the girl was a triplet. She wondered if that was the point of triplets, so you had one spare you could lose, two in an emergency. This made her feel vulnerable as an only child. She never stopped wondering what might have become of that girl if she had not died that day. What life would she have lived in Paradise? It could have been Ruby who died that day, it was only a step, a second of time and Ruby might have been the one lying on the bitumen with blood flowing from her skull. On that hot dreadful day, the girl's life stopped and Ruby's life continued, forever infected by the rippling of butterfly wings of the girl's ebbing life.

14

MADELINE

Madeline's phone vibrated. She checked the message and felt a sense of foreboding when she saw Steve's name on the screen. He was late, so maybe he was just letting her know. She looked at the message, *Can't make it, sorry Madeline. Steve.* Something inside her slumped as she read the text. Tears appeared in her eyes; she didn't know why but she felt like someone had kicked her in the stomach. It was stupid to think the worse like this, she assured herself, it was just a phone message, but she couldn't help her emotions. Maybe he was just simply held up; maybe it was nothing to worry about. He had reverted to the formality of her full name when he normally called her Maddy. She phoned him but it went straight to message bank. She didn't leave a message. She couldn't think of what to say. She sent him a text to ask if anything was wrong and then she waited, but her phone remained silent and motionless. She wished she hadn't sent the text. Madeline's depth of love for Steve had flourished under his careful tenderness toward her. She tried to hold back and be more measured but the more she tried, the more in love she fell. She knew it was dangerous. For a start there was the considerable age difference between them, and then there was the worrying business of how Peter was going to react. It wasn't only the difference in age, it was more that Peter and Steve had been friends at high school. She had no idea how Peter might react to this news. She was in limbo now, should she read anything into Steve's message? It was all so difficult.

Madeline thought she had sat in the hotel lobby long enough and felt the need to get out. She hurried away from the hotel; after all, she had pressing duties elsewhere. But as she hailed a taxi, she felt the discomfort of hope – a threatening black sky of disappointment. She could only hope it would last with Steve but she always knew what a dangerous landscape life was, when it relied on hope. But hope was the only choice in Paradise.

Madeline wiped the snot from her father's nose. She listened to the ping of the heart monitor and the rhythmic whoosh of the breathing apparatus as though his life, such as it now was, no longer cared for its accommodations but had relocated itself to the machinery keeping his body going. For the moment, it continued to remain in contact via the various tubes entering him at a number of junctures but threatened to, at any minute, disengage itself and perhaps wander the corridors of the hospital looking for some other more substantial body in which to reside. Madeline felt a constant panic that every whoosh of the machine or every ping of the heart monitor might be her father's last.

Madeline's father was dying; in fact, the doctors had already told her to expect the worst. A massive stroke had rendered him depleted of any chance of life. He had been in a coma now for ten days, and the doctors hadn't expected him to last this long.

'I've met someone, Dad.' She had been on her way to finally say these words to him over a week ago, having delayed it for so long. By the time she had built up enough courage to make the announcement, he had collapsed at his rifle club and been in a coma ever since. A part of Madeline was relieved as she dreaded telling him about her life. Of course he would have disapproved; not that he would have necessarily disapproved of the fact that she was dating a man the same age as her son Peter; he would have disapproved of her no matter what she did or didn't do. He was disappointed with her in much the same way as he breathed. It was automatic, his default setting with his daughter. He had even blamed her for her ex-husband's death, which had occurred when her husband had fallen off his desk while screwing his secretary. Madeline sensed that even though her father was now in a deep coma, he was still disappointed with her. She could smell it on him.

She tidied his blanket. 'He is half my age, in fact; he is the same age as Peter. I love him and he, I think and hope, loves me. I think we are going to make a go of it, Dad.' She spoke to him with confidence; unlike the way she spoke to him throughout her life, which was more like a scared little girl, even though for most of her life now, she had been an adult. He was unconscious and unable to answer. The doctors said it can sometimes help to talk to coma patients. She couldn't see how her talking to him could help, even if he could understand, he couldn't answer. This empowered her. She felt a little guilty because she still loved him, even though he had made her life miserable with his constant disapproval. She told him all about Steve but leaving out the text message and her dread that even as she spoke, the relationship with Steve might already be over.

'Peter said he would be in to visit with you later today, when he is finished work.' She sat back and sighed. Not only was her life marching toward a similar end to her father's, but due to his stroke and imminent death, she had to face the fact that she was next in the natural order of things. Her mother had died years ago, but she always felt that while her father was still alive, she was shielded from her own end.

She picked up her mobile and checked for any messages from Steve. There was a message from Sheila reminding her she had an appointment tomorrow. She waited in the antiseptic world of her father's private room for her phone to vibrate a message. None came.

15

RUBY

At the supermarket, Ruby was employed to stack shelves and take her turn on the checkouts. It was boring but it suited her for her first job. She was fresh out of high school and had few skills to offer any employer. She had started some night classes in administration and basic bookkeeping. After about a week, the Manager led her out to the stock room and gave her some tea.

'Ruby.' He stared at her, which she found calming. There was a lot about him that reminded her of her father. He was calm, authoritative and quite handsome. He liked to say her name. He spoke little, sometimes about the supermarket business, sometimes about how he had been promoted to Manager so early in his career. He looked away from her eyes. He looked at a pallet of tomato soup cans as he spoke. She sat in the cool silence of the pallets of stock. She felt guilty that her condiments section wasn't getting the attention it needed. She thought of the sauces and tins of vegetables that need replenishing. She thought of the gaps in her aisle.

Sitting there, she wondered if he might like to look at her toes. It was cool and dark in the stock room with the occasional shafts of light through the cracks from the ceiling and a blinding strip of white light from under the roller door at the loading dock. She glared at it and let the light take over her mind.

They met like this usually once but sometimes twice a week. He asked if he could hold her hand. It seemed to be all that was required of her. It usually lasted for an hour. She enjoyed her time away from the checkouts. She introduced one rule in regard to this ritual with the manager. Her section had to be fully faced – no gaps. On occasions during these times with him and between his long silences, she closed her eyes and thought of her dark stranger and for a precious moment or two she was free of the spider and so she allowed his searching hesitant fingers access to her. She stopped going to her night classes, even though she was doing well.

She, in effect, became the de facto manager of the supermarket. It fell to her to order the stock, manage the warehouse, organise the roster and to hold the Manager's hand a couple of times each week.

She recalled a conversation she had with her mother when she was given her new black bra.

Ruby tried not to think too much about herself as a sexual attraction, but as her mother had warned, she got used to the way all men looked at her and spoke to her and only occasionally did she take enough notice to get irritated by it.

Of course, the only male, apart from her father, who hadn't treated her like that was Todd; apparently, as it turned out, with good reason. Some of Ruby's parents' friends had at one time or another showed her special attention, especially when they had drunk too much at Christmas time, or other street get-togethers. They threatened they would reveal her to be sexually precocious if she dared to mention their behaviour. The men sometimes offered her money. But such threats and gestures were unnecessary; she couldn't see much point in protesting or telling her mother. She was quite sure her mother wouldn't have wanted to know. Ruby felt her mother would hold the good relations with the neighbours as paramount and would have blamed Ruby for causing trouble. But the real reason she remained silent was that she wouldn't want her father to find out. She still wanted to be his little princess.

Even though she felt uncomfortable about all this, she still never understood everyone's guilt. Body parts touching other body parts; it was only flesh and didn't seem that big a deal to Ruby. She had seen the girl lying on the road, dead, just a body, just meat, just road kill, nothing more, alive one second and dead the next. An animal tearing at the flesh of the young body on the road sometimes flashed across her thoughts.

In spite of the sexual interest Ruby caused, she somehow managed to remain a virgin until her sixteenth birthday, and even then, she still remained technically a virgin, but that's another story involving Hawkey, his friend Peter, and a dolphin. She found out early in her teenage life that there were secret ways to defer men from their insistences; ways her mother had described to her in the 'birds and the bees' talk she was given in her early teens, although much of this subject had been well and truly

63

covered in the school-yard. Ruby felt grateful to her mother, she knew her mother was doing her best to protect her daughter as Ruby developed into a young woman. After Ruby's first period her mother had put her on the pill and provided condoms, but Ruby never had a need for them. She could calm anyone who became insistent. She deferred having intercourse; she wanted to wait for when she might find someone she loved. Ruby entertained a romantic hope for her life. Unfortunately for Ruby, her first love was Todd, or so she thought at the time. The preparation Ruby had arranged in advance of sex with Todd was a waste of time.

The day after Ruby's fifteenth birthday, Ruby was taken into the master bedroom. It was the first time Ruby had been in her parents' bedroom for years, since she was a little girl and would run in and jump on her father on cold winter mornings. The room looked smaller than she had remembered. It was too pink, she thought. Her mother sat her on the satin bedspread and opened the bottom drawer next to the bed and pulled out a small dolphin toy. Ruby held it for a moment and thought it lovely, if a little worse for wear. It had lost most of its paint and felt oily.

'You know what this is, don't you?' Her mother asked, taking it from Ruby.

'Yes,' Ruby answered, as confidently as she could. It's a dolphin, Ruby thought, and wondered why her mother had asked her such a question.

Her mother pulled a tissue out of the box on the bedside drawers and rubbed the dolphin.

'It's in the bottom drawer, okay? You can use it any time you like, you understand?'

'Yes.' Ruby watched her mother place it back in the bottom drawer.

'You mustn't tell Daddy, though. It's best not to, he would only get angry, he doesn't understand things like I do. He still thinks you are his little girl, he doesn't see you are turning into a young woman. Get dressed now love, Daddy might be home any minute, and we don't want to have to explain things to him, do we?'

Ruby never used the dolphin until her sixteenth birthday when she needed it for a very specific purpose. It had a small motor in it. It was operated by turning its tail and this made its head vibrate.

After the news that Todd was a homosexual had circulated through school, Ruby cried for a few hours but then just stopped. He spent a long time in hospital with his leg suspended. Ruby visited him with a tray of teacakes she had baked for him but he told her not to come again. She thought she loved him and wanted to love him even more, but didn't know how. When it was over, her immediate feeling of loss turned into a kind of numbness; mere tears seemed pointless. She stopped crying just as abruptly as she had started. Her parents took this to suggest she wasn't as distressed as they feared.

For reasons Ruby couldn't understand, the break-up with Todd was like a death to her. She was flooded with feelings she couldn't explain, feelings that related back to the death of the schoolgirl. It was though her reaction to the girl's death had remained inside her, and only found a way out when Todd rejected her. Ruby's mother saw she was struggling emotionally and arranged for Ruby to see a psychologist whose particular speciality, as it turned out, was grief.

'I feel sometimes like my own life is dead in some way… like the dead girl's,' Ruby said, trying hard not to be over-dramatic.

'Really, how interesting.' The counsellor responded and made notes on her pad.

'It's a bit like I have to creep silently about in my life, so as not to disturb the…' She stopped and let her voice fade off. Right then, she decided not to mention the spider. It all seemed so complicated, requiring too much energy to sort through. 'I try to keep things simple, it is best for me to do that. Do you find that too?' She didn't tell the counsellor, but she felt as though she had lost her feelings, that they had somehow been pulled through her that day when the girl died in front of her. Holding on to the bus shelter only prevented her physical self from being dragged off. She knew, although she never discussed it with the counsellor, that she had always felt a dull aching guilt over the death of the girl. She couldn't say why, but maybe it was because it all happened so slowly. She saw it happening but she remained frozen and did nothing to stop it. She didn't even yell out a warning and after, it seemed to Ruby, there had been plenty of time to prevent it, but that she had been too fascinated by it all to do anything to help. When the car blurred, it rolled over the young girl and ripped her dress from her frail white body. Ruby saw each stitch of her school uniform tear one after the other in slow motion. She felt a strange happy satisfaction as she watched. She gazed at the young thighs and felt a strange but warm and pleasant sensation through her body. She could never tell this to the counsellor.

Ruby had continued to visit the counsellor every week for most of her life now; it was a habit, some kind of ritual that had taken on importance but not in any way that resolved her life. Ruby realised that in recent years, she had seen more of the counsellor than her own mother. In turn the counsellor seemed happy to continue to see Ruby as though it was of some comfort to her also.

'Do you have a twin or a triplet?' she asked the counsellor.

She had met up with Todd as agreed later on the day of her sixteenth birthday. She offered herself to him. This had been her plan. It would be her first time to have intercourse. She had made considerable preparations for the event, which had involved the dolphin and the two boys from her school. So she was ready for Todd but it all backfired and Todd laughed at her and then ran away. He ended up that day in the car, which crashed into a tree. Ruby couldn't help but feel that she had initiated this outcome. Apparently, apart from his physical injuries, Todd had to be induced to vomit so as to retrieve the driver's penis he had bitten off and swallowed whole during the impact of the accident. After a thorough wash and some pampering causing the rogue penis to stiffen opportunistically (as the story goes), it was returned to its owner, but rumour had it, the surgeon sewed it back on slightly turned, so it looked a bit like a corkscrew. Thus the boy's reputation for being a 'great screw' became legendary. Even Todd's reputation took on a new dimension. Jokes about Todd being a 'swallower', or 'when Todd swallows, you better hold on to a bus shelter', or 'what's the definition of a girl? answer, a guy who Todd has sucked off', or 'watch out, if Todd breathes in, he could suck the paint off a car', 'fur off a cat', 'fingerprints off a hand' etc.... As much as this amused the entire student body and many of the teachers, it only served to remind Ruby of her obsolescence in Todd's life and that this had been ever so.

She wondered where the little dolphin was. She wanted to have it in her collection. It was a symbol of her youth, perhaps of her innocence, or the loss of her innocence. But she never saw it again after the day behind the chook shed when she had wanted so much for Peter to kiss her. It was a gradual realisation that she was actually in love with Peter and not Todd but by the time she had figured this out, Peter was out of her life.

But all that was a long time ago now. Ruby had just started her new job at Easy Motors. She had business cards. She loved her business cards. They made her feel as though she had achieved something; that she was import-ant in some small way. She mailed a couple off to her parents, but couldn't think of anyone else to send any to. If she knew who had given her the English poetry book, she would have sent him one. She even thought of sending one to Hawkey at the crash repairer's next to Easy Motors, but decided against it.

Her first week at the car yard had come to an end. She hadn't sold any cars, she hadn't even spoken to anyone but she had watched and learnt from the other salesman and the Sales Manager and she was eager to make her mark, although she was worried she might not be able to. She concluded that her own smile would have to be sufficient. It was Friday night and the week had left her exhausted so she made a cup of hot Milo, showered, got into her pyjamas and snuggled into bed with her poetry book. She was excited about her new career as a Used Car Sales Executive for Easy Motors and she dared to think that it might be the beginning of something hopeful. 'You have your whole life in front of you,' she said out loud, 'and now you have a great opportunity to be bold,' she reminded her teddies. Before she had finished one whole page of poetry, and drunk half her Milo, she was sound asleep with the trace of a smile on her lips. And at that moment, also with a smile, the spider sat motionless, crouched and ready.

She found him hanging in silence from a rope tied to the staircase railing. She found him circling and warm. She collapsed on the cold marble, like her skeleton had failed her. He was pronounced dead at the scene.

PART TWO

16

PETER

Peter stood in his compact, well-designed Nu-Paradise® galley kitchen staring at his dishes (one white plate, one white cup). He had just hand washed them; it wasn't worth bothering Mr Dishwasher with two items. He leant against the white wall of his kitchen and looked out into the sunlit jasmine-scented internal courtyard garden while tussling with the notion of whether to dry or let drain.

Peter had superhuman powers and he wanted a woman. Not just any woman, but a mate with whom to live happily ever after. Peter was the kind of man who was built to pair for life, like swans or whichever animals and birds did this. Unfortunately, he'd already had two chances, two perfect examples of female womanhood (one of Ryan's often used tautological descriptions of the fairer sex) and he'd lost both of them; losing one was unfortunate but losing two, as the famous sentiment goes, was bordering on the careless. He lost Ruby when he was a teenager; he was devastated by this event and perhaps never fully recovered from it. Of course he was a teenager at the time, and he knew nothing of how you went about wooing and capturing a young woman's heart – not that he could claim much more wisdom in this area of life as an adult; proven by the fact that he had lost Belinda as well. He had no idea why she left. She had shown every indication of being blissfully happy. They both were. Then she vanished. Peter's superhuman powers were not the kind that enabled him to wear a terrific red cape, save the world wearing his underwear as outerwear and be rewarded by winning the girl's heart. His superpowers were more to do with his ability to see his own shortcomings. He had crystal clear X-ray vision when it came to identifying his faults. Sadly though, his superhuman powers had abandoned him in regard to figuring out why Belinda had left. He looked down and noticed a tiny mark on his shirt; he frowned, but not just at the mark. He frowned at a world where the moment you put on a freshly laundered and ironed shirt, life conspires and synchronicity cuts in and of all the places a splash can go, it just has to land on your clean shirt as if the two totally unrelated events are, in fact, related. Peter checked the mark in his reflection in the toaster and looked at his face. He had black hair, deep brown eyes, a sharp jaw and clear skin. He had no freckle legacy from Madeline's genetic pool, but he was the recipient of his father's matinee looks – or so he had been told by his mother many times. This gave him comfort on one level but caused him to frown on another; he wanted no legacy from his father. Nonetheless, none of this or any other redeeming quality he may possess was getting him any closer to finding a mate for life.

'You can never find what you are looking for' and 'everything you want you already have'. Two overworked platitudes used by Madeline and Ryan (parroting Madeline) to sum up Peter's dilemma. He understood they both were trying to be helpful but all they achieved was to increase his level of frustration exponentially. He didn't mention it but it did seem to have escaped both of them, his mother and his best friend, that they too were without a partner in their respective lives.

He watched the nurse in the apartment opposite iron her uniform; Peter had watched her perform this ritual many times. Life goes on, with restrictions, with caveats, with indifference, even at times with joy but it goes on. He re-focused on the dishes and made the only decision available to him, he decided to dry. He could never leave the dishes half done, or anything else for that matter; he could not live with loose ends and this is why not looking for Belinda and asking her for an explanation was so out of character for him.

Peter lived in a modern flat in North Paradise opposite a park where the most peculiar trees grew. Peter was an architect. He was considered by his firm to have excellent prospects, although it was still early days in his career at City and Urban Architects Inc. His company's main business came from government contracts, working under the mandate of tenders for PERP, a paradoxical acronym standing for 'Paradise Environment Renewal Program'. Ryan found it amusing that any place called 'Paradise' should need a renewal program. Pointing this out to Peter or indeed, anyone he came across, was Ryan's current obsession.

Peter was working on the new wing of the Paradise Mental Health Hospital, which according to the Minister of the Interior would be the best Mental Health facility in the world. Peter mused on the fact that only a politician would fail to see the incongruity of on the one hand naming a city Paradise, and then making a case for the urgent need to build a modern best practice Mental Health Hospital in which to lock up its troubled citizens. Notwithstanding this, Peter loved his job and he enjoyed working on the project. The partners of the firm were also pleased with the project; at the regular end-of-week Friday night drinks in the boardroom, the partners and associates congratulated themselves on the good works they were doing for the people of Paradise – albeit the ones that needed locking up. The enormous profits the company made out of this work were never overtly mentioned. Peter rarely stayed any longer than was strictly necessary at these functions. He wasn't very good at that particular form of small talk. He was savvy enough to acknowledge that in the long run, this deficiency might work against his career prospects with the firm but in the end, he couldn't help the way he felt and reacted. He had always harboured the ambition to perhaps one day start his own practice, but at his age and stage of his career, there was plenty of time for all that.

In the meantime, he could slip on his red cape and fly around a bit putting wrongs to rights. He could start with the Minister of the Interior, who seemed to spend quite a bit of time in the firm's executive offices and who lived a few streets away from Peter in North Paradise. The Minister was a man whom Peter described to Ryan as having purchased his smile from a used car salesman, given that his own was entirely transparent.

Peter was the kind of person who held himself responsible for everything. Or at least this was the 'gospel according to Ryan'. According to Ryan, Peter never limited his sense of responsibility to only those things within his personal control, but he included almost anything you could think of. Ryan accused Peter of an endless capacity to be concerned. Peter naturally denied this but couldn't help but feel, well, concerned over Ryan's observation; maybe there was some truth to it and if there was, that was concerning. Q.E.D., as Ryan was fond of saying. Of course Peter recognised the game and generously played into Ryan's trap, for the sake of their history, for Ryan's sake and for all the right reasons in respect to the rules of friendship. They'd been friends since pre-school, having met in the sandbox and immediately begun fighting over the only fire truck available. Ryan liked to be the world authority on all things Peter. That was Ryan's role. Peter's role was to let him.

'I am your only friend, do you know that?' Ryan intimated this was a bad thing. They had this conversation last Sunday night at Romeo and Juliet's, a neighbourhood wine bar. These conversations, like most of their observations about each other and life in Paradise in general, took place after more wine or beer had been consumed than was strictly optimal.

'You were the only one who answered the ad,' Peter countered.

'Don't you think you should have more friends though, don't you think that that isn't healthy? Don't think your mother hasn't worried about that too.' Ryan had mastered the use of the double negative; sometimes, depending on how many beers he had consumed, he could roll out triples and quadruples.

'I have never given the thought much thought. I suppose if I wanted more friends, I would have them. Maybe I am quite contented having just the one.' The one being Ryan, who it must be said was no cakewalk. Who was, in his own words, 'high maintenance'. Actually, Peter thought Ryan liked to think of himself this way, but in reality he wasn't as high maintenance as he thought, nothing like it. Ryan was lanky. He was all arms and legs and gave the impression he was not worried about anything, but of course that wasn't the case. His hair was prodigious and he preened it often but more as a nervous tick than the obsessive need to have it perfect. The attraction of girls dominated his conversation. But this was a ruse, Ryan was only interested in one girl, the perfect girl for him and he never stopped looking for her. He was a lot like Peter in this respect.

'What do you think women think of a guy who only has one friend? They think loner, loser, limp. You get it?' Ryan guzzled the rest of his beer.

'Do they?' Peter responded. 'I don't see you surrounded by a hoard of alliterating friends of either gender.'

'Yeah well it's a full-time job lookin' after you and besides, I drive a cab for a living. When people are out making friends, I'm droppin' drunks off in Hindley Street, so they can purchase a friend for a hundred bucks an hour, or two for one seventy five each including champagne.'

'Such is the cost of love,' Peter said.

'Love is extra. Anyway, I was just sayin' is all, it'd take the pressure off me.' Ryan slurred this out, the beer having taken over his mouth muscles.

'I'll keep it in mind, 'nother beer?' Peter picked up Ryan's empty.

Peter started to head for the bar.

'No need to do anything drastic of course,' Ryan yelled after him.

'No, I wasn't intending to.'

'Well, good.'

'Yeah, beer or no beer, or have we had enough?' Peter stopped and mouthed back through the closing gap of people between him and Ryan.

'Does the pope have a tarmac fetish?' Ryan yelled a little louder than was strictly necessary and this resulted in attracting the odd derisory look. 'And don't waste your time with the barmaid; she's in love with me.' He smiled at the few girls who had turned to check him out and ignored the men who were also glancing in his direction.

'Good for you, I'll give her a wide berth.' Peter countered. 'I bet she just can't get enough loud drunks in her life.'

'Absobloodylutely, why else would you be a barmaid?' Ryan responded, proud of his wit given his current alcoholic haze. He suddenly developed an alarming wobble in his left knee. He looked at his knee, as if looking at it might reveal its problem; nothing seemed evident, so Ryan looked back at the room full of people in case anyone might be checking him out – none were. His knee settled.

Dry or drain. Drain or dry. Peter allowed himself the luxury of tussling with this question, even though he had already dried them and put them away. However, for a moment he considered the proposition of dry or drain as a metaphorical question of the million such questions presented to any individual during any day, upon which a decision is required, and on which fate turns. These questions are never the most profound questions of the universe but then perversely, that's how life is, even in Paradise, Peter thought. When it all boiled down, life was a bunch of small questions requiring small decisions. It wasn't for the ordinary to ponder the extraordinary; there was enough to do to wrestle with the everyday. He had heard someone say, perhaps it was his mother, that none of the big answers can be found with profound deep thought, only bigger questions, and the more deeply you think about anything, the less sense it makes. In fact, Peter had argued this very question with Ryan after the usual number of beers at Romeo's last Sunday night.

'It's not for the ordinary to ponder the extraordinary; there is enough to do to wrestle with the everyday,' Peter mused.

'You can leave serious deep thought to me, I'm the cab driver,' Ryan responded, cruising the room with his eyes. 'Stick to your knitting, that's what I always say.'

'This would be the cliché fall-back solution?'

'Trust me, clichés work, so long as you don't over use them.' Ryan laughed at himself. Peter nodded acknowledgement, raising an eyebrow at Ryan's joke.

'But isn't that how they become clichés?' Peter countered then continued with his discourse. 'Of course, the big questions of life might well find their answers in the small questions. Get the small questions right and the big ones will take care of themselves, or not, depending on how many beers one has had. Take architecture for example.' Peter often regaled Ryan with the parallels between the business of architecture and life in Paradise. This was in spite of Ryan's abject disinterest in such matters, or any matter that was not pertaining to the attraction and bedding of the beautiful Paradise angels who frequented Romeo's on such a Sunday evening as this.

'As with life, in architecture,' Peter said, 'it is the little things that count, the detail. They count for form and function. It is the endless small components that make the whole greater than its parts.' Ryan yawned with affectation but without much expectation that Peter would, or even could, be dissuaded from his topic. 'Take life in Paradise for example,' Peter was now running his words together in a beer induced pidgin form of the language, 'wearejustfrecklesinthevastcosmic…' Ryan nudged Peter in the ribs and indicated a sighting.

'Angel at nine o'clock, check her out, she is stunning, how do I look?' Ryan had the habit of preening himself in anything shiny, this time it was Peter's beer glass.

'You look like a freckle to me, about to make a complete idiot of yourself,' Peter answered.

'Be brave and great powers will come to your aid, read that in the *Reader's Digest*.' Ryan recited this under his breath a couple of times before launching himself in the direction of the unsuspecting angel. Peter just watched and waited, safe in the knowledge that if previous outcomes were anything to go by, Ryan would be back in about two minutes and in time for his shout. One thing you had to admire about Ryan was that he never gave up or lost hope that one day he would meet the girl he would marry.

'Right, my shout I think.' Two minutes had passed and Ryan returned, grabbing Peter's glass, and headed back toward the barmaid.

Ryan plonked the beers on the table in front of Peter. 'How'd you go with the barmaid then?' Peter asked sympathetically.

'She was busy, I got the barman instead.'

'Oh. How'd you go with the barman then?' Peter asked.

'Huh! The bastard turned me down.' They looked at each other for a split second, laughed and toasted each other with their beers.

Peter was credited with good problem-solving skills in his work. The more complex the problem, the better he was at finding a solution, but then, he found the simplest questions of life could be unfathomable. Sometimes, the little decisions paralysed him; like what approach should be used to capture the interests of a woman at Romeo's that doesn't render you a boorish fool. He had met Belinda at Romeo's but that had been a total accident and as such, an exceptional situation. On his way to the bar to get another round, he tripped over her bag and fell heavily at her feet. On the way down, his head hit her knee and the blow had knocked him out. He woke in hospital with her at his side and that is where she stayed, by his side, up until the day she vanished. Obviously, he couldn't repeat that again, even though Ryan had thought it was as good a plan as any, maybe better than most.

Peter sometimes sat in silence in the fading light of his apartment and considered how the endless thread of the 'fall' continues to colour life. You fall from grace, you fall in love, you fall head over heels in love, you fall out of love (or Belinda did), you fall into a deal, or a house, or a car you never expected to find and so on. It seems a lot of the turning points in life come from the synchronicity of the ubiquitous fall. He thought this might be new ground for discussion with Ryan when next they were at Romeo's. It was the kind of philosophical examination Ryan hated as it distracted him from the job of meeting girls. Not that Ryan ever met any, but then as he often complained, how could he with Peter rabbiting on about life etcetera – according to Ryan, this was a total girl turnoff.

17

HAWKEY/STEVE

Hawkey sat in a grey room looking at the sign on the wall, which read, *If you lie to your Psychologist, you are still telling the truth*. He waited for Doctor Robert Reynolds to come in and sit in his big leather chair, hit the button on his timer to start the half hour session and save Hawkey's life. Hawkey had a story, and he was about to tell it to Doctor Reynolds, the consequence of which would be that the good doctor would dispense a few a-huhs and couple of hmms and then some predictable pyschobabble advice. Hawkey had sat in front of many psychologists, including the one in Paradise jail, but that was only to get an hour free a week from being someone's 'girl-friend', which was the reason he had developed the story in the first place. It was also the reason for the content, essence and the intimate loop.

Hawkey respected his own story, so he didn't mind repeating it, although he no longer needed it, as he had long ago left jail, and would never return. He thought his story unique, and he hoped imaginative and complex. He had made every attempt to avoid the narrative trap of complication for the sake of it and felt that he had by and large achieved that objective even though the story was made up. Although, no fiction is entirely made up, there must always be an element of truth to it – but as any author will argue, you can't tell the raw truth, no one would believe it, you have to water the truth down, you have to fictionalise the truth – so except for the bits that weren't made up, which was most of it, Hawkey's story of buggery was still a work of fiction and thus contained many truths. Hawkey loved the rolling vistas of logic and paradox. If he had had his way, Paradise would not be the name for the city; Paradox would have been his choice. Anyway, Hawkey believed his life was his own doing, and no one could argue, himself included, that up to his jail time, he had fucked it up. So in spite of the good intentions of Doctor Robert, Hawkey had his own agenda. He loved his profession as a crash repairer on the Great Southern Road, although he recognised his job was concerned with facade, much like the city's new name. He was tall and blond and good looking, which made him a favourite amongst his fellow inmates. He had a good defence though; his X-ray blue eyes could look into your soul, and this risked the destruction of both his soul, and the soul into which he looked. These days he never used his school days nickname except when telling his story, and more importantly, more crucial at this point in his life, he was well down the path to saving himself.

'What's the difference between a psychologist and God?' Hawkey opened.

'Yes I have heard it before; God doesn't think he's a psychologist,' Doctor Reynolds replied, adopting his professional 'heard it all before' demeanour.

'But he does think he is God,' Hawkey said, staring deep into the doctor's soul, such as it was.

'Hmmm,' Doctor Reynolds mused. 'I am inclined to tell that joke against psychiatrists more than psychologists. I hold that psychology is where human hope remains active and seminal. Some have accused me of an excessively popular approach but I believe everything is relevant. Shall we get started?' The doctor's phone rang and he made a gesture to Hawkey to hold for a minute while he took the call and walked over to the window, out of which the works-in-progress on the new wing for the Paradise Mental Heath hospital could be seen in full swing.

Hawkey knew why he had his story. He knew its purpose and he didn't need a bunch of academic 'do-gooders' telling him what was in effect obvious, although there was a part of him which enjoyed watching them get themselves all serious about deconstructing and analysing it. Hawkey came to the conclusion that out of all the professions, psychologists took themselves the most seriously, with the possible exception of parking attendants if 'parking attending' could be said to be a profession. And the professions which seemed to take themselves the least seriously were dentists (this was the case for the one in jail, who was the only dentist Hawkey knew) and butchers. Although to be fair, Hawkey hadn't completed a comprehensive survey; such a thing would be difficult to accomplish in jail while you are being buggered to within an inch of your life, not to mention extraneous. He also thought that car salesmen were the sleaziest of all professions, closely followed by politicians, especially if the current Minister of the Interior was included in the survey. Hawkey considered architects among the noblest – but that was as far as he had gotten with his survey of the professions. Hawkey often wondered about his school friend Peter, who he thought had attended Paradise University to study architecture. In Hawkey's view, Peter was one of the noblest people he had known in his life and he had not needed to become an architect in order to achieve his nobility. Hawkey and Peter separated after an eventful incident behind a chook shed with a girl called Ruby when they were all sixteen and in the same class at high school. Hawkey left school soon after that event and lost touch with Peter, but had heard occasionally about how well he was doing.

Hawkey could never rid himself of the guilt that his stupid, selfish, unthinking actions, when he was a nine-year-old, had caused and which resulted in the devastating death of his triplet sister when she was run over on the Great Southern Road. It was his job to look after her and he failed her. He believed that this resulted in him losing his way in life.

'Now you are aware that I am researching a book about people who feel disenfranchised from life in Paradise, perhaps due to an early trauma of some kind, and how this affects their feelings of self-worth. I am also interested in the discussion and any causal link with the impact or otherwise of the city's name change on people's expectations and outcomes of their life after their respective traumas,' the good doctor recited.

Hawkey nodded.

'I am very interested in your case,' the doctor said to Hawkey with a less than convincing smile and unnecessarily emphasising the 'your' in his statement.

Hawkey saw the smile and raised it with a grimace. A lot of poker, in one form or another, was played in jail and not always with cards, and rarely as a game.

Hawkey agreed to meet the doctor to tell his story, perhaps, he considered and hoped, for the last time, as a condition of his probation. He didn't mind telling it. In fact it didn't hurt for him to remind himself of his story. His story enabled him to appreciate his current good fortune. Coincidentally the doctor had a story too, and he insisted he tell his to Hawkey first. The doctor's story was like Hawkey's: practised, rehearsed and necessary, although unlike the doctor's, Hawkey's story was balanced in breadth and detail and enhanced (Hawkey hoped) with the romanticism of odyssey. But this wasn't the essential difference between Hawkey's story and the doctor's story. The essential difference was that Hawkey knew the truth underpinning his story, while it seemed obvious to Hawkey that the doctor thought that having his story was sufficient, an end in itself and that it need not contain any essential truths. But it wasn't for Hawkey to point out this absurdity to the eminent psychologist. And it wasn't for Hawkey to point out the danger of telling a story like this to vulnerable people. Hawkey was no longer vulnerable; well, not tragically.

The doctor expected his story would qualify him to Hawkey, so Hawkey would feel he was in 'sympathetic' company, that they shared something in common. The doctor was also trying to establish the importance of 'story' to isolate incidents that otherwise might adversely affect one's psychological progress through life. This was a pet theory and clinical strategy of Doctor Reynolds. The doctor's story was short and it went like this more or less. *The little pre-psychologist Robert Reynolds, nine years old at the time, was staying with his mother on a farm that was covered by bright ruby-red grapevines, on the outskirts of Paradise – then still known as Adelaide – during school holidays. He sat on a log at the edge of a pond hidden in the bulrushes amusing himself as was his habit, catching tadpoles and putting them in a jar of pond water. Breaching the sanctity of this moment, he heard a strange but very familiar noise. He put down his homemade net (made of a wire hanger bent into a circle with a handle and then covered with one of his mother's stockings), and his jar of tadpoles, and crept toward the noise. His breathing held, he picked his way through the bulrushes, feeling the sucking mud oozing between his fingers. Then through the undergrowth he saw her, his mother, as he knew it would be, as the source of the recognisable noise. She was on all fours in a partial clearing of bulrushes on green and yellow flattened grass. Her knapsack was strapped to her back, and with her pink cotton dress folded back over her knapsack, it gave her a humped-back appearance. With each jolt to her body, her knapsack wobbled, much like the hump on a camel wobbles as it slopes along in a caravan. Robert's mother was sandwiched between two men, neither of whom was Robert's father, although one was recognised by Robert to be the Ring Master from the visiting circus currently set up at the local oval. Robert had been taken to the circus the night before by his mother as a treat for being a good boy and for staying out of mischief during his holiday, something his mother apparently found difficult to achieve herself. Robert was aghast at the sight, particularly the vast white cellulite-dimpled vibrating expanse of his mother's buttocks, not a sight he would expect to come across in his daily toil.* It was a sight that Hawkey imagined would have a profound effect on the doctor's attitude to sex later on in his life, but this was conjecture on Hawkey's part and not worth a discussion at this stage.

The doctor seemed keen to invite discussion about this story, so Hawkey, while admitting to not being a literary critic, made the observation that he thought the story suffered from a lack of subtlety while crudely attempting to shock, and rather played too heavily for sensationalism. It seemed not to be the real story the doctor should be telling but the story he used to mask the one he couldn't bring himself to tell. Or perhaps the doctor was yet to experience the story he should be telling and had to either make this one up or borrow it from someone else and embellish it to satisfy his immediate needs. The doctor made no comment but continued to make notes as Hawkey spoke about the doctor's story.

Hawkey continued, filling the clear air with his gravel voice, by acknowledging the knapsack was a nice touch of detail lending some authenticity, even if he doubted the nine-year-old Robert had seen many sloping camels in caravans in his time; perhaps at the circus, to be generous with licence. And it was pretty obvious to Hawkey that it wasn't so much that Robert saw his mother in this position, albeit as traumatic as that would have been for a nine-year-old, but that it was the fact that she was enjoying herself. This was evidenced by the production of this singular high-pitched noise she produced through her mouth from somewhere deep in her throat as related to Hawkey in the longer version of this story. The noise familiar to Robert was the noise his mother made whenever she was in raptures. A noise that hitherto was the noise she made playfully wrestling with her son on the carpet, or the times she disappeared behind a closed bedroom door with Robert's father for his version of wrestling with her. It was this 'enjoyment' noise and the cellulite which combined to cause the young Robert the greatest trauma, and it was this which interrupted the Zen-like rapture of tadpole collecting, that only a nine-year-old boy can appreciate, at least as far as Hawkey's interpretation of the doctor's story goes. This was the thrust of the discussion Hawkey had with the good doctor about his story. It did occur to Hawkey that her noise-making seemed a little unlikely given that she supposedly had her mouth full at the time but Hawkey wasn't inclined to be picky on the point and he chose to keep this criticism to himself. Anyhow, give or take, this was the story the doctor used to provide himself with special licence to be talking to Hawkey. Hawkey thought the doctor might need some professional help himself, not the least of which might be from a story editor, or even another psychologist, if it came to that. At that moment the doctor's mobile phone rang again and interrupted proceedings. The doctor looking at the incoming number and decided to take the call. He held his hand up to indicate Hawkey should hold that thought.

18

TOMMY

Tommy had to come home early from work. He was sick again. He managed to pick up some tin beer at the Tonsley Park Hotel drive-thru near his flat in Clovelly Park without passing out. He had to rest outside the cafe where Ruby often had her favourite pineapple crush drink and where he bought biscuits. But that was when he was eating. He made it back to his flat and struggled up the stairs, holding on to the rail and trying to keep hold of his tin beer with his shaking hands. About half way up, Lemon Guy who lives on the top floor was coming down. Tommy didn't look at Lemon Guy, no one looked at Lemon Guy, he wasn't the kind of guy you wanted to make eye contact with, he took it as an invitation to beat the crap out of you. And Tommy was too sick to take in Lemon Guy's stink. 'Well if it isn't Franz.' Tommy was never sure why Lemon Guy insisted on calling him Franz but he wasn't the kind of guy you challenged; Tommy wouldn't have thought him capable of reading anything more substantial than a comic, so literary allusions were well out of his reach. Tommy stopped, held his breath swallowing his nausea and bowed his head to let Lemon Guy pass. But it was no good. As Lemon Guy reached Tommy, he clocked Tommy right in the face. Tommy's legs buckled, and he crashed to the floor. When Tommy opened his eyes, his nose was full of lemon smell and blood and Lemon Guy's face was only centimetres from Tommy's face. Lemon Guy spat at Tommy. 'You killed my cat, you cockroach.' Lemon Guy shouted this into Tommy's nostrils. Tommy didn't ordinarily use his nostrils for hearing, but in Lemon Guy's case, he felt compelled to make an exception. Then Lemon Guy smashed Tommy again with his head and that was when Tommy felt his nose buckle, making a sound like plastic snapping. It seemed unlikely that a discussion about neighbourly harmony would be fruitful right at this moment. Tommy felt his nose fill with blood, which surely would put to an end any ambitions Tommy's nostrils might have entertained as listening devices. As it stood at the moment, they were flat out fulfilling their basic design function of air in, air out. Tommy didn't know it was Lemon Guy's goddamn cat. It was true then, Tommy thought, he had killed Lemon Guy's cat and this confirmed his worse fears about himself. Tommy was a killer.

The first thing Tommy hoped was that no one in any of the flats had heard his nose snap. Especially Ruby. His regular noisy breathing as he walked up the stairs every day was bad enough. He would be embarrassed even more now, if she came out to see what that snapping noise was and found him lying on his back with blood bubbling from his nose, tin beer all over the steps and Lemon Guy standing over him. Tommy really didn't need that. And he didn't need Lemon Guy head-butting him and converting his nose into a lumpy fleshy bloody mess either. He was already not feeling good. But it would be worse if Ruby came out and saw him being beaten up by Lemon Guy. Tommy would feel defeated if that happened. He would feel he had let her down. He must never do that. Tommy believed it was his job to look after Ruby. Ruby had no idea Tommy was her self-appointed guardian angel. Billboards with the self-promoting smiling Minister's face in Paradise said, 'everyone has a guardian angel'. Not that Tommy was capable of saving anyone, himself included. Truth be known, Tommy could have used a guardian angel himself. Tommy had to hope that Ruby also had a real guardian angel, so that her safety wasn't totally reliant on him. Even so, as pathetic as Tommy knew he was, if he saw Ruby was in danger, he would do what was necessary to save Ruby. Sacrifice himself, if that was what was required (it wasn't as though this existence of his was much to write home about).

Some things you know about yourself, and Tommy knew he could sacrifice himself to save Ruby. And let's face it, Tommy was a killer, that was a proven fact and if he had to, he ought to be able to rely on that trait if necessary. He would kill anyone who put Ruby in danger.

Lemon Guy kicked the beer from Tommy's hand and all the tins broke from their plastic sleeve and crashed down the stairs with an unholy clatter. Tommy would have to wait for the beer to settle before he could open a tin, and he was really thirsty. Nothing was easy for Tommy. Whatever could go wrong, did. He was plagued with bad luck. The beer was critical. It was all he could take in these days. Blood dripped from his nose onto the concrete steps. He felt embarrassed causing a mess on the steps which everyone had to use, even though the building had been scheduled for refurbishment under the PERP programme. He felt he had let himself down again.

Lemon Guy scrunched one of Tommy's hands into the concrete step with his heavy army boots as he passed. Tommy felt the bones crack. Lucky it wasn't his right hand, the one he used to write his stories. Tommy crawled up the two flights of stairs to his flat, fell into his bathroom and started throwing up. He didn't need to be throwing up. He knew he had to try and keep things inside himself. He had stopped eating biscuits. He was losing fat fast now. He already looked like a stick insect, but now a stick insect that sweats and cries, and has a nose the shape of a mushroom slice and a hand that looked like it had been stuck in a giant's mouth and chewed. He hoped that Ruby in flat three hadn't heard all the noises. He worried that Ruby's quiet life might be disturbed by his small unnerving sounds. He didn't want to scare her.

Tommy was scared himself, so he knew what that was like, although he wasn't scared in any particular way, like of Lemon Guy. He was pretty scared of Lemon Guy, but anyone would be. Tommy was just scared in a universal way, scared of life, scared of synchronicity, mostly synchronicity. What scared him about synchronicity was that it was impartial, disinterested and unpredictable and, as such, more wretched than something that intends harm, like Lemon Guy. Synchronicity. It wasn't as though it singled you out for specific retribution in a way that suggested you might deserve it for your sins, or crimes against the Universe. No, it didn't do that. It came along and shat on you for no good reason because you were in the wrong place at the wrong time, like some kind of coincidence monster. Because, let's face it, someone is always in the wrong place at the wrong time, otherwise there wouldn't be such a thing as a wrong place or a wrong time, but there was, and Tommy was always there. Synchronicity wrecks your life and then moves on as though you were not important, just a freckle on someone's leg in the Universe; like you just happen to be in the way. And it leaves you with an enormous debt. Tommy felt the everyday business of life was about dealing with the consequence caused by your own presence. Tommy felt half his problems were as a result of just being. Tommy figured everyone had this 'universal scaredness', in varying amounts. Although Tommy felt he had more of it than most and with good reason. He felt it in Ruby too when he stood across the Great Southern Road to watch her at work at the supermarket, before she started selling cars for a living, or when he saw her sitting on the steps of the flats eating grapes and sunning her beautiful legs. He wished she wouldn't do that; he didn't want Lemon Guy getting any ideas, or looking into her eyes. You couldn't look into Ruby's eyes without crying. Looking into her eyes could rip your heart out. With a guy like Lemon Guy, well, it could tip him over the edge. Tommy had shadowed Ruby for a long time, for years now. That was his job, his life's work. But he was sure she wasn't aware of his presence, he didn't want that. She didn't know him. He didn't dare tell her who he was. Tommy had loved Ruby for all this time and would love her forever. He would look after her. He owed her that. He would kill her himself, if that was the only way to save her, but she would be the last to go.

Tommy tried not to think too much about killing things and he thought he was getting better but when he realised how much of a phoney Doctor Robert Reynolds was, it was like something inside him clicked, and he all of a sudden started sweating and waning. It was like his cerebral waters broke, and emptied in a sucking spiral out of his head and down through his body. He couldn't explain it any other way. In fact, that was how he explained it to Doctor Reynolds. Or did he get that from Doctor Reynolds? He couldn't be sure. He had relied very heavily on Doctor Reynolds and his counsel. Tommy was losing about a kilo of fat per week – similar to a bag of wet sponge cake. The sweat ran off him in rivulets. He hoped like hell the sweat would equal the weight loss, and that it was fluid he was losing not his actual self. He hoped it would all stop soon. He tried to read articles about weight loss, to see if any of them say, 'don't goddamn worry if you sweat a lot or if you suddenly start losing weight', but none of them did. He tried not to worry but it would have helped if he had someone. It would have helped if he wasn't always alone in his flat or in his bastard building, or his car; being in his car was the worst. But there was something wrong with the building too; it sweated, and didn't like its tenants. Inanimate objects could be killers. Tommy suspected everything. But then Tommy had good reason to suspect things had malevolent intent, because everything did. He had firsthand experience of this – things could kill, cars for instance, especially cars. All he wanted was a normal life, a normal life in Paradise. Unfortunately, Paradise provided him with no clue as to what a normal life was, or how you went about having one. This is where he had expected Doctor Reynolds to help him, but after years seeing the doctor, including reading every line of the doctor's first book, that was just a goddamn blow-out.

19

HAWKEY/STEVE

To Doctor Robert Reynolds, Hawkey was prime material. Hawkey, at the age of thirteen, along with his sister Allie, had witnessed the death of his father in a rather bizarre and vaguely documented circumstance. The courts took the view that the death had been caused by unknown and suspicious factors, but there was no evidence to point the finger at Hawkey himself. Hawkey and his twin sister knew the circumstances and they remained silent on the matter. In fact, it wasn't this event at all that had affected and changed the course of Hawkey's life but another one entirely, one he never spoke about, and one he hadn't even witnessed first-hand. He saw no reason to disabuse the doctor from making whatever assumptions he saw fit about Hawkey's supposed trauma. After all, it was only in service to his probation that he agreed to the discussion at all.

Hawkey wasn't a talker by nature; with the exception of his story, he never had much to say to anyone. He thought most of what was said could just as easily be not said for all the contribution it made to life, and in his experience most sentiments could be conveyed by a simple nod of one's head, or for the contrary, the absence of a nod. Hawkey agreed with the graffiti scrawled across the smirking face of many of the Minister of the Interior's billboards around Paradise, 'after all was said and done, there is a lot more said than done'. Hawkey had achieved an economy of communication. So then, this was Hawkey's story as told to the good Doctor Reynolds.

'There's that paradoxical story about Superman, which you heard in jail,' Hawkey started.

'*I* heard.' The doctor corrected him, emphasising the personal pronoun. Hawkey had the habit of referring to himself in the second person, something he had by and large eliminated from his speech except when he was telling his story and on occasions when he was either nervous or sexually excited. On these occasions, he would lapse back into the habit.

'*I* made up in jail,' he corrected himself, 'which made *me* feel sad. It goes like this. Superman is walking sanguinely down the street and trips on something and accidentally falls against a bus. As he's the strongest man in all of Paradise, the bus jolts off down the road and runs into someone and kills them. In your, *my* own case, I know, like Superman, I am not the kind of person who intends any hurt – but this doesn't mean to say that you don't somehow or sometimes cause hurt, by doing nothing more than being who you are. To cause pain in this world or to fail to prevent it, you need do nothing exceptional beyond existing, and in that existence, do nothing exceptional.'

'We must try and speak in the first person,' Doctor Reynolds pointed out with that rhetorical demeanour represented by the recognisable authoritative doctor *methode* of speaking to patients using the royal *we*.

'Certainly we must,' Hawkey agreed with deadpan delivery.

'Go on.'

'Well there was C and rupert (small r) and me, the three of us, three teenagers huddled in a row. It was a cold mid-morning, in front of a front door of some expensive house, in North Paradise. You're pretty sure it's North Paradise and not Prospect. It doesn't matter, it's an expensive suburb. It's break and enter – like scientific discovery and life, not like burglary, although the distinction will be impossible to explain to the police. This too fast?'

'No, it's okay, I'm taping you as well, remember?' Doctor Reynolds held up the tape recorder.

'Okay, if you really want this the way it should be, I have to tell it this way, it's how I thought about it in jail to block the moments, you know? It's more form than content, you understand? (Although the content comes from somewhere and is where the key is to be found.) And grunting, there's a lot of rhythmic grunting. I thought of it over and over and over. I said it over and over and over. It needs to be told in the second person, okay? There was a lot of fucking. The use of the second person was essential to the exercise to achieve the necessary disassociation.'

'Yes, I know, tell it how you want, that's more important.'

'Okay, it's graphic but then no more than yours.'

'Yes, that's good.'

'You ready then?'

'Please go ahead, take your time.'

'You can't think why you are here in front of this North Paradise door. In fact, at that moment, it strikes you it doesn't matter and you feel your anxiety flood as though cerebral waters have just broken, and emptied in a sucking spiral out of your head and down through your body.' Hawkey started to rock rhythmically back and forth like a kind of pendulum as he moved into his automatic storytelling mode.

The doctor made a special note of the 'cerebral waters' metaphor. 'Interesting imagery, what do you think it symbolises?'

'Earn your money, doctor.' Hawkey said this without looking up or breaking his physical position, as though he had reached some kind of trance state which the doctor had now broken. Hawkey had worked hard to chisel out this descriptive phrase and he was proud of it, he thought it did a lot of work.

'Do you mind if I use that description as a direct quote? But please go on.'

'You sure you want all of this, because once I start, it is best I keep going, one long line, nonstop, it's like a monologue, it is a monologue, a *tour de force*, emphasis on the *force*. You have to do your bit here as well; you have to imagine me being held down and buggered. All the way through so to speak, you got that picture in your head, because it won't make any sense without it?'

'I want you to tell me everything, exactly the way you want to, the way you have rehearsed it, I won't interrupt again.'

'C is fiddling with the lock on the front door of someone's home. He contends he can pick locks but he always ends up losing his temper and smashing the door in like some clumsy breakthrough in the Grand Unified Forces theory. For some reason you don't understand, you imagine aliens on the other side, sitting with portentous anticipation and humour, always humour, waiting for C's boot to crash through the door. Meanwhile you're here, with your companions, in shafts of cold daylight, three uneasy gulls in a line like a Greek chorus. You think of breaking into song. You don't know what song, maybe 'The hills are alive…', there's more absurdity.

'Next to you is rupert, he's in the arts, an 'art placer' he says. He creates art and places it. The art, he claims, is in the placement. 'Whatever', you think. And C, a polymath and self-proclaimed doctor of philosophy, claims his philosophy doctorate is based on not thinking deeply. He says none of the big answers can be found with profound deep thought, only bigger questions, and the more deeply you think about it, the less sense it makes, which he argues proves his theory. 'Q.E.D.', as he is fond of saying, if prosaically. They call you Hawkey or the Hawk; nicknamed after Stephen W. You share his first name, and science was your subject at school, you excelled at school in physics, since then you have read philosophy, and also ethics – so you know what you are doing is wrong on one level and you also know that it has no intrinsic meaning on another level. You wait for C to lose his temper. Standing patiently, you try not to think about the consequences. You hope that your interruption into the absent lives of this house will not cause any harm. It is not your intention to cause harm or to interrupt the natural order of life but to observe it; you wish you could guarantee no interference in their lives, but you are all too aware of the observer affect. You are nonetheless compelled to immerse yourself in other lives in order to confirm your own existence, so you are careful.'

At that moment the doctor's mobile phone rang once more. As was the case before, he held his hand up to indicate Hawkey should hold his thought again.

20

TOMMY

Tommy started a story in his striped essay book. He wrote, '*Lord Twinings, the tea guy, overhears a conversation at the tennis club about a mad Frenchie called Marie Antoinette*'. Tommy scribbled faster hoping the story would begin writing itself. '*and this gives the Lord the idea for a new sponge cake product. The Lord decides 'teacakes' for a name and comes up with the slogan, 'let them eat teacake'. The Lord congratulates himself on how catchy his slogan is*'. Tommy put his pencil down, although he preferred not to finish a sentence with 'is', it was clumsy and it made him feel ill, well more ill than he already felt that is.

Sweat dripped on the lined pages. Tommy thought it was from his eyes. He closed the book. But he had made a start and it felt interesting. Tommy liked big ideas. He enjoyed a dramatic gesture in his writing, if he could manage it, a flourish, the equivalent of an architectural folly, as it were. But he was never satisfied. He worked laboriously at his words, chiselling, changing, re-working, but still he never felt he achieved anything. Mostly he rarely got a sentence out before the idea seemed small and useless, and a reflection of himself. He once related to Doctor Reynolds during one of their sessions a saying he had read by a French writer which the doctor immediately made a note of; the saying was 'we don't see things as they are, we see them as we are'. This depressed Tommy; if this were true, he knew his writing would never amount to any more than him, it couldn't. How could he avoid himself in his work, how could he escape himself? Huh! He couldn't even stop himself from dripping on his work. How could he write a character more intelligent than himself, more emotionally stable than he was, more eloquent? How could he even write the truth, what truth, whose truth? No one would believe the truth anyway, he assured himself, but fiction that didn't contain truth was obvious. This much he knew. He had read somewhere that there was no reality, only perception. He could never tell the real truth because he could never know it. You can only be aware of what the part of you that knows what you are aware of, knows. You can't know if you have another part you don't know but that knows things you don't know and informs the part you do know in some way. Doctor Reynolds continued to make notes as Tommy talked about this dilemma but made no material comment.

Tommy suffered from the feeling he had let everyone down. He never meant any harm. He had figured out for himself that things happen and, invariably, they were a function of who you were, not necessarily what you intend. Just being Tommy was enough to bring all manner of grief to the innocent. Tommy realised that in Paradise you could cause hurt unwittingly, by doing nothing more than being who you are. To cause pain in this world or to fail to prevent it, you need do nothing exceptional beyond existing and in that existence, do nothing exceptional. Tommy remembered Doctor Reynolds had said this in one of his textbooks. He was making some kind of point that Tommy now was having trouble remembering. But the sentiment had stuck in Tommy's mind and he copied it out and pinned it on his wall. Tommy never meant any harm to anyone. He wished he could not be himself. The world and all its cats would be safer. Ruby would be safer. He was bad luck. Bad luck for himself and others. One of the Minister's posters around the city said, 'you cause your own luck in Paradise'. Tommy wished he could believe that, but then that was the problem, he did believe it. Unfortunately, the luck he caused was all bad.

For many years, up until recently, he was grotesquely fat, then it, his fat, started to disappear with the sweat. He felt Doctor Reynolds and his phoney story about his mother being fucked in a clearing was the cause of his weight loss. Admittedly, Tommy had embellished the doctor's story somewhat but this he did out of his search for meaning. The point of the doctor's story highlighted to Tommy the need to find your real story, and that he and the doctor too, had not, and until you do, your inevitable destruction is, well, inevitable.

Tommy could only blame himself for getting fat in the first place. Tommy had been so fat he couldn't get clothes. And he wrecked things; his car seat, which he had to replace with one of his kitchen chairs, and his stool at work, which they made him pay for. But that was okay, that was what happened when you were Tommy, fat Tommy – but now he was losing his body weight and it was Doctor Reynolds's fault with his stupid borrowed story.

Tommy missed his sister, Tippy. Tippy lived on the other side of Paradise. Tommy was seventeen before he appreciated how important sisters were. He only had one, not two, like some. His sister had a job on the weekend at the North Paradise Football club. She rubbed footballers down before and after a game every Saturday. She told Tommy she massaged high up their oiled buttocks; it was her job. Tommy was glad she had something she liked to do. He was proud of her, not for any particular reason, but just because she was his sister. A sister is a unique and special thing, they are irreplaceable and you can never have too many, in fact it helps to have a spare in case you lose one or find you are no longer in touch.

Tommy was somewhere around his thirties, he couldn't remember exactly, but he felt a lot older. He didn't think he should feel so old. Being fat had been really bad for him but now he wished he had his warm fat back again, or some of it. He felt he couldn't get anything right. During his research about weight loss at the Paradise library, he had read that when people dropped body weight rapidly, it was something bad. But that wasn't all there was to worry about. There was also the blood he kept spitting up, and the blood that dripped from his nose spasmodically, and not always from being head-butted by Lemon Guy either. He wanted to find out more about the blood but there was always this farmer on the only computer there at the library, trying to figure out how to use the thing, and monopolising it, and getting some girl there to help him. He overheard them one day and found out her name was Allie. She was beautiful, Tommy thought, and he wished he could get someone like her to help him sometime. But that would never happen.

Tommy sat at his desk, with his hand and nose throbbing in sync; he started writing again. '*Lord Twinings has a brother who thinks of himself as an inventor. He invents this thing, a tampon, he calls it, for no particular reason. He just likes the sound the word 'tampon' makes in his mouth when he repeats it to his brother, the Lord. His tampon has no obvious commercial application. He just dangles the thing in the air as though a use for it will suddenly occur to him. It looks like such a handy thing even if he couldn't immediately describe a function for it.*'

'*Tampons won't be an easy sell.*' Tommy writes this at the bottom of the page as a footnote that he might use later, but then he felt exhausted. No blood spots on this page – 'Just when you need goddamn symbolism, there isn't any,' he murmured to himself.

Tommy felt momentarily better one morning. On the way to work, he imagined he slammed into three people. He hit one on a pedestrian crossing; the guy was taking his short-haired dog for a walk. Tommy missed the dog deliberately, although, normally, Tommy didn't favour short-haired dogs. But he had decided to try to stop killing animals. That was something he could do, or not do, as the case may be. He also hit the guy's briefcase. When Tommy got home later that day, there was a new dent, and half an Elysium spread sandwich stuck in the grille of his car.

That night he sat at his *Laminex* table and wrote words describing his day, the people he imagined hitting and killing, the inkbottles he had filled, and the dead bee in his car. Dead things are lighter than when they are alive. He started in the middle of his exercise book, in the very centre, to start fresh, just in case he had a new idea brewing. He didn't, but you never know.

After writing for two hours, he called his sister. Tippy said, 'Why don't you kill yourself Tommy, if that's what you want.' And then she told him not to call her any more. He hadn't said anything about killing himself. He wrote that in his book and felt sad. He felt a great sadness. The bandage on his hand needed changing. He didn't blame his sister, she had tried to help him for years, but he was beyond help.

Next night Tommy couldn't sleep. He started writing on a fresh white page, with no sweat drops. He knew if he could just find the thing inside him to write, he could save himself. All he had to find was his story, and he knew he would be goddamn all right. He had told this to Doctor Reynolds but the doctor didn't hear him. He heard him but he wasn't listening, which Tommy thought odd for a psychologist. The doctor was too busy taking notes for his book or some speech he was preparing, or taking calls on his mobile. All he ever said was, 'Ahuh, ahuh, hmmm, ho hum.' Tommy tried again at his tampon/tea bag invention story. He wrote, '*Lord Twinings's brother is swinging his tampon invention about and he accidentally lets go of it and it lands in his brother's cup of black tea. Lord Twinings preferred his tea black with a slice of lime at tennis as it was more refreshing than with milk, and not as astringent as a slice of lemon. The Lord was notoriously fussy about tea. Lord Twinings looked at his tea with his brother's tampon in it for a long time.*' Tommy tried to write it all down before anything dripped on the page, but he didn't manage it. The story was not working; it contained no truth. It was just imagination driving it. Like when he imagined killing people with his car. Tommy's story was not sustainable without truth. Tommy needed to find fiction that had truth – imagination without truth was nothing more than a catalogue of ideas. This fiction had no truth, but he hoped it might lead him into the story he felt was just under his skin; a story which lurked and bubbled and threatened to erupt like a purple pustule.

Tommy knew he had to find his story and fast; time, his time, was running out. Don't philosophise, just write the story, let the reader worry about the philosophy, he told himself. Tell the story and let the story do the telling, he repeated often, in fact he wrote this on a piece of paper and stuck it on the wall in front of him, next to the doctor's quote about seeing 'life the way we are'. He hated writers whose prose dripped with hidden meanings, esoteric clues, subtexts under allegorical subtexts; it was all too much work. Why don't they just say what they mean? He had read some short stories by a writer some time ago; he can't remember the writer's name, only that he lived on W57th Street in New York. Tommy couldn't remember why he remembered that detail, but Tommy liked this guy's writing; it was funny in a black kind of way, although Tommy lost some respect for him when he discovered he was a creative writing teacher at Columbia University in New York City. Tommy still liked his writing though because he wrote about things that didn't exist, but made you believe they did. Tommy's main ambition was to write comedy, as comedy was the only way to dissect the world and reveal truth, or so he thought. The trouble is, every time he tried, it came out serious, full of truth-searching empty philosophy but no actual truth. Not funny at all. 'Comedy is hard', as the saying goes, but dying was something Tommy was having no difficulty accomplishing.

21

HAWKEY

Doctor Reynolds concluded his call and nodded to Hawkey to continue.

'Synchronicity is impartial, disinterested, so you don't know that C will soon die, and you will go to jail for nine months where you will be TRAPPED, HELD, FED, NURTURED, ADORED, RELEASED. You'll smile at the symbolism of it all, but only a long time after. Not during. During, the only thing that smiles is not your face.'

'Very clever.' Doctor Reynolds said this spontaneously, but then realised he had interrupted and felt embarrassed.

'As C continues his work, you stare hypnotically, soft-focus like, at the lock, and at that moment, you make a decision. You try to suspend your anxiety. The decision you make is to tell the truth, it's what you wanted since you had a father like you had, who always reckoned you were lying (and he was right) and clipped your ears the way he did. You'll survive jail and sometimes you'll wonder; you were there? You weren't there? – It's the paradox of presence. You'll think it wasn't so bad; it's a modern family full of modern moments. "Fuckin' hurry, I've got to go," urges rupert. C's boot goes through the door splintering the lock. It makes you wince. You wander in savouring the moment. The air smells cold. You don't know these people whose lives you are just now entering. It's exciting, like the pungent sticky scents flowing from a body you are exploring for the first time. Entering these people's lives feels both tantalising and familiar. You wish. What? You don't know what you wish, but you have a longing, which you don't understand. You've had this longing for most of your life, you realise. You wished you knew what you wished for in life. Where is happiness to be found if not in wishing? You are hushed, you don't want to corrupt the new moment but then rupert farts, which is his habit. He scurries off looking for the toilet. rupert has to crap. When he gets in, he goes. Some time ago he announced he would not be flushing any more. He says he wants to leave his calling card; a turd by rupert, like it's some piece of art, placed, brown in white, large with parallax – ART with a small 'a'. C disappears upstairs, he'll be looking for the master bedroom. Boudoir, he calls it, like he knows French, it is just absurd farce. He sniffs female under-wear, it's unimaginative, a sign of impotency, in fact you find it disgusting. He's heard the arguments but he still does it. He's back down with two pairs of soiled knickers. He sinks into the fat sofa with the knickers on his face. He inhales with power yet with sensitivity, like a beast straining and sampling the scents, confirming the quarry across the Savannah or a wine-maker nasal-sucking the fruity vapours off a feisty red at *R. T.* You have to admire technique; your father taught you this.

'C reckons he can determine the age of the woman and where she is in her month by the scents in her underwear. But then he also reckons he can pick a lock. You like to infiltrate the lives of your new family, find some-thing, share their secret. All families have secrets, born from moments; you need secrets to be a family. In theory, you are supposed to be stealing the television and the video, looking for cash or jewellery but you are not inter-ested in this, you've never stolen anything, except food on occasions. Apart from the lock, it thrills you to leave the place as you found it: "Who was that masked man?" you whisper. You are looking for something intimate. This is what you crave, to osmotically creep through their lives and belong in their family without touching the sides, just seeking their moments. It's like the powerful feelings you draw from the secret you and your sister share, which you didn't understand until after puberty sometime. Your father understood the secret, and you and Allie came to understand it, then you excluded him. It was this exclusion that withered him. He died humorously from shrivelling, the loss of the hydrating secret. You took the secret away from him; you knew he would die, excluded from his family secret. He became lighter. You told no one and nothing could be proved. People lament incredulously after their house is burgled, they say, "It's not the television or video or the Henschke (you go for the product placement), it's the fact that someone has been in here, in our home." They mean in their family, from which the only escape is death. And it's not so much that someone's presence has been in their home and maybe stolen stuff, it's that it is still there, like an unwanted miasma. This you regret – you would like your presence to be wanted. You would like to be present in your own life for a start.

'"There are two women in this house, a mother and a daughter. The mother is about forty-two, sexually active and still very fertile and willing. The daughter is young, and shy about her sexual appetites," says C with his two nostrils in two separate crotches of two sets of panties. He says this as though he thinks his interpretive skills are highly developed. You throw a photograph of the mother and daughter at C from the bookshelf. He picks it up and pokes his nose out from under the soiled panties, looks at the photo, and exclaims his accuracy, as if the photo has proven him right, and as if he hadn't already seen it. "Q.E.D. Hawkey, Q.E.D.," he proclaims, in the matter-of-fact tone people effect when they use the Latin abbreviation. "I'm hungry." C gets up, pushes the knickers off his face and back on his head. He opens the fridge looking for comestibles. C reckons vagina odour makes him peckish. He doesn't realise it's supposed to, but not for food. That's the trouble with C, his philosophical *raison d'être* is arse about face. rupert is still in the toilet, putting in *le grande* effort. You whisper the word "effort". You feel an irritation, a concern, a sharp pain, you definitely feel a sharp pain. You absorb the tension of being in someone's home and the possibility of them returning with you still there. But like Superman you just don't always mean, nor can you control, the outcome; you can't undo your presence. You notice how the everyday business of life is predominantly about dealing with the consequence caused by your presence. It's breaking, entering and discovery, like life… you cop the consequences. You browse the collection of books. People are their books. People say "what you read today walks and talks tomorrow". People use their books to say the things about themselves modesty forbids. They hide things behind their books, their money, jewels, airline tickets, passports, their Will and private letters. Sometimes they'll put private correspondence behind the free standing family photo in the silver etched frame that shows them rollicking together on a grey beach, their noses covered in zinc cream, they look forced, the photograph often including an awkward adolescent stranger. Everything is contrived, you understand this, you wish it wasn't so. Next to a book called *Metamorphosis* and behind a hand-bound book of middle-English poems, featuring fourteenth-century alliterating epics, a textbook on mathematics lying across the top suggesting a coupling, you find the letters. A small bundle held together with a perishing rubber band. You peel out the top letter. They've been there for years, maybe decades you like to think. You notice the fragility of the paper, crackling. The paper is paper-thin, you note. rupert is out of the toilet; you didn't hear a flush. You visualise the turd in the water and consider how art, like science, like philosophy, like your life, is not static but dynamic. You recognise that rupert's art is different now to how it was a few minutes ago. Like at first it was hot and shaped a particular way as it squeezed from rupert, like a distorted baby's head just out of the birth canal. You don't know why you are visualising all this detail of rupert's proclivities but you think it is for rupert's sake, or your own. You glance at rupert, he stares fecklessly back then turns to C who has made sandwiches with all the stuff piled out of the fridge and on the table. You feel the uneasy feeling again. You hope rupert washed his hands. You sit on the fat sofa and delicately undo the first letter and hope the others don't make too much mess. You read the letter. It has no date but is old, exchanged between the husband and wife before they were married, before the first secrets between them had taken shape. Letters establish intimacy which secret lovers can own, a gluey gossamer forming layer upon layer of secret binding history, like a Danish pastry, like families, like brothers and sisters. The letter is full of sex. You read it aloud to C and rupert, but they are both too busy eating sandwiches and crunching into squeaky pickled onions. Her letters were the best, C was right, she was willing. She was very willing when she wrote these letters. You read into it a naivety; you wonder who this young woman has become. You wonder if her hoped-for sexual ache has been satisfied or has it grown and expanded always remaining frustratingly ahead of ful-filment availability? The letter reads, "you think how such hope is always imperilled. You know what those jubilant crowds did not know, but could have learned from books: that hope can lie dormant for years and years in furniture and linen-chests; that it bides its time in bedrooms, cellars, trunks," and bookshelves just like this one containing the letters. The letter makes you hot. You feel your cock awaken, but you don't want to share the existence of the bulge in your pants with the masticating twins, so you head upstairs like a bull elephant in must. You lie on the king-size bed; the room looks like a cave, there are two cats sleeping in the corner of the room, they stir, then ignore you and settle back down again. You undo your belt and slide open your fly, gently, so your cock feels the butterfly-like dancing of your fingers outside your pants. You want it to expand as you release your zipper. It's out there; you feel the cold air swirl around the shaft; *a stranger in a strange land*. You don't touch it. You close your eyes and run the letter through your mind. You can hear sounds from downstairs but you don't let anything disturb the moment. She wrote to him about finger fucking herself, her language surprised you but then you remember Isadora in *Fear Of Flying*, and how she was quite partial to finger fucking in the absence of a satisfactory alternative. You prolong the heady full feeling of your erection by wondering if the woman at the time of writing her letter had read Jong's best seller, and if it influenced her own writing. Everything in Paradise is derivative, referential – ideas, architecture, music, writing, everything, including sex, perhaps especially sex. Where will the *new* come from in the future, you ponder? You instantly, but only for a second, understand the mighty theory of Chaos and how you are nothing to anything but everything to nothing. You feel the sharp pain again. You slip out of your jeans and underpants; you brush your erection in the execution of undressing and feel the titillation race around the head of your cock. You acknowledge, but try to ignore, the throb this causes. The erectile tissue pulses with spasm, it mimics a tiny thrust. You describe this as the primitive procreation reflex, a vertical steaming drive shaft balanced on a set of large ball bearings. You smile at the clumsy visual and note how "clumsy" perfectly describes male sexual fantasy, even the act itself seems brutal and all shudder.

'You are paralysed with pain. You can't move. Something is piercing your eyeballs. You can't open your eyes. You feel your hands tied roughly above you. The excruciating pressure lifts from your eyes. You open them and wait for the speckled spots of colourised pain to subside before you focus on the leering face of a man. He holds a piece of cotton string just above your face. You realise this is what he held across your eyes. He laughs and tells his wife how he used to win bets with his schoolmates, how he could keep them from getting off the ground with nothing more than a length of cotton held firmly over the eyeballs. You notice a leathery blonde woman is finishing off tying you to the bed. She's not the woman who wrote the letter, you're sure of that, she's changed. He checks the ties on your hands and you flash back to your father who promised you how much fun it would be to be tied up and tickled in special places. For years, you and your sister thought this was what a feather duster was for, it was only later you discovered you could also dust with it. It's your own family secret, yours and Allie's. It's your story.

'You stumble home. You can feel the dried blood between your legs. The police are waiting; you don't get the chance to wash. You like to be clean.

C and rupert must have heard the people coming in and escaped out the back. You think they didn't have time to warn you, or they didn't know where you were, or they didn't think too deeply about it. And the people probably thought, someone's been eating in their kitchen, and someone's been sitting in their sofa, and someone is sleeping in their bed. C, you later hear, was hit by a car, which was hit by a bus, while effecting his escape; unfortunately not a philosophical bus but the number 42 to Paradise Central. The story goes that the bus sort of jumped from a stationary position, like some other force was behind it.

'You thought of the wind slapping your eyes high above the ocean. They didn't call the police right away. They looked at you. She watched your erection subside, you felt silly, you wished it stayed hard. You felt her general disappointment. You tried to will it back up for her. They tied your ankles up and out over your head, it forced a smile and made you nauseous. Afterwards she engaged the device on the floor; it reminded you of the dolphin only it was large and not mechanical. You could see her on top of it with him helping. She bucked like a brumby at the end of the bed. You could see her through the territory your erection once occupied and was starting to reclaim. You watched sweat fly off her rotating breasts, you saw her scream, you saw their secret, you saw her story. For a blissful second you felt present, even warm and happy, like with Allie, sharing a moment with a modern family.' Hawkey stopped.

'That's it. That's the speech, end of buggery.'

The doctor didn't look up; he continued to write in his notebook. Hawkey looked around the office and out of the window at the gardens of the Paradise Mental Health Hospital. He saw the workmen building the new wing. He saw a large sign indicating this was funded by the Minister of the Interior's special Paradise Environmental Rejuvenation Fund. He saw a couple of guys in suits with hard hats, poring over plans and talking to another man dressed in working gear. Hawkey felt a sudden need to sigh. He thought of Madeline and felt depressed. The doctor continued with his notes, oblivious to Hawkey's sudden feelings of despair.

22

PETER

Peter's apartment was a shining example of the re-birthing of an old building, although North Paradise was one of the A-grade suburbs and illogically was one of the first suburbs to benefit from PERP.

Peter gave the fridge door a good hard satisfying polish and flippantly snapped Mr Dishwasher with the towel. He draped the towel over the oven handle. He grabbed his sports bag, slipped on his leather jacket, tied the garbage and, on his way out, dropped it into the wheelie bin. It was Saturday and the best day of the week; the day he played football for the North Paradise Football Club. He had played for them since he left high school. He played centre, the engine-room of the game as they say. He was quick and his ball skills superior. He had been named Club Champion for the past four years running. On the days they played at home, his day and preparation were full of ritual. He always left at noon, walking through the leafy streets of North Paradise to the ground. He loved the dappled winter light on the pavement, which evoked childhood memories of the same. He wore his leather jacket every time for luck, and he kicked a rock or something along the way. When he arrived, he undressed and had a shower, wrapped a towel around himself and climbed onto Tippy's massage table sucking in the nostalgic scent of liniment, allowing it to mesmerise him into his pre-game trance.

Tippy had been the club's masseuse for three years. She was good at her work and wasn't shy about being a girl in a room full of naked men whose language at times bordered on the obscene. She remained aloof from it, as though she acknowledged she was in an environment of secret rituals, and that she was accepted so long as she remained invisible. She rarely spoke; in fact, apart from a limited greeting and 'turn over' or 'you're done' accompanied with a slap on a thigh or buttock as a punctuation point, Peter couldn't recall her saying anything to anyone. And yet he still knew vague things about her. In the rooms, she was ignored; not rudely by the men, but because that is the only way it could work. She for her part stuck to the rules, and accepted her invisible but professional status.

Peter loved his massage. Tippy started with his legs; she worked them to get them warm, using plenty of liniment and kneading with her fingers. She worked his calves, then up his thighs to his buttocks. As Tippy pushed and shoved Peter's muscles, he fell into a kind of liquid euphoric contemplation, a Zen-like experience where there were no small or large questions of life to ponder. Peter was vaguely aware that Tippy had a brother named Tommy, who was sick, or fat, or skinny; Peter couldn't remember exactly but there was some suggestion he was not right in some way. Tippy never spoke of this, nor had he asked, it would have been a breach of the code. Tippy was very pretty and had a striking body. Peter, like the rest of the team, had to maintain a stoic vigilance in order that no embarrassment occurred. There were times when there had been incidental touching of his penis, when this occurred, she made a clearing-of-the-throat sound and then continue with the massage in some other place on his body, as though nothing had happened.

Lying in his liniment-soaked daze on Tippy's table, he recalled a thought he had had passing the Colonel Light statue on his way down to the bridge over the River Torrens. Setting aside his budding success in his chosen profession, he had thought his life lacked meaning. This might have been a bit grandiose; maybe what his life lacked was fun. Ryan had suggested Peter's life was a big blob of nothing, Ryan not one to embellish his words. In fact, Ryan, never one to let a good idea rest, suggested that calling Peter's life a big blob of nothing was gilding the lily. Burying the knife a little deeper, Ryan further suggested that if Peter could achieve the level of 'big blob of nothing', it would be an astonishing improvement; Ryan never quite mastered the social contract of collaborative lying. One of Ryan's New Year's Eve resolutions was that for the month of January, he would eliminate the word 'but' from his conversation – he claimed that 'but' signalled a lie had just been told or was about to be told. Peter could not see that this resolution changed much as Ryan always seemed blissfully unaware of the value of being circumspect. He always just blurted out what he thought regardless of any sensitivities, which is what made him both annoying and charming. Anyway, the long and short of all this was that maybe Ryan was right, and it was time to start getting on with enjoying his life more.

He was very close to a car accident once, his mother shielded the worst of it from him, but he heard the screeching and the death crack of young bones snapping like twigs. He was only nine years old at the time but he had suffered nightmares for many years after the event. His mother insisted throughout his life that he count his blessings. He found this concept debilitating, it was like watching himself constantly, as though he had to maintain an active awareness of everything he did in order not to lapse into taking things for granted. 'Count your blessings' was exhausting and ultimately unsuccessful in as much as it was self-defeating; you can't appreciate your life if you are always checking to see that you are appreciating it. At university he topped the state, then he met Belinda and thought he would be happy for the rest of his life – these were at least two blessings he could manage. Of course during the months after Belinda's disappearance, Ryan had been at him about this very subject for some time. 'You need to lighten up a bit, you're dead a bloody long time.' Ryan was only ever a platitude or two short of a cliché at the best of times. 'You know what your problem is, Mr Gloomy? You think too much, especially about thinking. Here's an idea, why don't you buy yourself a car? Go for a test drive, who knows what might happen. You have to have some fun, that's all you need, just fun, you could have fun in a new Beemer or something sporty? Belinda's gone and she's not coming back,' Ryan would insist. But maybe Ryan, and Madeline too for that matter, were right. He supposed he had to agree with Ryan up to a point. Not that a habit should be made of agreeing with Ryan. Well actually, there wasn't ever much opportunity to agree with Ryan, most of what Ryan said was impossible to agree with unless you had just swallowed a full bottle of tequila and a desk calendar. Nonetheless, fun, he thought. Could it be that simple? Fun was the substructure, the building block that was patently missing in his life – substructure was second nature to him. Substructure was the stuff of architecture. So okay then, fun seemed like a place to start. Fun; he remembered saying it out loud earlier that day on his walk along the river as the Popeye-named boat cruised by. Several of the resident homeless propped up against the rotunda seemed alarmed at the interruption to their own monologues. He said it again, 'Fun', even louder and wondered if this is how it started, how you ended up walking the streets having whole conversations with no one in particular.

With the scent of liniment rising from his legs, he continued to retrace his steps of earlier that morning when he had crossed the grass and walked along the pavement behind the university. He had skipped over a hubcap, which contained a fresh dog turd. This set his mind whizzing, as Tippy worked deep into the tissues of his left hamstring. Did someone put the turd in the hubcap and then leave the hubcap right there in the gutter, in Paradise, third quadrant just left of Alpha Centauri, a light year or two down the road from oblivion? Or did the dog just happen to shit where the hubcap was lying? And miraculously his turd ended up right in the middle of the hubcap, centred, not just to one side but right in the high diddle diddle as Ryan would have said. Or did the dog look around for something to shit in? Or was the dog specifically motivated at the sight of a hubcap? And what would be the statistical chances that this has ever occurred before anywhere in the universe, or would occur again or even that it occurred at all? Life, Peter thought, was full of seemingly unexplainable coincidences; calculations, his mother called them. It was an undeniable fact that staggering, mind-blowing unbelievable coincidences happened each day, like this dog turd in this particular hubcap – if it wasn't for coincidence, nothing would ever happen, at least not twice. Everyone has a coincidence story. Just because something was statistically improbable does not mean it was impossible, quite the reverse – an event can be either possible or impossible, it can't be both or neither, as Madeline would extemporise any chance she got on what was her favourite subject. Was this fun though? Ryan's eyes would be glazing over about now, so not the kind of fun Ryan would approve. Was Ryan right, did he think too much? Peter felt unhappy with himself on so many fronts.

Fun, fun, fun. A pretty stupid word really, fun, the more he repeated it in his mind, the more ridiculous it sounded – for a start you didn't automatically have any, just from the business of saying it. He knew it wasn't going to be that easy.

Peter's personality, he had to admit, was more on the serious side of reserved, and he knew he was not convinced that *fun* alone would be the efficacious antidote Ryan's simple view of life offered. Nonetheless, some fun would not be a bad thing, he supposed. And who knows, developing a sense of fun might make him more attractive to the world somehow, particularly to the opposite sex; not that he was unattractive he hoped, but it wasn't like he was being crushed by a stampede of women lately. Lately, he'd be lucky to be ignored by one.

Tippy slapped his thigh. 'You're done.'

23

HAWKEY/STEVE

Hawkey acknowledged he had grown up in a broken family and it had caused him difficulties, but he believed that it was up to him to get over it and make his life work and that everyone, as best they could, must try to do this, simple, Q.E.D. He owed this to his dead triplet sister. He had 'paid his debt to society'. Of all the break-ins he effected, and there were too many to remember, the only thing he ever stole was an old book of Medieval English poetry about some gallivanting Green Knight. He no longer had the book; he put it in Ruby's letterbox. He thought she might find some peace and beauty in it. He was too embarrassed to include a card and reveal himself to her and wasn't sure she even remembered him. He was happy to see her the day she came to borrow a ladder but he couldn't bring himself to enter her life. He had already done that a long time ago and had come to realise that entering people's lives was not a path to understanding your own. Even worse, it had unintentional consequences for the innocent people he had infected with his presence.

Hawkey knew he would never return to jail, and in this respect he was very lucky. Siting in Doctor Robert's rooms that day, he felt both warm and cold. He anticipated with anxiety his meeting with Madeline in the city later that day. He then made several decisions. He decided he would never repeat his story again. He would drop his nickname and only use his real name from now on. And he made a seminal decision about his future. He was grateful: grateful to get a second chance, grateful for his new life, grateful he got through jail unscathed, grateful he now knew how he was to spend the rest of his life, just grateful. In some of the Minister of the Interior's television commercials, he liked to remind the people of Paradise, 'You're not doing *life* in jail, you're doing *life* in Paradise.'

Steve acknowledged that while he had let one of his sisters down, he still had Allie. He had to make sure he never let her down but she had gotten on with her life. She had left Paradise for a small farming community about

106

two hours from Paradise. She worked as a computer programmer for the local district business association. She married a young farmer she met one day sitting at one of the long benches at the Paradise community library. He was swearing and muttering under his breath at the computer he was trying to make sense of. Allie leaned over him to help. Later that day, sitting on a log under the blue sky, she told him everything about her life. They married, then settled into a stone cottage, a replica of one the farmer had seen in a library book on Keld cottages. Steve was proud of her; for one thing, she was not doing *life* in Paradise.

Allie contributed to the profitability of her husband's farm with the use of a program she wrote to manage the animal husbandry side of the business. The impact was to ensure a healthy mathematical guarantee of genetic diversity. She started a family, but after her first child, she made the decision not to have any more. She was relieved she hadn't given birth to triplets; it was too easy to lose one. Steve saw her often; they met at the Centennial Park cemetery where they stood silently at their triplet sister's grave.

Steve visited the gravesite at Centennial Cemetery frequently, even compulsively; much like an alcoholic attends regular AA meetings as a reminder of how life can so easily and quickly go wrong, like the car accident which killed his triplet sister. The afternoon of the fatal accident, Steve had left his sister to walk home by herself. He shouldn't have done this. Allie was sick and hadn't attended school that day. Steve had been buying sweets and a pineapple crush to quench the heat of the day at the cafe, further along the Great Southern Road, down from the Tonsley Park Hotel. He was spending money he had stolen from his mother's purse when in the distance he heard the screech of tyres and the metal bang. He was supposed to be looking after his sister; it was his job.

He preferred the cemetery on wet cold windy days. It didn't matter to him how cold and soaked he got, he would stand at her grave for hours, letting the rain lash at his face and run down his cheeks and inside his shirt. Then one very wet day, while standing a little distance from the grave, he saw someone he recognised. Someone from his past. He did not approach her but the event confirmed to Steve that he was not alone in his story.

Steve's story had saved him. It had saved him in jail, but it had also saved his life. It didn't redeem him, nothing could do that, but it did save him.

He did not feel so disenfranchised; he had never felt unloved, his sister had always loved him, both his sisters had loved him. It was a mistake, but he was young, he didn't understand how the smallest action could have such an expanding and final outcome: how synchronicity can conspire to destroy you. He did feel the destruction caused by the loss of love and he believed this had set him on his wayward course, a course of blame and guilt. It was his story that enabled him to change his life.

He hadn't seen Ruby again since high school. At least not until he saw her from a distance, standing at his sister's grave in the pouring rain and then again when she walked into the crash repair shop and asked to borrow a ladder. He stood up and looked at her and all he could do was nod. It was comforting to see someone from his past. It was comforting not to feel quite so alone in Paradise. Although in recent months, he had experienced what it was like not to be alone. He had met Madeline. But that was now turning into a problem, which must be attended to.

Before he left the doctor's rooms, the doctor felt compelled to comment, as though this convention was necessary.

'Very interesting.' The doctor's voice jolted Steve's concentration back. Steve checked his watch; he was supposed to be in the city to meet Madeline in half an hour.

'I notice there is no mention of your dead sister in your story, only you and Allie?'

'She's dead.'

'Well yes, I understand, but why isn't she mentioned in the childhood references within the story?'

'She's dead.'

The doctor looked at Steve for a moment, then started writing more notes in his pad.

'You understand I made up rupert with a small r, and C don't you, they are fictional names and characters?'

'So long as *you* know they are made up, that is what is more important.'

'Is that not what I just said, but even so, how made up are they?'

'Yes, quite.'

'As a matter of interest, do you know what the most sought after commodity in jail is? See if you can guess.' Steve stood ready to leave.

'Cigarettes?'

'Use your imagination, doc.'

'Love?'

'Petroleum jelly.'

'Oh, I see.'

'Actually you aren't completely wrong. In jail, love is a jar of petroleum jelly, perception is everything as you lot like to say.'

'That cotton thing, does that really work?' the doctor asked as Steve turned his back and left.

Outside the doctor's office, Steve felt relief. His depression had eased as the decision he had now made about his future took hold; he felt a burden had been lifted. Of course this was not from anything that could be attributed to the psychologist or the session he had just completed, after all, he had recited his story many times and never had this elated feeling. The sun shone hard on him. He heard the noise from the building site behind him and the traffic on the Great Southern Road in front of him. He now knew that he would not meet Madeline at the hotel, which in fact was the decision he had just made. His decision was about his life. No more story, time to get on with his new life and create a new story, one in which he celebrated his life. He knew to achieve this, everything must change. He was an adult and must take up his place in society however paralysed it appeared to be to him. He would have a conversation with Madeline about his decision, but when he was ready, and he had the words rehearsed and in the right order. For now, he sent a text to her telling her he wasn't coming to the hotel, then turned off his phone.

24

TOMMY

There was a middle-aged lady who lived in Tommy's building. She lived in number five, opposite side of the stairwell, down one floor. Tommy called her Flat 5 Lady. She watched television but only detective and crime shows, mostly re-runs; you could hear the Mike Post theme music of the various shows emanating from her flat, day and night. She'd been acting weird lately. Tommy didn't think he liked her much but she was the only person in the building who took any notice of him, apart from Lemon Guy, but Tommy could do without any attention from that maniac. Flat 5 Lady was company for Tommy, sort of. She kept cats: one at a time. But then sometimes more, it was confusing. Tommy had to stop himself from thinking about killing them; he had to stop himself thinking that a lot. Once he ground up some glass and put it in half a kilo of mincemeat. Green glass was hard to grind, a lot of people wouldn't know that. Another time he swung a lump of wood around his apartment, like he might practise a golf swing, only instead of hitting an imaginary ball, it was an imaginary cat. He threw the mincemeat out, then realised some stray might eat it, so he had to retrieve it from the dumpster and got covered in rotting food. Lemon Guy saw him, and called him a filthy cockroach; this is what Lemon Guy called him when he wasn't calling him Franz. Lemon Guy was mental but with an unexplainable literary bent. The whole thing, the thinking about killing, the grinding of the glass and the sifting through the dumpster just made him feel so useless. He had to keep thinking of new ways to kill just to keep himself interested. But Flat 5 Lady kept buying new cats like it was some kind of game or maybe they were the same cats, he couldn't tell. It made him feel empty and sick and it was a distraction from his writing. He had to find his story and urgently. He knew he didn't have forever. Tommy hated cats. He couldn't see why anyone would have one, even Lemon Guy. Cats despise you for who you are, like humans do, and cats are useless at protecting your place as well, they don't goddamn care, again like humans.

A dog can love an evil-smelling fat bastard. But not cats. Dogs will lick you even when you are covered with rotting food, and they will protect you, even when you are hardly worth protecting. Tommy would like to have a dog, but he couldn't look after himself, much less a dog.

On top of all the problems Tommy had and the lack of help from Doctor Reynolds, he also had a shitty job. His job was to fill inkbottles for fountain pens. It was the kind of job fat people got. Most people think fat equals stupid, so when you are fat, people treat you like you are stupid, and that is the kind of job you get too: a fat stupid job. Tommy thought he might write this down somewhere, it had a ring to it. But he didn't. His job consisted of sitting in a dingy factory at Edwardstown, five minutes from his flat, north along the Great Southern Road – in *shedland*, as Tommy called it. The shed he worked in was freezing in winter and stifling hot in summer. Tommy noticed how he couldn't keep warm even when it was forty degrees in the shed. He would sit at his station with his old blanket around him freezing and sweating, filling bottles with ink for goddamn characters with fountain pens. It was a crappy job, but he did get lots of time to think about his writing and also to watch Merry Mary. Merry Mary worked on the bench opposite. Even she had noticed Tommy had lost weight. She said the other day, 'You losing weight?' That was the first time she ever spoke to him but she didn't look at him when she said it. Tommy looked away. He watched her breasts bulge when she screwed the caps on the bottles. He'd think of her when he masturbated. Doctor Reynolds thought this was quite natural. She was the only girl Tommy knew close up, not counting Flat 5 Lady or Ruby, although he didn't really know Ruby, not to speak to anyway. Tommy had never spoken to Ruby and never would.

Anyway, there is at least one good thing about losing weight. Tommy could masturbate now with his hand. He was now able to reach himself. Before, when he was too fat, he had to use an old tea towel, he held on to each end with his hands and wrapped the middle around his penis and then worked it back and forth like you would do polishing your shoes, only in reverse of course. A while ago before he started losing his weight on a day when he had felt okay, he thought of asking Merry Mary to have a beer with him. He was going to, but just when he was about to, he started losing all this goddamn weight and he thought she wouldn't be interested in him if he wasn't fat like her.

A few nights back, Flat 5 Lady knocked at Tommy's door. He looked at her through the eyeglass in the door and made out he wasn't in. When he saw it was her, he wished it was Ruby. He let his stertorous breaths condense on the door as he watched her standing there. He thought she was going to accuse him of killing her cats, although he didn't know why he thought that because he hadn't killed any of her cats. She was dressed in a clothy red dress, which showed her uneven cleavage. She had a mad-hatter velvet hat with a large feather sticking out of it: maybe it was a quill. He just wished he could wear that hat. She had put too much make-up on, but that's what you would expect. She wore the same lipstick colour as Ruby, only much thicker and it ran over her lip line. While he was watching her through the peephole, he thought she didn't care about the goddamn cats; she wanted to be jumped. Of course she did, she was middle-aged and leathery. She probably thought, 'Someone like him would be happy to jump a middle-aged leathery woman like me.' He leant his cheek against the door for a while; some blood-stained dribble ran out of his mouth. It smelt peculiar, but good to him, like all his body smells. Then he looked through the peephole again. She was still there. She was scratching at a piece of dead skin on one of her fingers. She kept sticking it in her mouth, trying to catch it between her teeth to tear it off. He went and got a tin beer from the fridge. Then, because he was exhausted, he just sat against the door and every now and then, he looked to see if she was still there. She stopped working on the skin after a while, and disappeared. Shortly after he heard Lemon Guy scream out like he was in pain or something. Tommy peered through the peephole and off to the side he saw the strangest sight. Lemon Guy was lying on his back on the landing being held down by Flat 5 Lady; she did this with nothing more than a piece of cotton string across Lemon Guy's eyes. She held the cotton down either side of his face and it was making Lemon Guy scream with pain but he didn't seem to be able to move. Tommy watched as Flat 5 Lady looked over to his peephole and smiled at him. Tommy got it that she was doing this for him. She was showing Lemon Guy that a middle-aged leathery lady was not to be underestimated. Tommy started breathing quickly, he thought it was great; he admired Flat 5 Lady. She then removed the cotton string and Lemon Guy jumped away from her. He looked at her like he was real goddamn scared. He staggered about, still blinded, and stumbled up the stairs to his flat. Flat 5 Lady sat on the landing looking over at Tommy's peephole smiling and started working on that tired soggy piece of dead skin some more. He looked at her and looked at her cleavage. He guessed he could do her. Water ran out of his eyes. He went and got another tin beer and some nuts. He put the nuts in a bowl with some extra salt, opened the door a crack, and slid out the beer and nuts, then closed the door again. He felt a lot of affection for Flat 5 Lady; anyone who could do that to Lemon Guy had to be admired. And if he had to, he would jump her, if that was what she wanted. Funny thing was, if he saw Flat 5 Lady crossing the road, he'd probably slam into her. Nothing personal, it was just who he was, and because of who he was, that was the kind of thing that happened to him.

He stole some ink. He was expecting the police to visit him any day now. He didn't steal it for himself. He didn't have a fountain pen. Tommy was not a character like that. He stole the ink for Flat 5 Lady, for her quill if that's what it was. He wrapped the ink in Christmas paper and got one of those ribbony things from the newsagent and put it in her letterbox. He wanted to do the same for Ruby but he couldn't interfere in her life, so he didn't. He was really cold: cold in his flat, cold in his head. He was so god-damn cold. He'd have to do something soon: he'd have to make a decision. Other posters around the city featuring the Minister of the Interior said, 'You have to play the percentages in this life. Paradise rewards gamblers.' This poster was on the top of the Paradise casino on North Terrace over the central railway station. Tommy knew he would soon have to take a chance, before it was too late.

He slid over to his desk, pulled his exercise book from the drawer and started to write shakily, '*Lord Twinings releases a new range of teacakes which he calls ancien cakes. They are a big hit.*' (Tommy's research in the Paradise library paid off.) '*The Lord expands to new and larger premises. And shortly after, he invents the tea bag. He would later tell the press, "It just came to me, out of the air." He thinks this is a great joke and he doesn't tell the press he got the idea from his brother's tampon invention, when his brother accidentally slung it into his tea cup. He had a blue argument with his brother over the invention. The Lord argues that no woman is ever going to stuff a tea bag thing where his brother was suggesting, it was plainly ridiculous.*' Tommy scribbled over this last sentence. The two brothers were at odds over the invention; one saw the invention as releasing and the other as absorbing – both were right.

Someone put photos of women with blood smeared over their bodies in Tommy's letterbox. He looked at them; it made him dizzy. He knew this would happen one day. It made him think of Merry Mary and how he'd like to do her, and then maybe kill her, run over her as was his usual method. The photos reminded him that he was a killer. He didn't need that.

Tommy got shocks when he touched things at work; from the toilet handle, the seat, even the button for flushing, so he stopped flushing. In fact it had been years since he flushed. He left things, his things, in other people's toilets – he felt guilty about it. It was the electric shocks. He was too scared to touch Merry Mary, even if he was allowed to.

In the past six months Tommy had lost three quarters of his body weight. Yellow skin hung off him like waves of tripe. He thought he should go to a doctor. He went, but he felt too sick and had to leave before he threw up on the magazines. He could try again, when he felt better. But he never thought of it then. Recently he had started vomiting whenever he ate. In the end, he could only drink. He drank tin beer but it couldn't be cold.

He thought Flat 5 Lady had got another cat but he decided not to kill it. She kept letting it out into the stairwell whenever she heard Tommy ventilating his way up the stairs. He couldn't be bothered with her cat. He almost hoped he'd see Lemon Guy again.

Flat 5 Lady slipped a photo of her breasts under his door. He was at his spyglass and saw her do it. He thought he should ask Merry Mary out. He could practise on her, then try Flat 5 Lady and maybe he would be okay, but he'd be too scared about the shocks. Maybe he should just ask Flat 5 Lady in and let her show him what she wanted. He needed to feel better though. He needed to get warm first. He wouldn't want to let Flat 5 Lady down. He was sick of letting people down.

25

PETER AND RYAN

Ryan and Peter were floating in a tinnie on the south end of Paradise Lakes, originally known as West Lakes, due to its location of being more or less west of the city and having a man-made lake which, in fact, used to be a swamp before PERP sanitised it. Peter and Ryan spent the morning floating under a sky marked with wispy scudding clouds, as Ryan was moved to observe. Earlier, before Peter had properly started his day with a coffee, Ryan rang contesting that it was a beautiful Sunday morning and they should make the most of it by hiring a tinnie and filling in some time before Ryan's shift, which started at three. Peter agreed, although without Ryan, Peter would never have bothered. He would have instead finished reading the weekend papers and wasted the rest of the day doing not much of anything, maybe watching the nurse opposite ironing if she was around. Peter's superhuman powers extended to his ability to waste a lot of time.

They were supposed to be fishing, but neither of them knew the first thing about fishing, and it was doubtful that there were any fish in this lake. So they spent the time drinking beer and picking at a big platter of seafood Ryan had picked up from Stanley's fish cafe in Gouger Street before it closed its doors for good. They watched the yachts race back and forth with exhausting and incomprehensible purpose.

'So what's the point of all that then?' Peter asked, looking at the yachts swishing by.

'None. I would guess,' said Ryan.

'No point is the point I suppose,' Peter said.

'Pointlessness has a point.' Ryan punctuated his point with the sound of a ring-tab pop of his next beer. He handed it to Peter and got another out of the esky for himself. 'If not, then there would be no point to your life, as a case in point.' Ryan busied himself scratching his left leg.

'Women then?' Peter ignored Ryan's sarcasm and decided not to wait for Ryan to stop scratching his leg.

'Yeah, women,' Ryan replied and continued scratching as though he had discovered something odd about one of his freckles.

'I suppose a strategy is what is needed?'

'You think too much,' Ryan said. 'You need to loosen up, let your natural style do the work.'

'Good to know I can always fall back on my natural style.'

'You can't find anything you're looking for. It's a well-known fact.'

'Correct.' Peter scoffed. 'I certainly didn't find Belinda.'

'You know what your problem is, Moley?'

Peter looked out over the lake's waters toward Paradise Hills. He once took Belinda up to the Paradise Waterfall. They had had a wonderful day. Belinda had prepared a picnic lunch and Peter sat on the blanket in the picnic grounds and fell in love with her and got bitten by a Paradise tick.

'You live in the past.'

'What?'

'Yes, you live in the past. That is where your present and your future are stuck. Belinda has gone, mate. Gone. Finito. She left you, she's not coming back. Get over it; time to drag your present into the now and give your future a chance. For a start, snag yourself a Paradise angel, the world's your crustacean my friend.' Ryan lifted a polystyrene plate loaded with oysters and held it out to Peter. 'Crustacean?' Peter declined.

Peter had heard it all before. He had heard it from Ryan and from Madeline and he was smart enough to know it himself. Madeline talked about the Great Sadness, but Peter had his own sadness that lived under the Great Sadness, and one of them was re-naming Adelaide as Paradise. Peter wanted Adelaide back.

'Do you ever feel your hopes are dashed?' Peter asked the indefatigable Ryan.

'Not when I'm mucking about with boats, Moley.'

'Nothing kills a bad product faster than good advertising,' Peter said. 'The Minister of the Interior has been tireless in his endless promotion of the benefits of living and visiting Paradise and as a consequence, achieved nothing more than drawing attention to its failings.'

'I've drunk too much, I'll have to cancel my shift today,' Ryan said. He pulled out his mobile and started dialling. 'Did you buy a new car yet? I saw a nice one on a small lot along the Great Southern Road the other day, had your name on it.'

'Really.'

'Yeah a little cutie. Just what you need, and it would save me from having to transport you everywhere for free in my cab.'

'I suppose I could take a look, no harm in that, but even if I had a car now, I would be too drunk to drive you anywhere.'

'Typical,' Ryan scoffed. 'Look for the car lot next to the crash repairer, a red Beemer, it is right at the front, you can't miss it.'

Peter hadn't gotten off to a great start with women. There was the excruciating chook-shed day with Ruby, whom he hadn't seen since. It was a day he regretted, and will for the rest of his life; he owed Ruby a kiss from that day. And Belinda, of course, the whole Belinda moment was big.

'You don't hear much about lover's balls these days,' Ryan said out of the blue. 'I remember that mythical ache you get from not having sex when you are a teenager. We had it all through high school, or at least that is what we told the girls.'

'Of course there is no actual scientific evidence proving the existence of lover's balls,' Peter said.

'Yeah, but I remember we were always bending over in dramatic agony.'

'Or dramatic irony,' Peter scoffed. 'No one was convinced.'

Peter couldn't remember anyone from school, well, hardly anyone. He remembered Hawkey, who he formed a friendship of sorts with, but lost touch when Hawkey left school soon after the incident behind the chook shed. Hawkey had been close to his remaining twin sister Allie, especially after the accident. From time to time, Peter thought of his school friend and wondered what he might be up to these days, and if he was married, or with someone, and what kind of a life he was living. He was reminded of the death he witnessed on the Great Southern Road when he was a nine-year-old boy. He remembered how the next day at assembly after the car ran over the girl from his class, which was Hawkey's triplet sister, they had a moment's silence. Immediately after the silence, they had their milk, which was by then warm. To this day, the smell of warm milk brings back a complex cache of memories of the dead girl, the heat of the Great Southern Road, warm cucumber sandwiches and his mother's perfume and sticky tar and most of all, Ruby.

Ryan jumped awake with a snort and looked at Peter in a way which suggested he had not snorted.

Peter was quite sure Hawkey wasn't one of the guys he discussed lover's balls with anyway. He wasn't the kind of guy to invite that kind of discourse. In fact, for the longest part of their friendship, they never spoke a word to each other.

'You remember Hawkey?' Peter asked Ryan.

'Doin' time in Paradise jail, I heard.'

'Yeah, but since then, he'd be out now?'

'Blames himself, I reckon.'

'Blames himself for what?' Peter asked Ryan.

'Everything.'

'Don't we all.'

'Lover's balls eh?' Ryan mused. 'You know it's real bad for you, you can get cancer from it and die within a week.' They both laughed, which caused the boat to rock precariously.

26

TOMMY

Flat 5 Lady was standing over Tommy in the bathroom. She helped him up and leaned him over the sink and washed the sick and blood off of him. He couldn't remember how he got there or if he had run into Lemon Guy again. But he didn't feel any pain so maybe he was just sick and Lemon Guy had nothing to do with it. He didn't think Lemon Guy would try anything if Flat 5 Lady was around. She helped him to his bed. She was really surprisingly strong.

Between his waves of nausea, Flat 5 Lady started talking to him, but it was like she was in a cheap film and the sound was not good. Tommy couldn't understand anything she was saying. He wished she had subtitles, but then he thought he was too sick to read quickly. She undid his pants and pulled them down but she got them all caught up with his shoes, so instead of taking off his shoes, she just got his pants down to his knees and gave up. He hoped the building wouldn't catch fire. She also changed the bandage on his hand. She cleaned out the maggots.

She pulled down his underpants. He felt the cold air. He hoped his underpants were clean and he hoped that there wasn't any smell from his cock. It sometimes smelt funny; it used to when he was too fat to reach it. It went putrid a couple of times and he had to get a nurse from the Paradise Hospital to help. 'Nurses are angels,' Tommy thought and their uniforms were always so well ironed. He wondered if Flat 5 Lady had been a nurse at one time. She looked at his cock and pressed the end of it, like she was trying to prod it awake, or like it was a button that automatically opened something; a remote control perhaps? He would write if he could. *A tanned girl in English Avenue walked past a loading dock of Eat Cake Inc., and the roller door opened and everyone looked at her as though she had done it, but she hadn't. And none of them, the girl included, knew that there was a remote penis operating in the area.* Tommy had stopped writing, and that did something to him, something not so good. He started crying. He felt very embarrassed. He tried to thank the old lady but his voice was too scratchy and his throat was full of vomit. She left him alone.

He hated the flats. He hated his life. He felt exhausted all the time, even while he was asleep he dreamt how exhausted he was and then woke up even more exhausted. Nothing ever made any sense. He was surrounded by debilitating absurdity and he was the centre of it. He didn't want it to happen in his flat. He was tired of imagining killing people on the road. Just thinking about it was soul-destroying, but he had to keep on thinking about it. He believed if he didn't, he might lose concentration and actually kill again.

Tommy had to stop going to work; he couldn't stand any more shocks. Merry Mary sent him a get-well card and it made him cry. But he might have already been crying. He was now crying pretty much non-stop.

His sister wouldn't talk to him. He called her to talk about getting lighter but it was no good, she hung up on him. He couldn't blame her. She had her own life massaging footballers.

He was spitting up green tissue and blood. The tissue smelt like how his cock used to smell when it got putrid. He tried to write again.

'*Later in the early nineteen hundreds, tampons finally started selling but not until a chemist opened. The Lord's brother had to wait for the chemist to open.*' A few weeks ago, Tommy thought about getting some medicine. He drove into the city to find a chemist in Hindley Street. He drove past a lot of chemists to get there, but he wanted to just drive around for a while. He wandered up and down the chemist aisles trying to find medicine. He had no idea what he needed. He saw a woman who looked familiar. She was buying tampons; she wore a yellow hat.

He tore up his exercise book with the little energy he had left. The tea bag story was stupid. Untrue, like him. He could see now there was no point to it. 'There's no goddamn point to me,' he yelled at the top of his voice, which used up all his energy.

He seemed to have stopped losing weight. There was none left to lose. He couldn't leave his bed. He needed the blanket to stop himself from floating up. He was so light. Flat 5 Lady came in every day and gave him buttered teacakes, which were absolutely heavenly, she said. Ruby had made them for him when she had heard he was unwell. They were the only food that didn't make him nauseous.

After he had finished one of Ruby's teacakes, Flat 5 Lady held his cock and waited. At least it felt warm to him when she did that. She bought her device in and secured it to the side of his bed. She engaged it, and bucked like a brumby. He watched the sweat fly. He watched her naked breasts bounce preposterously. She looked French with her hair up. She seemed to enjoy it. He hoped she did. Afterwards, she dunked a tea bag in a cup in front of his face; he sipped at the warm sweet tea. He felt sorry for her, sorry that his cock did nothing when she held it, she deserved more from him. She was trapped in her own sexual cubicle, and he got the impression she thought he might get her out. But he couldn't. He wanted to. He wanted to help people and not be a burden. It wasn't even as though he wanted to for himself; he wanted to for her sake, it would have been some contribution to someone else's life he could make – after all, he couldn't do much for Ruby, not in his current state of health. He thought maybe Flat 5 Lady would call a doctor for him, but she didn't. He couldn't blame her, she was mad herself. It was the flats or it was her life that made her mad. Her life was full of secrets and disappointments. Like all lives in Paradise; everyone was trapped in one way or another, in one secret or another, in one disappointment or another, in one adage or another, in the promise of hope. He could sense her story was a gluey gossamer forming layer upon layer of secret binding history, like a Danish pastry, like families, like brothers and sisters. Tommy felt sorry for her because she was a failed person, like himself, but he was also a killer. There was something about her desperate airs and graces that hinted she had come from a better life, like she might have lived in North Paradise or Prospect, and once, a long time ago, when she was young and her skin was smooth, her life might have been full of expectations. Now she found herself living in a crappy flat in Clovelly Park, nursing a killer and holding his penis, controlling a maniac, and waiting for PERP to start work on the building, which everyone knew was never going to happen.

The blood was getting worse. It oozed out of his mouth and made a mess on the pillowcase. He stunk again. He stunk so much it was unbearable. But strangely, for the first time in a long time, he felt good. He felt the best he'd felt for weeks, maybe years. He had found the story he needed to write, the story that could save him. It was a pity that it came when he was too weak to write any more, but he was happy to be feeling good. He felt so goddamn good, he felt sleepy. He had Flat 5 Lady to thank for his story emerging, and for keeping him alive long enough to find it.

Just before he drifted off into a promising sleep, he remembered the cat he killed which was just an accident. He ran over it with his car, and he heard it squeal, and its bones crush. He ran around to see what had happened. All its teeth were bared at him, like it was blaming him and not its goddamn self for getting in the way. The cat was just in the wrong place at the wrong time. Or Tommy was again. It smelt like lemon. It was Lemon Cat. And he had to re-live the nightmare. It wasn't his fault; it was synchronicity. It felt like synchronicity was stalking him.

He didn't mean to kill Lemon Cat. He never meant to kill the young girl. She just stepped out in front of his car. He was too young to kill. He didn't know you could kill with cars. It was goddamn synchronicity. He saw her step out, he felt that everything went into slow motion as he hit her, and she disappeared under the front of the car. He felt the bump as the tyres rolled over her. Paradise could be hell; some people enjoyed this paradox, without really understanding how profound an effect it had on their lives. He had killed a young nine-year-old girl. The police called it an accident but Tommy never felt like it was just an accident.

Tommy's body closed down into the heaviest sleep, as though all his life he had been waiting to have this sleep. It was dark. He made the mental observation that there was no great white light.

27

PETER

Peter and Ryan had both drifted off into their own silence in the boat. Peter worried that sex might have been the reason for Belinda leaving. His father never spoke to him about sex although Peter would have died of embarrassment if he had, but as it turned out, Peter's father was eminently qualified to discuss the subject. Regarding his sexual education, Peter found out the usual way; he panicked his way through. The trauma of the day behind the chook shed with Ruby and Hawkey and that damn dolphin wasn't the best start to a boy's sexual odyssey.

'Remember Ruby?'

'Of course.'

'You know, I had an agonising schoolboy crush on her for years.'

'Yes everyone in the school knew that Moley... Remember the old rabbit punch?' Ryan said.

'Rabbit punching was the preferred punishment of the day at school.'

'Yeah, that and Chinese burns.'

'Oh yeah, Chinese burns, I'd forgotten about them.' Peter smiled at the memories flooding back.

Ryan popped the ring pull on another two beers and passed one to Peter.

'I never did tell Ruby how I felt about her. I suppose you didn't have those kind of conversations when you were a teenager. You don't know how to. Don't you find that sad?'

'Bugger me,' was Ryan's only contribution to Peter's question, apart from, 'there's nothing as much fun as mucking about in boats, Moley,' quoting *Wind in the Willows* for the second time. Ryan started paddling with his arm over one side, causing the boat to move in a circle, round and round they went, but why Ryan felt this was necessary right then was not immediately obvious to Peter. Peter found going around in circles unsettling in more ways than one.

About two years ago, Peter had met a guy from school who turned out to be the younger brother of a woman who was a grief counsellor and whose house was one of the houses broken into by, of all people, Hawkey. This grief counsellor visited Hawkey in jail a couple of times and had recommended him to a psychologist friend of hers, a Doctor Robert Reynolds, after Hawkey was released. Peter knew Doctor Reynolds. He was the senior consultant at the Paradise Mental Institute and Peter had had a couple of site meetings with him and the engineers, on the new hospital wing. Peter had some vague recollection that this grief counsellor woman had also treated Ruby when Ruby was a teenager. Where was Ruby today, right now, he wondered? Peter questioned what he could possibly say to Ruby though, if he ran into her again. He was so ashamed of his behaviour that day behind the chook shed; he doubted she would have ever forgiven him. He certainly hadn't forgiven himself.

He had always regretted not telling Ruby how he had felt about her; maybe it would have changed everything, for both of them. Ever since, he found he couldn't help himself from telling the girls in his life, who he might be taking out for the second or third time or sometimes more, how special they were, and how he felt about them. He knew he shouldn't always do this. He knew they sometimes looked at him as though he was weird. To be fair, it didn't work, but he just couldn't help it. He couldn't make that mistake again.

'How many girlfriends are you supposed to have?' Peter asked Ryan, who was wiping some spittle from the side of his mouth with his sleeve.

'It's not for me to make you any more depressed than you already are, but the usual number for me is one a day and two on Sundays.' Ryan said this between gulping down the last of his beer, crushing the can, and finishing with an operatic burp that sent a flock of cockatoos scattering from a nearby eucalyptus in someone's backyard; a burp to rival his snort.

'I thought Belinda was it for me. It never occurred to me that she wouldn't be.'

'Fascinating though this is, don't feel you need to tell me every little detail of your life, Moley.' Ryan squinted his eyes into a ridiculous face.

'You are hopeless, you know that about yourself?' Ryan asked but didn't seem to require an answer.

Peter picked up the oars and began to row back to the jetty. Bloody hopeless, a lost cause, Peter thought to himself. Ryan was right about him.

Peter knew he was trapped in his own personality. His heart only ever wanted two women, first Ruby, and then Belinda. He had dedicated everything to both of them. He had tried to date post-Belinda but it didn't work. He just wasn't the kind of guy who would be satisfied with casual relationships. It was just who he was and he didn't suppose he could change that about himself.

Peter knew he never really stood a chance with Ruby. She was his teenage unrequited love. It never concerned him that he had only been sixteen when he fell in love with Ruby. Romeo was supposed to have been the same age and Juliet even younger, and no one questioned their love.

With Belinda, he thought he had found someone on whom to vent his endless capacity for love and who loved him in return. But he was wrong, and he lost Belinda. He lost her on a number of levels. He found it impossible to stop wondering why this had happened. Madeline said it was meant to be, he was meant to be with someone else, although she urged him to try to contact Belinda and see what might be done. He never tried to find Belinda. She had a sister, he could have contacted her, but the sister was mad, and anyway, Peter just couldn't see the point of it. If Belinda had decided to leave and left, then that was the decision made.

Summer days had long passed, and winter's low afternoon light crept through the quiet shadowy rooms of Peter's flat. Peter felt the chilly air swirl and settle around him. He stood naked in front of his mirror, evoking his superhuman powers, which enabled him to leap tall bouts of self-assessment in a single bound. He asked himself, what was he like? Was he okay? He wanted to be okay at least. But what kind of a catch was he? How did women see him, for example? What was their first reaction? What was their second reaction? Did they have a reaction? Should he be thinking about this as much as he did?

He lifted his penis for a second then let it drop. He always considered this tube of flesh hanging off him to be quite strange, even alien, as though such a thing had no place being on a human, certainly not on the male of the species. He thought men were the least qualified to be in charge of a penis. Penises were complex. They caused life-long confusion by confining men's responses, while at the same time effecting a disingenuous liberating facade. In other words, a penis acted as both a binary trap and a freedom, not unlike living in Paradise, Peter had observed. A penis infiltrates and informs every aspect of a man's behaviour, but counters its demand to be taken seriously by ensuring that men are never allowed to think about it circumspectly. Peter noticed the goose bumps covering his skin as the chill advanced upon him, but he did nothing to warm himself. It was over twelve months since Belinda had vacated his life.

Setting aside the appropriateness or otherwise of his penis, he came to the semi-confident decision that he was okay, with his clothes on – naked was another matter altogether. He wondered how his life's events had changed him. He peered at himself, even squinting, as though squinting would either reveal or shield the truth. There didn't seem to be any discernible physical changes but he knew he was changing and not just physically. Madeline had obsessed over these kinds of philosophical questions of life. Now he found he was following in her and Socrates's footsteps: 'An unexamined life is not worth living' – difficult though, if the examination reveals little substance. Perhaps Belinda had examined his life and determined she should move on. Was that it?

He'd learnt to survive. For a start, he'd learnt how to dress himself – that is to say, he could with reasonable confidence make fashion choices without choosing shirts and ties that clashed savagely. The trick here was that he had figured out how to shop – that is to say, he figured out how he should shop. Without the guiding and impeccable colour-matching talents of Belinda, he realised he would have to develop a shopping philosophy. He shopped in particular proven places and let the shop assistants he trusted put his wardrobe together. By way of a method, he had done this twice since Belinda left, at the beginning of summer and then again at the beginning of winter. He thought this was far more practical than Belinda's method, which didn't really comprise anything remotely resembling a method. She would shop as she went, ad hoc, for herself and for him. It wasn't unusual for him to get home from work to find a new jacket or a couple of shirts in his wardrobe. Another reminder that he didn't have Belinda in his life any more was the business of his underwear and socks. These things had never reached his conscious level; he simply always somehow had them. Sometime after Belinda left he noticed how so many of his socks were now single and had lost their match, and that his jocks were disintegrating. He realised that these things needed to be attended to and that Madeline, and then Belinda, in some unspoken act of passing the baton, had taken care of this part of his life. This made him feel uneasy;

he had allowed these things to be taken care of for him, as though this was some male right, certainly an embarrassing admission for him as a male and, he now concluded, unacceptable. He now had to look after himself, so he developed his shopping philosophy – an architecture effected by a critical path, as he liked to describe it. Perhaps more management than was warranted in this area of his life, but it ensured his life was organised and didn't descend into some kind of wardrobe chaos. He wanted to prove to himself, if to no one else, that he was capable of looking after himself, not that he had much choice in these matters. To give credit where due, this had been Belinda's argument.

Continuing in the spirit of self-management, he learnt how to cook, not that he did much, but he could if he got sick of takeaway, as he did every now and then. Cleaning and ironing he had always taken care of himself. Other changes in his life included not having to spend time on the subject of marriage or starting a family. These topics had been constant preoccupations for him during his happy days with Belinda, but now he had no need to spend thinking, or planning, or discussing time on any of these subjects. There wasn't anyone with whom to discuss them now, if you didn't count Ryan, and it was best not to. For a while he and Belinda had discussed things like going overseas to live for a time, or perhaps buying a house. They spent a lot of time discussing these subjects; what they would do, when, how it would fit with careers, where they might buy a home, would they build or renovate, when they might start a family? These are topics that only have relevance if you are a couple. They both agreed any-thing was possible, but whatever they did together, they would *be* together, they would be a couple, a team, best friends and in love, and it was the grandest feeling. Belinda luxuriated in it. You could just tell. Lately though, consistent with Peter's examination of his life, he had started to think that perhaps this was his perception of their time together, and that his per-ception was quite some distance from his reality. Perhaps he was guilty of seeing and hearing and feeling what he had wanted to be true; he had seen his life the way he was, not the way life was.

'Rakish.' He looked at himself in the mirror and this was the word he decided, if generously, that best described him. If you cock your head to one side and squint, well, you can get close to rakish, he thought. But if you try this outside your flat you will skate right past rakish and end up as the village idiot, especially if you are naked at the time. He looked okay and there was sufficient rakishness left to almost have a Peter O'Toole, *Lawrence of Arabia* kind of feel. Well maybe this was a little ambitious. He had a good physique, a legacy from his football training, and his penis wasn't any stranger looking than it was meant to be, he supposed, and of course he didn't have any of his mother's freckles. He did feel he might be showing some preliminary signs of weighting up around the middle; more crunches at training will take care of that, he thought. He had started watching the saturated fat intake – the pizzas from Bella's had to be curtailed. He checked his reflection and sucked his stomach in. When he did this, he could see definite traces of a six-pack, well a four pack for sure. At least with the four pack, he didn't have to hold his stomach in all day. He felt very exposed and self-conscious standing this long in front of a mirror, naked. What if someone was watching him? Someone always was. He looked around the bedroom, then through the door to the lounge. There was no one there, of course; it was just a reflex response born out of an acknowledged pathetic desolate hope. He looked out of his window and across the courtyard to the nurse's flat to see if she might be watching him, but her flat was in darkness. He grabbed a clean pair of jocks from his drawer and his running shorts, slipped them on and pulled on a sweater.

Peter considered himself fortunate to have a career he loved, and apparently one for which he had some talent. He placed little store in the office rumours about his future associate partnership prospects as it was years away at best, and he still wasn't sure he would stay with the firm in the long term. In any event, he had some competition for promotion from his colleague Maria, whose talent he felt far surpassed his. But he was yet to turn on his rakishness, which would no doubt bridge the gap, not that he felt in the least like he was in competition with Maria; she had a way of making him feel very relaxed and unusually clever. In fact, Maria always seemed to find him funny or interesting, or both; she laughed easily with him. The birthday card she gave him, whilst not declaring she was going insane with sexual desire for him, was very thoughtful and sweet. Peter liked this feeling. It was after all *a* feeling, and a good one. Feelings, good or bad, were few and far between these long days, he felt.

'We can't all be Romeo and Juliet,' Ryan said in relation to nothing in particular, the day they painted the floor of Peter's flat.

'Do you think they're a good example?' Peter thought out loud.

'What, you don't think so?' Ryan answered.

'I'm not so sure. There is something about them, which is, well, a bit bland, don't you think? At any rate, they are not even together any more, they are dead, and let's not forget fictional.'

'Bland? Bullshit.' Ryan was not one to dwell on the subtexts of life. 'Possibly, only possibly though, as a couple they were possibly a bit bland. But apart, and in their own right, they were anything but bland. No way bland.'

Ryan was referring to Baz Luhrmann's film and in particular the two stars, Leonardo DiCaprio and Claire Danes, although you would have to know Ryan well and the way he thinks in order to know this was what he was talking about. Peter knew Ryan's thought processes pretty well.

'Of course as a couple they were very much for each other, against over-whelming odds, projecting in, not out, as it tends to be with two people as in love as they obviously were,' Peter added, which somehow explained it all, if only to Peter.

'Bugger me Moley, how'd you get to be such an old man?' Ryan slid down against the wall and rested his paint brush on the side of the paint can and opened a couple of beers. 'Time for a Kit Kat.' He handed a can to Peter. 'Who's the sexiest woman in Hollywood? Nicole would have to be up there, don't you think? I always think of her when I am nobbing someone,' Ryan said.

'That's bizarre.'

'Have you seen that young Tunisian actress, she was in whatsitsname, you know, the movie with camels, and that guy you see all the time on British dramas who can sing good soccer songs. And I think I saw her in a documentary as well, about an animal maybe, or maybe an island, or maybe it was an animal on an island. You know her?'

'No, do you?'

Ryan was always talking about people no one had ever heard of, but he rarely remembered anything of significance about them that could lead to figuring out who he was talking about.

'Do you mean to suggest that this guy sings soccer songs well, or the songs he sings are good?' They both felt they'd known each other for cen-turies, so making life as difficult as possible for each other was an essential plank of their mateship. It's the way you talk when you are painting a floor with a mate, and half dozen cans of beer have already been consumed in the pursuit of the meaning of life.

'If I knew what I meant, I'd have you say it,' Ryan scoffed in return.

Peter was aware that men often think about women other than the one they might be making love to at the time. But he did believe the day you were consumed totally and only with the woman you happen to be making love to, and that worked, that was the day you'd found your partner forever.

The whole Belinda scenario, with the engagement ring and the growing old together was starting to feel so, well, stupid. So like 'hello, is anyone there?', as Ryan loved to say. Ryan watched way too many LA teen movies. It had been a long time since Peter had thought about the diamond engagement ring he had abandoned to one of his kitchen drawers. It must still be sitting there, in the dark, in its box, waiting to be released. It was starting to seem a long time ago since Belinda had vanished, but his memory of that momentous day was still crystal and agonisingly clear.

It had been his birthday. Now it seemed so long ago, it felt like he was another person then. That evening, he stood in front of the door to their flat, ready to surprise her. Just to think of her would make his eyes glisten. He had reached into his pocket to feel the ring. He ran his fingers over its cool smooth surface. It was modest, though not without charm and *some* distinction, he had hoped. It represented all his savings and was to have been the symbol of his future with Belinda, however old fashioned that seemed. And it *did* seem old fashioned, but what the hell. He believed he was out of his league with Belinda, but she seemed not to realise this herself and so there he was standing in front of the front door, ring in his pocket, about to propose to the girl with whom he intended to spend the rest of his life. That was it for him. He had sucked in the clichéd deep breath to steady his excitement, ran his fingers through his hair, turned the key and stepped inside.

For one sickening confusing moment, he wasn't sure he was in the right flat, in fact he couldn't be sure he wasn't in some soap opera television show, caught in some televisual cliché. The place was empty. Not empty, like as in, Belinda was out, but empty. Everything in the flat was gone. He stood in the entrance, which opened to the living room. He knew instantly. *Now* he knew. His legs felt like pylons sunk into the floor. He could physically feel his life draining through him. His eyes darted around the darkening space, he was trying to take it all in. But there was nothing to take in. Even the phone had been disconnected, and unhooked, and removed. All that was left in the room was a square of fluff where the sofa had been. He stared at it for a while. The fluff took on considerable importance; it was, after all, the only thing he had in his life right at that moment. The fluff of life, he muttered, as tears flooded his eyes. Later he remembered staring at the toothbrush sitting there out of its element on the kitchen sink, on top of his pile of clothes, on top of the note she had left. He couldn't think. He was empty. He was numb. Later that night he returned the ring into its velvet box and threw it into one of the kitchen drawers. He promised himself no one would ever see it.

Peter could say he was pretty much over Belinda now. He was confident he had moved on from her. He heard some time ago through Ryan, who had met one of her ex-workmate's sisters, a dental assistant to the dentist Ryan found when he hit his mouth, in particular his tooth on his steering wheel, doing what he never fully explained, and had to go to a dentist urgently, that Belinda had moved to New York to get married to an Australian writer teaching creative writing at Columbia University. She lived on W57th Street, and had something to do with the Russians and tea and deli sandwiches. The details were a bit sketchy – Ryan claiming the influence of a local anaesthetic, a mouth full of tampons, fingers and instruments of war, as he explained it, in his mouth, no doubt overstating everything, prevented him providing Peter with any further information or even clarifying the information he did get. Peter felt sick all over again. It was so inexplicable and so unfair and finally over. Her opportunity to one day tell him why now seemed to have gone forever. He now had two unanswered events in his life to do with women. The first was to do with Ruby – he failed to kiss her when he should have, which could possibly have changed his life. The second was Belinda, who left without explanation, taking his life and his future with her.

The unanswered questions of his life were getting larger and more distant from any potential answers. Lately he found himself wondering more and more about Ruby, who was his first love, but he put this down to the fact that most of his time these days was spent alone. Maybe it was time for him to start using his superhuman powers of self-appraisal for something more positive; after all, he was who he was, apart from some things he might do or not do around the margins of his personality, he was pretty much a finished project. All he lacked was the wisdom, which only comes with living your life, and he felt he was getting plenty of that lately.

She found him hanging in silence from a rope tied to the staircase railing. She found him circling and warm. She collapsed on the cold marble, like her skeleton had failed her. He was pronounced dead at the scene. The knot had fractured his larynx, broke his neck, then asphyxiated him – death was thorough.

PART THREE

28

RUBY

Ruby woke to a distant shout in the building. She heard a male voice yell, 'There's no goddamn point to me!' Her spider stirred smugly, as it would. Ruby broke out into a dizzying sweat.

Ruby had been at Easy Motors for over a year. She sat on the toilet seat at the rear of the showroom looking at the back of the toilet door. It was covered with photographs of naked women. A number of the girls had moustaches drawn on their private parts; one had a pair of glasses drawn on her nipples. The flies buzzed around Ruby with indifference – they didn't land on her; they just seemed to watch her. One of her feet rested on the soiled toilet seat cover she had brought along in her first week at Easy Motors. It was discarded on the floor amongst the stained *Playboy* magazines and various automotive journals. She had become immune to the stench of urine. She tied the tube around her arm and pumped her hand a couple of times to get the vein to stand proud. She punctured the scar tissue with the needle and pushed down on the plunger. She felt the heat flood her body. The Sales Manager kept her supplied with the heroin. He let her shoot up in the toilet and took the money out of her pay packet. She was doing well selling cars; he told her this many times. She was cooperative and the best sales girl he had ever had, even better than the last girl, he had said.

Selling cars had turned out to be easy for Ruby, with the help of her little friend H. When a potential punter came in and ran his fingers over the contours of a car he liked, Ruby would appear next to him, open the door and let him slide inside. She would take him for a test drive, stopping at the back of the yard under the giant fig where she would lean over and use her mouth. She knew what men wanted. She had known this since puberty; her mother had explained it to her – although, to be fair, perhaps her mother had not expected Ruby to utilise this information in quite this manner. Back in the showroom the Sales Manager signed the punters up to the sale, and arranged finance, and added on insurance. In the event they tried to get out of the sale, the Sales Manager would remind them that it would be unfortunate if their wife were to find out about the special service they had received out the back. Ruby sucked different men off two or three times a week on average. She didn't know how many, maybe more. She had no idea how many cars she had sold. It didn't matter. Only the heroin mattered, it was the only time she felt life stir inside of her. Heroin kept the spider quiet and satisfied.

This is not how it all started. In the first couple of months she didn't sell a single car. She thought she was going to get the sack one day when the Sales Manager left a note on her desk asking to see her before she left for the day. She sat at her desk and felt so empty and useless; she knew she was going to get fired. Black long legs kept rising in her throat and threatening to choke her. She wanted to cry and fought against the tears and nausea. She couldn't imagine what she would do now. She felt so alone and exhausted. She looked without much focus through the glass front of the showroom and across the Great Southern Road. Cars blurred past in both directions; she saw, without it registering, a figure that seemed to be looking back at her. He stood next to the bus stop. She lost her focus and her battle to stop tears in her eyes. The figure blurred through her tears and disappeared from her sight.

The long shadows of the wintry dusk had started invading the showroom early and by the time it was five o' clock, she stood in the dark, in front of the Sales Manager's desk, with goose bumps across her skin. Despair was flooding her body. The spider was getting stronger and stronger.

'Do you want me to leave? I just can't seem to get anyone to buy. Maybe it isn't for me. I've really tried to sell the red BMW; it's such a nice car.' She said this to the Sales Manager in his tiny dark office at the back of the building. The other salesman had gone for the day. She stayed back every day to the last in the hope that someone might come in, and somehow she would get them to buy a car; but she had failed to sell even one car.

'I think you've reached the bottom, Ruby. I think you are very depressed. Do you think people want to buy a car from someone like you? What shall we do with you? This can't go on, you know that, don't you?' Ruby nodded her head in agreement; it was all she could muster. He switched on his desk lamp, which had the effect of making his head shine. 'Look, I've got something for you, to cheer you up. Are you game?' He sat behind his desk, his fat stomach bursting through his shirt buttons, his smile extending over his layered neck. This was a man you would never buy a used car from, she had often thought, and yet he sold many, more than anyone else. He gestured for her to sit down. She took a seat but felt so tired with it all, she could have easily just curled up in the corner and gone to sleep between his rusting Christmas tree and the large garish trophy with its melodramatic spike shooting out the top.

'You need to make the best of what you've got, Ruby lass, if you want to sell cars. Men do like you. Don't you know that? Just relax a little. Let them like you. You know, in selling, you've got to give them what they want. I think you know what men want, honey. You have to use your 'unique selling proposition'. It's basic selling strategy, darlin'.' He laughed his slimy laugh while looking at her breasts. 'Or should that be your USPs? Plural darlin', you get my meaning?' He looked at her, then at her breasts and repeated this several times until she worked out what he meant. Her eyes dropped to the grimy floor. 'Those are your unique selling propositions, baby, you get it?

'Look I don't mean to frighten you, Ruby, I'm trying to help you understand that success for you is guaranteed in this world, you have to share your attributes, you know what I mean? Be generous. You are lucky you have me as your boss. I understand you. I understand how the world works and I'm here to help you, okay? You do want to be successful, don't you?'

Ruby nodded. She felt a little relief surge through her. It was, after all, always comforting to have someone who was willing to help. She wanted someone to believe in her. She had no one in her life who fulfilled that role. She hadn't seen her parents in months and even then, there was a distance between them, as though they didn't want to be involved in her life, as though someone might hold them responsible for their daughter's life. If she didn't know better, it almost seemed she embarrassed them. She couldn't blame them. She felt an overwhelming affection for the Sales Manager who had given her a job, and a chance, and was still willing to persist with her in spite of her lack of success. I must not be scared, she said under her breath.

'Trust me, Ruby, I have something for you that will help you relax a little, see things more clearly, you understand? Once we get you nice and relaxed, I think you'll be very surprised at how easy it'll be for you to sell cars here, and you must start selling cars, Ruby. You do understand that, don't you?'

She watched his hand slip inside his jacket pocket and pull out a little plastic bag. He opened his drawer and searched at the back for a small leather pouch. He kept smiling at her the entire time. He undid the pouch and took out a spoon and syringe. She watched him prepare the white powder with complete indifference. The flickering light from his cigarette lighter licked the bottom of the spoon, and mesmerised her in the shadowy office. She felt she could have just sat there for the rest of her life and watched. She wished that was possible. She saw the white powder bubble up. She watched him suck the mixture up into the syringe. She saw the girl lying on the Great Southern Road with blood flowing from her head and she felt the white line between her and the girl tighten and pull her toward the body. She wanted to stop resisting its pull.

'Come here my little darlin', I've got what you need. This will change your luck. Trust me, I promise.'

Ruby dragged a chair to the side of his desk and sat more or less facing him. He took her arm gently and caressed her pale soft skin, then rolled up her sleeve and wrapped a rubber tube around her arm above her elbow. He twisted it tight. She watched him tap her vein, and she saw the vein stand proud.

'It's a beauty, my love. You're going to love this, it will make everything better and solve all your problems. You ready?'

Ruby, not taking her eyes off the vein, nodded. She watched the needle move toward her skin, and then felt the sting as it slid into her vein. The feeling of total relaxation spread out through her and she felt her eyes close, and her mind stop, and the pain cease.

She woke in cold darkness. She felt heavy and her neck was stiff from the way she had been lying on the carpet. The Sales Manager was asleep on his sofa in the corner of the room. She tried to stand up but felt a pain between her legs. She lifted her skirt and saw dried blood on the carpet and smears on the insides of her thighs. Her panties had been removed. There was a stinging sensation inside her. She checked herself closely but she couldn't find anything, even though she felt as if something was inside her. She found her panties underneath the desk and slipped them back on. She tried to stand but had to pull herself up against the desk. The Sales

Manager woke with a start. He jumped out of the sofa; it was the most she ever remembered him moving. His sudden movement startled her and caused nausea to rise in her throat and the spider begin to stir.

'You all right?' he asked with panic in his voice.

Her mouth felt dry. She thought to ask him what he had done to her, but she wasn't sure she could speak.

'You had a good time little one, didn't you?'

Her head started spinning and she felt she was going to fall. He grabbed her and sat her back down on the sofa. When he stood up in front of her, she noticed stains on his pants.

'I don't feel so good.'

'You're going to be okay though, aren't you?'

'I guess. What happened?'

'What do you mean? You got high then you fell asleep, that's all. I hope you aren't going to be ungrateful now. You know how much smack you had? It cost money you know, and you have to know how to get hold of it. I did you a favour, okay? This one's on me.'

'Yes, I'm sorry.'

'Good, you'll be okay, you just need some sugar. I'll get us a coffee, okay? You can go into the bathroom and clean yourself, you know, clean yourself up a bit, okay?'

'Yes, give me a minute.'

'No, now. It's late and my wife will be expecting me. I have to go, so go now.'

Ruby nodded, struggled to her feet and fell down again. He got her up by lifting her under the arms and stood her up. She could barely focus and she was worried about the intense pain between her legs.

'Look, I'll take you out to the toilet. You can sit out there until you feel better. I have to lock up.'

She nodded and as he helped her out the office she saw how all the pencils and markers from his desk had fallen on the floor near where she had woken, some of them were in a big bundle held together with a rubber band. He was a messy pig; everything in his office was filthy, she found herself thinking.

After a couple of hours sitting in the dark, she got out of the toilet. Ruby stumbled home toward her flat. She barely felt the freezing wet wind against her legs and face. She had no recollection of reaching the bus stop on the Great Southern Road. The rain-blurred lights of the traffic mesmerised her. She looked at the spot where the young girl had been hit and died. She just wanted to lie down on the same spot. She just wanted to sleep. She closed her eyes and stepped off the kerb.

29

MADELINE

At the Stamford Hotel Glenelg, in front of the water slide, across from the beach, Madeline met an opera singer. Madeline often visited the hotel's lounge for a quiet drink after her visits to Sheila's *Paradise Found* beauty salon. Going to the salon was work on all sorts of levels and the hotel's lounge offered a place to recuperate. On this day, the opera singer sat at the next table. They exchanged smiles. They sat silently and self-consciously for as long as they could manage. Finally, the compulsion to break the silence exceeded the need to be silent. They started talking. They felt a camaraderie, and before they knew it, their conversation had taken on a life of its own, containing a surprising energy and spark. Feeling expansive, Madeline invited the opera singer to join her at her table and they ordered a bottle of white wine. Almost immediately the opera singer started relating a story to Madeline. If asked, neither the opera singer nor Madeline would have been able to account for the spontaneous story bursting out of the opera singer, but Madeline found it fascinating and didn't question the reason for it. The story surrounded the opera singer's recent visit to London. She told Madeline how she became so cold shopping in New Bond Street that she decided on a whim to treat herself to high tea. She chose Brown's Hotel, in Albemarle Street. The opera singer explained to Madeline how a girl, Allie was her name, was also having afternoon tea, sitting at the next booth. In a strange and surreal moment, Allie accidentally knocked one of her teacakes off her tier. In cartoonish slow motion, they both watched it roll toward the opera singer. The opera singer said how it felt so profound somehow. This rolling teacake heading for her seemed like a random moment in the universe but full of meaning, although what meaning she couldn't say. Madeline didn't want to interrupt but she felt that this was the case with all synchronistic random moments, and that all that was lacking was someone to interpret the inherent meaning. The opera singer told Madeline she gasped operatically when the teacake rolled along the carpet, heading straight for her. She and Allie watched it hit her foot and break open. It released its thick raspberry jam between her toes. The opera singer told her story with such dramatic operatic flourish that Madeline found herself gasping at the mental picture of raspberry jam-infused toes.

Neither the opera singer nor Allie could have known that the outcome of this innocent teacake rolling across the worn purple carpet in Brown's Hotel, Albemarle Street, London, would ricochet with life changing effect, halfway around the world; to be more specific, Madeline's world.

The opera singer told Madeline how she and Allie fell into easy conversation. They soon discovered they had both grown up in Adelaide, and both lamented the name change to Paradise. That day in the lounge room of Brown's, two strangers chatted about the most intimate things with each other. Perhaps the honesty of their conversation was reliant on the fact that they would go their separate ways, and in all likelihood never see each other again – or perhaps there was an immediate chemistry between them, which happens sometimes between strangers. Even the waiter, sporting frayed cuffs, and who served them their tier of cakes and creams, sensed an occasion. He celebrated in the connecting chemistry between the two women. He felt exhilarated in a way he couldn't explain as he quickly came to the rescue with paper towels to slurp up the jam.

The flow-on effect of this serendipitous meeting between the opera singer and Allie resulted, a year or so later, in the bringing of Madeline and Steve together again. One innocent teacake had the effect of changing Madeline's life in a way she would never have imagined possible. These connections, while as fragile as a butterfly's breath, seem also simultaneously cast, as though fated. Madeline's policy was not to argue the toss with destiny versus coincidence. All she could do was respond to life as it unfolded and, as she had always tried to do, make the best of it.

The spontaneous intimacy between Allie and the opera singer eventually led Allie to speak about her brother, Steve. Listening to this unfolding fascinating story, it wasn't long before Madeline had worked out that this Steve, Allie's brother, with his enigmatic nickname of Hawkey, was indeed the Steve who was her son Peter's schoolboy friend. The opera singer and Madeline both gasped at the coincidence of it all, and both remarked while ordering another bottle of wine just how small the world was. Madeline remembered the quiet boy her son had introduced to her once at a parents' day. He had had an impact on her. His politeness and good manners impressed her. She remembered how good-looking he was but also she felt touched by his awkwardness. She remembered how he had always referred to himself in the second person. She found this odd at first, but then like Peter said, you get used to it after a while.

The opera singer, now slumping a little under her own weight and the effects of the wine, told Madeline all about Allie, and Steve, and their story. Madeline found it shocking but also entrancing. According to the opera singer's memory of her conversation with Allie, Steve had survived it all and was out of jail, and had a job as a spray painter at a crash repairer on the Great Southern Road. He was doing well and had been featured in a local newspaper as being one of the best in his trade. He had learnt his skills during his time in jail, where it was said his rehabilitation was accomplished. Allie had related her story with considerable pride, and described the agony of losing her triplet sister in a car accident on the Great Southern Road.

Madeline could not get the story out of her mind. She felt connected to both Allie, whom she had never met, and to Steve, whom she had met only briefly a long time ago. After all, she had been a witness to the accident which took their sister from them and which had affected her own life so profoundly. Within days of hearing the story, she found herself looking up the crash repair address in the phone book (she needed work done to her car after Peter had scraped the passenger side door on a railway sleeper down at Victor Harbor recently). She needed the services of a crash repairer and she had been meaning to stop at one of the shops on the Great Southern Road for a few weeks now. But why not seek out Steve and give him the work? It all seemed so practical. In all honesty though, it was more than just needing a crash repairer. She felt butterflies in her stomach thinking about seeing him after hearing his story, although she couldn't say why she felt this way. It was all very odd. Peter and Steve had been good friends for a time. In fact, Steve had been Peter's only friend at school as far as she was aware. She knew she wanted to see him and she knew she was going to.

She found Steve's crash repair shop. It was next to a car yard called Easy Motors. She was only a short distance from the car accident site and this, as it always did, made her think of Ruby and that terrible day.

As Madeline stepped out of the car, he approached her. She recognised him. He had grown, filled out, muscled out – he was no longer the awkward teenager, now he was an awkward man. He didn't remember her at first, but then when she told him who she was, he smiled down at her, with a smile that literally ended, if ridiculously, between her legs. She winced at the crudeness of this feeling but she couldn't deny the truth of it. They started talking; well, Madeline started talking. Steve, she thought, had things to say, but no way of saying them. It made him all the more attractive because it made him vulnerable; it was like trying to help someone struggling with a stutter. Not only did he take her breath away and make her feel things she couldn't explain, but he had turned into a tall blond smouldering hero type as well. She could feel that bodice ripping with every second she stood next to him. She watched his body move like fluid under his white, fastidiously, if incongruously clean overalls given he worked with paint. He inspected the damage to her passenger-side door. She could not explain these feelings. He placed his hand gently on the body, caressing the peaks and valleys, and lifting the paint with his fingernail, examining it like it was the most important flake in the universe. She went home, undressed and fell back on her sofa and felt rapture.

30

RUBY

'How you feeling today, Ruby?' Ruby walked into Wendy's office, and sat on the leather chair in front of Wendy's desk.

'Good,' Ruby answered while smoothing her skirt.

'"Good?" Are you sure about that? You know I have been seeing you for years now, and it's been many years since the accident. Do you feel you have made improvements?'

'I guess so... Sure.' Ruby tried to find something inside her that could be considered an improvement, but she couldn't. The heroin was the only thing in her life now which provided any relief.

'I know someone, a psychologist like me, only I specialise in grief management and I think you might need a more broad examination. He's quite brilliant. I was wondering if you would agree to see him. I think he might be able to help progress you further. Perhaps more than I seem to be doing. What do you think? We have covered your grief related problems and I think you need more than I can offer.'

Ruby shrugged her indifference. She could only think about getting back to the office for another hit of heroin and feel nothing again. But before she could score from her Sales Manager these days she had to sell a car, and the only way she could do that was if she took the customers around the back of the yard. The Sales Manager was getting harder to please. He was withholding the stuff from her when she needed it. He was demanding she sell more and more cars, and that included helping him sell to his own clients by blowing them in the showroom or in his office. Once he closed the showroom early and let her shoot up in his office, and then two men turned up and took turns fucking her on the bonnet of the car they were buying. The Sales Manager sat in his office doing the paperwork.

'His name is Doctor Reynolds, Doctor Robert Reynolds.'

'Uh huh.'

'So you will see Doctor Reynolds? I should tell you he's writing a book;

it's his second book actually. He's interested in people's life stories, Ruby. He thinks we all need to find our story; it's a key to who we are and to surviving trauma in our lives. It's a coping mechanism, he contends. He is examining if we all form or follow our story unconsciously. Do you think you have a story, Ruby? I think it will be worth your time. I think you will find him a brilliant, caring and sensitive man. I am having dinner with him tonight. Can I tell him you will see him? He may be able to help you find your story. I can let you borrow his first book; it might be of some help?'

'Sure.'

Ruby stared off into the middle distance. She looked through the wall out into a field, the sun was shining and she ran and skipped across the field through the flowers. She saw a figure in the distance, a boy she felt she recognised. She stopped and put her hand up to shield her eyes. She strained to see who he was but she couldn't tell from the distance.

'Ruby, are you taking drugs?'

31

MADELINE

After Steve had completed the work on Madeline's car, Madeline didn't see Steve again. She had no idea of how to see him, even if she should, or even why. But if she did see him, she couldn't imagine what was to be gained. She was at a loss to figure out why she was even thinking about it, so she let it go. Then two weeks later, he knocked at the back door.

He stood in front of her. The sunlight was backlighting his head so his face was in darkness. She imagined his white stallion was probably grazing on the front lawn as he stood in her doorway. His sudden appearance caused her nervous system to ignite, or jump, or electrify. It did something which defied description. Her mouth dried and she panicked that she might not be able to speak without a gasp. Why was she reacting this way? This was not like her. Her first impulse was to kiss him. She could smell on him a faint and not unpleasant smell of cold milk. This reminded her of early mornings, dropping Peter off at his primary school. She insisted on walking Peter to the gate every day. She knew he hated it. She liked the cool smell of milk being drunk by the school kids before school started.

'Madeline.' This seemed like a long sentence for Steve, but it said everything either of them needed. When he said her name, she felt nothing would ever be the same again.

'Hi.' It all seemed so surreal, the conversation such as it was, sounded like dialogue from a black and white movie, where the men wore white suits and smoked French cigarettes, and the women were beautiful, photographed in soft focus, in the shadows thrown by venetian blinds.

She stepped aside and allowed him to enter.

She followed him in to her lounge room. He said nothing, but looked around inspecting her life. He picked things up and put them down gently, in exactly the same place, as though he didn't want to corrupt her world with his presence. He ran his fingers across the books on the bookshelf. She thought he seemed to be looking for something, something about her, her life, perhaps her secrets, whatever they may be, she thought. She felt giddy. He pulled out a book and inspected it; *The Plague* by Albert Camus, one of her favourites, although it had been years since she had read it. He looked at it thoughtfully for some time as though it triggered a memory he was having trouble understanding. He peered behind where it had been, and along the back of the rest of the books, again as though he was expecting to find something. She remembered some private letters she had hidden there for safekeeping. Her passport was hidden there as well, behind *Gulliver's Travels* and *Robinson Crusoe*. He moved effortlessly around the room, caressing everything. She felt his touch.

'The bathroom,' he whispered. She could hardly hear him. 'Would there be a clean towel? You like to be clean. I want to be clean, I have just left work,' he said correcting himself. She had the impression that this was the most he ever spoke in one go and that he was nervous with using words, or sentences or sounds.

Madeline felt simultaneously nauseous and exhilarated and petrified, and several other emotions she couldn't identify, as everything seemed to be colliding inside her. She wouldn't in all honesty ever have imagined herself in such a situation in her life. She couldn't imagine what Sheila would make of all this, and how much she would give to hear this little tale. Madeline found it all so incredible herself. It was not something she could ever have hoped for, or prepared for, she had no template of how to respond. In the life she had led, it wasn't possible to have this kind of experience, to feel this way, but she decided she loved it. She decided she must live her own mantra of making the best of what life throws in her direction. Thoughts of her husband flashed into her mind. She wondered if he had felt like this with his other women. If he had felt like this, then she couldn't blame him. 'Yes,' she answered, barely finding her own voice.

He hesitated and looked at her, as though he was telling her something about himself.

Madeline touched his lips with her finger to stop him talking, if indeed he was ever going to.

'I know,' she whispered.

Madeline stroked his hair with her fingers.

'It's through there, the bathroom,' she said and pointed the way. 'I will get you a towel.' She surprised herself with her own matter-of-factness but something inside had taken over. The opera singer had told her about

Steve and Allie, and how they both had been treated by their father. While there was no intimate detail revealed, it still had fascinated Madeline. She felt a very strong affection for Steve and she couldn't wait to touch him.

As she moved to the linen press, she tried to swallow but found it impossible. She knew how much it seemed like a preposterous plot from one of her racy novels. She wouldn't believe it herself, if it wasn't happening to her.

He waited at the bathroom door for her to hand him the towel. 'Do you have a nail file?' he whispered.

'In the bathroom cabinet,' she answered, as absurd as the question seemed.

He stepped in but left the door ajar. She found herself standing there for moments, not that she could think of anything else she wanted to do, or anywhere else she wanted to be. She couldn't move, she didn't want to, she felt a heavy feeling in her limbs. She was content to listen to the water running and breathe in his steam. She saw herself as a young girl lying on the back lawn on a hot night. She felt the tingling sensations over her body working their way into her, awakening her, as if from a dream, as if somehow from her life.

Steve became a constant in her life; although she decided to keep it their secret. Madeline felt Peter might not be able to handle their relationship. Peter, she thought, had enough to cope with in his life without finding out his mother had taken up with his best friend from school.

32

PETER

Madeline sat in the hospital reception area waiting for Peter and looked at her mobile again but there was still no message from Steve. Having Steve in her life seemed absurd on so many levels but she couldn't help herself, she was addicted to him, and she hoped he was as addicted to her. The last message she had received from him was worrying her but she had no real reason, nothing explicit that supported the need for worry. He still had not responded to her text to him when she asked if anything was wrong. Her phone remained silent, and in that silence she dreaded the worst.

'What's the matter, you look like you are crying?' Madeline said, concerned, as Peter came through the hospital's revolving door. Peter stiffened as Madeline wrapped her arms around him and kissed him on his cheek and accidently brushed his lips, leaving a wet smear. She couldn't kiss him without wetting him, or marking him with her lipstick. He spent the next few minutes trying to wipe off her wet without appearing to do so. It was a moment he could well live without in his adult life. His mother was an enigma to him. He didn't understand her. It concerned him that he did not know much about how she lived or what she felt about her life. He knew general things but not details. And it wasn't that he lacked interest, or hadn't asked, he had, but still he couldn't say for sure what she did, or what she thought about. She was simultaneously coquettish and needy. It was confusing. More than that, it was pretty damn annoying. He had grown up with her, yet never felt close to her. His father he knew even less about, but this didn't concern him in the same way. He felt close to his grandpa.

'Hi. No, just the dust out there got in my eyes,' Peter explained.

'You got the can't-help-its? You let things get to you. You have to watch your oxygen intake.' She wrapped her short arms around him and hugged him. Peter was having trouble reading her. It alarmed him a little. His mother had always been the strongest influence in his life, but lately, she just seemed annoying. Perhaps that was a bit strong; could it be he was just growing up, or worse, she was getting older? He didn't know. He had sensed that something wasn't quite right with her. She seemed frail, or sad, or needy, Peter thought.

'I'm as strong as ever,' she said, reading his thoughts, 'don't you worry about me, in fact in some respects, I've never been better. Your father did me a huge favour. Look at me, not bad for a woman in her forties, don't you think?' She stood back and turned side on. It was almost as though she expected a wolf whistle or something.

'I bet I'm in better shape than you naked.' She laughed.

Peter smiled awkwardly. Why did she say such things? This wasn't a thought he wanted in his head.

'Look,' she pinched the skin on the back of her hand. 'Look at that, still young skin, do you see?'

He couldn't figure out what she was saying to him. She sometimes did the most bizarre things. Or not so much bizarre, he supposed, more just surprising. He felt guilty though; she was his mother and he should know her well enough not to be surprised at anything she did or said.

'Anyway, it's your grandpa that needs comfort. Do you want to go straight up to the ward?' She checked her lipstick and teeth in her compact mirror. They were standing in the entrance to the Adelaide Hospital; for some reason the hospital had retained its name, as though its business took precedence over the aesthetic nonsense of what it might, or might not, be called. And the matter-of-factness associated with such a place excluded it from having to submit to political expediency. Peter's nose detected the faint smell of antiseptic, and he heard the squeaking symphony of nurses' white shoes as they hurried about their duties. His mother continued her grooming, while hospital staff and visitors continued to surge around them like corpuscles around a blockage.

'Yes, I'm here to see grandpa.' He was irritated by having to say this, why else would he be here?

'You sure you're strong enough for it? He doesn't look so good, you know.'

'Of course, what are you talking about?'

'Nothing, it's just that, well he looks smaller. You'll see, lighter somehow.'

'Well I want to see him, that's what I am here for, and I am not a child. I am sure I will manage.'

'Okay, I wasn't sure, that's all.'

What wasn't she sure about? That he wanted to come? Or the reason for him coming? His mother very often spoke in riddles. He wondered how he'd managed when he was young, only understanding about half of everything she ever said – not that much had changed in that regard.

'How long are you staying? I have some news for you.' She headed off toward the lifts. He had to scurry along after. 'At least I think I have some news,' she mumbled to herself.

'What news? Is everything okay?' Peter always felt so drained with Madeline. His brain seemed to slow up and he was always lagging behind. It was like when she took him to school as a child, his little legs could never keep up with her, and still now, as fit as he was, he was still trying to catch up to her.

He wished he could be back in his apartment, in his white serene surrounds, sitting in his cane chair looking out into the atrium, and watching the nurse in the apartment across from him. He loved to watch her go about her life; he found it soothing seeing her iron her uniform. He wondered if she was a nurse here at the Adelaide Hospital. Maybe she was looking after his grandpa? Strange how he felt an intimate and comprehensive connection with a complete stranger he had never met, while his relationship with his mother was much less clear.

'We can go for coffee after, if you have the time. Did you walk here?' Madeline asked.

'I walked along the river,' Peter responded.

'You want me to drive?' he offered, for no real purpose other than to fill the void while they went up in the lift.

'No thanks,' she answered with a scoff in her voice, suggesting Peter would be the last person on earth she'd let drive her car.

'Just because I have written off several of your cars in my youth, there's no need to be like that,' he said, smiling.

'The last time you drove my car, you banged the car door against a sleeper and I had to get it spray painted.'

'Oh yeah, I forgot about that. You get it fixed? You never sent me the bill, how much was it?'

'That's okay, it wasn't very much. In the end it turned out to be quite lucky.'

'Oh, okay, but I still want to fix you up for it.'

'It's okay, Peter; I have been well and truly fixed up already.' She couldn't believe she said that, but she smiled inside just the same. They both kept their eye on the display indicating the floors as they went up. 'I won't come in. I've been with Dad for an hour or so. I will meet you downstairs, but take as long as you like with him. He is in a coma but they say it helps if people he knows sit with him and talk to him. Tell him something personal, they say that helps too. Tell him a secret, if you have any.'

The elevator stopped and the doors opened. Peter stepped out leaving his mother searching for the 'door close' button in the lift. He saw her check her phone, as the lift doors closed.

Peter wondered what he should think about his mother. It was the first time he had ever noticed her check her mobile phone and he couldn't think of anyone that might call her. He did not know her friends. He did not know her enemies, not that he imagined she had any. He knew nothing of her life and it was something he felt guilty about. He realised at that moment he didn't even know her mobile phone number. He always called her on her home phone and if she wasn't there, as she often wasn't, he just left a message. There was never any business between him and his mother that was so urgent it couldn't wait.

Peter wiped at his grandpa's eyes and used a tissue to wipe the spittle from the side of his purple mouth. The memory of Ruby washed over Peter to the rhythmic ping of the heart monitor.

'Well okay grandpa, I want to tell you something; something no one else in the family knows; something you will enjoy finding out about, so pay attention now.' Peter leant forward on his seat to get closer so he could whisper to his grandpa. What he was about to reveal to his grandpa was not for public consumption.

'*So grandpa, you remember Ruby from school, I was in love with her and you saw her once I think and you liked her. Well Ruby was my first, you know, well maybe I need to qualify that, she was my first sexual encounter, not that much happened but it all happened behind the chook shed at Ruby's house two houses up from ours when we lived in English Avenue.*' Peter watched his grandpa's eyes for any flicker of acknowledgement but there was none.

'*It was a bizarre experience. In the end it didn't turn out to be that difficult to break, you know, her hymen, scary but not difficult. Thankfully, it didn't seem to hurt her too much, at least I hope it didn't. Later she told me it felt a bit like the stinging you get when your mum dabs Dettol on a graze. It took several attempts before we managed it… before*

I managed it, Hawkey had to just watch. You remember Hawkey, we hung out a bit at school. He didn't talk much, he did some time for break and enter but I think he is okay now. You liked him too, do you remember?"

Peter could hear a low gurgling coming from his grandpa. He didn't know if this was his way of responding to what Peter was saying or his body going about its business of dying. Peter thought he might fluff up his pillow for him but he didn't know if that was a good idea, so he didn't. The sounds of the hospital continued as white noise in the background and he felt safe, crouching next to his grandpa.

'Anyway, I had no idea how hard to push, we'd never done this before, Hawkey or I, in fact, neither of us had even seen a girl's private area before. Hawkey said he'd seen his younger sister Allie heaps of times, but I didn't think that counted, although why I would have thought that defies sense.'

Peter spoke with animation, but it was like he was caught up in the memory, lost in the recollections of himself as a sixteen-year-old boy. *'I still remember the humid summer and the smell of chook poo and how comforting the clucking hens sounded. Ruby lay on her back in the tall dry grass, her dress up over her hips, her panties off and her legs spread. She was sixteen. In fact it was her birthday and later that day we were supposed to be attending her party. Ruby was already well developed as my father often pointed out to me. He would say, "the boy that picks that cherry, will be a hero… a hero, boy, a real hero". It was my father who first made me look at Ruby, you know, in that way. Father talked about her womanhood a lot, and how well developed she was. I guess he meant she already had breasts. She had fantastic breasts, I guess, for her age, and she was already the most popular girl at school with all the boys. None of us could stop looking at her, talking about her or, later, thinking about her. But none of us had gotten near her either. The closest any of us got, was seeing her in her bathing suit at the pool – that year every boy in the school signed up for swimming. She stood out amongst the other girls, so much so that even the girls watched her. The boys would dive in the pool and come up right in front of her as she sat on the edge of the pool with her legs spread open and dangling in the water. It was a game, played with Ruby's consent, or so we thought. The object of the game was to try to see and count the tiny hairs poking out from either side of her bathers between her legs, then to return to the other side of the pool to say how many had been seen and counted. I didn't do this; I was too scared, but Todd Brian, the school's swimming champion and richest kid in school, reckoned he saw and counted six. This was the school record and remained so in perpetuity along with his time for the hundred metre butterfly, his specialty stroke, at least that is what we thought his speciality stroke was but how wrong were we? Todd was involved in a car accident later that same day as it turns out, you might remember all that. He was the passenger in a car that smashed into a Stobie pole on Blackwood Road at one o'clock in the morning. The papers said his body skidded across the wet bitumen several metres from the car. He was unconscious on arrival and had a penis in his stomach.*

'*Before we got to the business of breaking Ruby's hymen, she let us see her breasts. My father was right, she had spectacular breasts although it wasn't as though I had seen others to make comparisons, but they were round and white, and I was amazed to see how big her nipples were. They were at least double the size of a fifty-cent piece. She let Hawkey lick her nipple and then told me to do the other one, which I did. It didn't taste like anything in particular, but I liked it anyway, it was rougher than I expected. So was Hawkey's, although he had to tell me this later, I wasn't going to suck the same nipple as him. Anyway, I figured you could pretty much assume they were going to be alike.*

'*I say hymen but in truth, neither Hawkey nor I had any idea what it was or that it even existed before Ruby told us what she wanted us to do to it. Her mother told her all about it and gave some books to Ruby, which she passed on to us. Hawkey and I learnt more from Ruby in those two weeks about life and sex than we had so far managed from the mumbling about the topic from our respective fathers and the* Playboy *magazine circulating in the boys' change rooms. For a start, I found out that masturbation was normal; although I couldn't find anything in the books about how often per day it was normal, so I still had that to worry about. Also, I found out that there is a thing called a wet dream, which I was worried was a result of me masturbating so much that I had busted something or had caused a leak or a strain. So I didn't have to worry about that any more. I also found out that girls also masturbated, which I thought was just unbelievable, although I can't think why I thought that, except maybe I couldn't quite see how they would do it. The only thing the books said about it, apart from the fact that they do it, is that they do it "occasionally". This worried me again, I didn't know how many times a day "occasionally" meant, and if there was a problem if you did it more than occasionally, however many times that might be – in my case, a lot. I wanted to ask Hawkey but I was too frightened he might say he didn't do it that much, and then I would have something wrong with me for sure. Other boys at school were always going on about "tossing", but with boys, you can't ever get from what they say exactly what they do.*

'*Ruby announced to me that she wanted her hymen broken on her sixteenth birthday and that I could bring a friend if I wanted, so long as it wasn't anyone dumb. She had thought about it because she suggested Hawkey, although she didn't call him that but I knew who she meant. She described him as the boy that doesn't talk. I didn't know if she thought it might take two to do it, or if I might not turn up if it was just me, or if* she wanted two boys for a specific reason which I didn't know and couldn't figure out. Anyway, I asked Hawkey if he wanted to, but it wasn't easy because he never spoke, he just nodded mostly. I mean I had no idea what Ruby wanted, what I was supposed to do, and if she might end up pregnant or not. I have to admit to being very nervous but also excited as you would expect. I mean we were going to be able to get a close up look at Ruby's private girl parts with all its hairs on display, about which the only thing we could say for certain was that there was at least six hairs. I think I even broke my own record in those few days before her birthday for tossing off, and I just had to hope I wasn't doing any lasting damage.'

This did seem like a strange subject to be telling your unconscious grandfather, days before he would probably die, but Peter had always had a close relationship with his grandpa and the story just seemed to be pouring out of him and if anything was going to have an impact on his grandpa, a story like this was surely going to do it. Peter had never spoken a word of this to a soul in his life. Madeline had said that he should tell his grandpa something personal. He hoped that no one came in to his grandpa's private room while he was talking, especially not the nurse across from his apartment. The chances are, she had seen him watching her and already thinks he is a pervert of some sort.

'Ruby told us she liked to be touched between her legs; she liked to be tickled there, so we were to bring something soft to tickle her with. Hawkey couldn't think of anything so he said "grass" suggesting that he would just break off a piece of grass and use that. I wasn't sure Ruby would want grass between her legs, so I pulled the feather out of an old Indian head band I used to play Cowboys and Indians with when I was a kid. I thought it was soft enough, in fact, I know it was because the moment I thought of it for Ruby, I also thought of it for me, and I used it to rub up and down my dick but then I had to stop because it was now full of my stuff and I had to worry if this would make Ruby pregnant, even though I'd scrubbed and washed it hard. I washed the thing so much it lost a lot of its feathery bits and looked weird and sorry for itself, but I couldn't find another one anywhere, apart from off one of the chooks in Ruby's backyard but I couldn't sneak into the chook pen and start chasing chooks around without having a good reason for doing it, and I couldn't think of any. So the feather I had, had to do, it still worked just as good on me although I had to stop in case I got my stuff on it again. I don't think it would have survived another wash. Even though it was pretty clean, I still had to worry if one of my sperm was still hiding in it someplace waiting to get inside Ruby but I had no choice, I didn't have anything else I could use, and I didn't think Ruby would go for a piece of grass.

'*I studied the books really hard but still I was very nervous and still didn't know what I was supposed to do or why Ruby wanted it done. This last thing, she explained sort of, she said she didn't want her first time to hurt like her mum had told her it might. This just didn't make any sense but Hawkey and I both nodded as though we understood but I didn't and I don't think Hawkey did either. She said she was doing this for Todd sort of, as though this would explain everything to us, but it didn't. And it feels nice, she said. I guess I liked it when she said that.*

'*She let us touch her breasts, which was good and it made me really hard, so hard I had to stay pretty much bent over the whole time. Both Hawkey and I touched and tickled her breasts as best we could, although after a while I didn't know what else to do with them and I thought she might be getting bored with Hawkey and me touching her and licking her nipples, so I started to tickle my nipple (that is, not my nipple, her nipple but the one I was in charge of) with my feather, which she let me do, so I guess it was all right. Hawkey was sucking his nipple and after a while she pushed him off of her, so I guess she was getting sick of it. He broke off a piece of grass and started to tickle his nipple and she didn't stop him, so I guess I was wrong about the grass, although maybe, I still thought, she wouldn't want it for between her legs. She let us do this for a long time and she just laid there with her eyes closed. Hawkey and I looked at each other not knowing if we were supposed to keep doing this or not, but I guess we both decided to just keep doing what we were doing and let Ruby say when to stop and what next to do. We both kept looking at her box and wondered when we could tickle her there with our respective tickling items. She had an amazing amount of hair, much more than Todd ever counted. Todd was in for a big surprise.*'

Just at that moment a male nurse put his head around the door. 'Everything all right?' he asked.

Peter nodded yes and hoped he hadn't heard any of this story. It would be difficult to explain why he was telling his grandpa all of this. He didn't know why this story was just flowing out of him. It was as though it had been there all the time and now in this situation, he was finally able to let it out. His grandpa had always been interested in what happens to people. He was always asking Peter to tell him what was going on in his life. Peter always felt like he was disappointing his grandpa not to have any great stories to relate. He would have been too mortified during his teens to tell his grandpa this story but now it seemed like just the sort of story that his grandpa would appreciate and it was doing Peter some good in a way he didn't quite understand. Perhaps it was like it was some kind of burden he was getting rid of, but one he didn't know he had until he started getting rid of it. He continued on with this story, which seemed to be something of a basic key to his personality and to his adult life. It was a form of therapy. He leant over and brushed some of his grandpa's hair to one side.

'*When we would be allowed to move between her legs wasn't the only problem we had, we also had our erections to keep hidden, but the main problem was that Ruby's mother was home and might get suspicious at any moment and come out and see what we were all up to, although there was always something slightly suspicious about Ruby's mother. She seemed always to be smiling at me in a peculiar kind of way, as though she knew what I was thinking and how I felt about Ruby. Anyway, when we arrived at Ruby's house, Ruby had some tea ready for us which she poured, while her mother passed us a plate of teacakes she made special for the occasion she said. What occasion was she talking about? Ruby's birthday I guessed, although there were no candles or Happy Birthday spelt out in icing on the top of them. I didn't know what would happen if she found out what we were actually about to do and if she did come out to investigate. I didn't know how I would be able to run with an erection, after all there aren't many occasions when you are called upon to run with an erection, so it wasn't as though we knew how that would go. Hawkey and I hadn't discussed this and so we didn't have a plan. I was enjoying doing this stuff to Ruby but I was feeling sick about it as well. After a little more tickling of Ruby's nipples, she opened her eyes, which looked funny to me, and said to me to use my feather down there. She told Hawkey to keep doing what he was doing with his piece of grass to her nipple because it felt nice she said, and if he wanted to, he could run his grass up her neck and over her face and then back to her nipple too. He did this once because he probably thought it was better to just concentrate on her nipples, which were about double their size from when we started. But even so, Hawkey and I exchanged looks. I could tell he was really sorry he didn't think of a feather like me right at that moment. I shuffled down on my knees to Ruby's hips, careful not to unbend myself, especially as I felt a little squirt come out so I knew I would also have an embarrassing wet patch. I started to tickle Ruby between her legs and she opened her legs further so I could get a better go at her. I noticed the end of my feather had gotten all wet and I remembered that this is what happens to girls who are aroused, which was the word for it; I remembered reading in the books. I also knew that this is where you stick your dick in when you are rooting, or having intercourse, although I couldn't see any specific hole where this might be achieved. I even leaned right over between her legs to get a better look but I still couldn't see an actual hole through the hairs and I thought maybe they only get their hole when their hymen is broken, but I also couldn't see anything that looked like a hymen either, not that I had any idea what one might have looked like.*

'*Ruby's skin turned a patchy pink colour and she started breathing funny and even more so when my feather went harder at her and when my fingers and knuckles were touching her as well. I have to admit that I was doing this deliberately, I couldn't see why the feather should have all the fun, so I sort of let my fingers touch her area and when I did this my hand got really wet and it felt fantastic. I spurted for a second time in my pants and this time a lot, so now I had the problem for sure about how I was going to get home, and especially past Ruby's mum without her seeing a wet patch on my pants. There was something about Ruby's mum that if I had a wet patch, she would notice it for sure. She was that kind of person.*

'Ruby touched my hand but didn't stop me; she just turned her head to one side and even moaned a little. I was sure she liked what we were doing, although Hawkey, I could see, was concentrating so much on watching what I was doing, his piece of grass was missing Ruby's nipple but it didn't seem to matter to Ruby, she was moaning and even said yes a couple of times, which I knew meant she was really getting carried away. One of the cartoons in the Playboy *at school had a girl yelling out yes when the guy was tickling her with a feather duster between her legs; actually this is where I got the idea for the feather in the first place.'*

A large sigh or exhale came rushing out of Peter's grandfather, which shocked Peter for a second and he wondered if this story was causing his grandfather any problems. But then he didn't do it again so after a while Peter decided to continue as he was getting to the climax.

'So right at that moment, Ruby produced a strange looking thing from the grass. It was wrapped in plastic, which she took off and then I could see it was a small dolphin, although it was looking a bit old with some of its paint missing. She gave it to me and said put it in. I took it from her and looked at Hawkey, and instantly I got really worried and wished I had just stuck with a piece of grass like Hawkey. Hawkey looked away and went straight back to tickling his nipple with his grass. Ruby opened her eyes and asked me what was wrong and I didn't answer, I just looked at this dolphin and prayed I would figure out any second what to do with it. She said it's her mother's, it's a vibrator and you can push it in so she wouldn't get pregnant and that her mother said it was safe. I nodded, sort of, and put it between her legs but that's all I did, I didn't know what else to do with it. She said go on do it, hurry. I panicked and said do what, where, it was so embarrassing because obviously Ruby had expected I would know what I'm supposed to do, from the books she gave me or just from knowing but I didn't, I felt sick, sicker. But she looked at me and smiled, and took it from me and said like this and then she put it between her legs in just the right spot and it slid in a bit. She grabbed my hand and put it on the device or vibrator as she called it and said like that, just there, it feels good. So I took hold of it and sort of just held it there but then moved it around a little but I

didn't push on it, I didn't know how deep a hole she had there and I didn't want to hurt her or do any damage to her. But she said push, push it in. So I pushed and it went in further but then stopped. She said you'll have to push it hard now. Now I panicked, I didn't know how to do this but she said please, so I squinted and gave it a shove but it didn't move. She said that's it only harder this time. So I squinted again and this time I really pushed it in and it held for a second then went easily in nearly all the way. I was amazed at how far it could go in there. Ruby moaned which seemed more like she was sort of crying out, actually I nearly cried out myself, I might have done. Her noise scared me so I pulled it out and she closed her legs and rolled over. Hawkey and I looked at her and didn't know what to do. As I pulled it out, I must have moved its tail and it started vibrating in my hand. I turned its tail and it stopped. She seemed so sad lying there in the grass. I wanted to cuddle her but I didn't. I wanted to kiss her but I didn't do that either. Right at that moment I really loved Ruby, in fact that was the moment I fell in love with her. She sighed a couple of times and then said thank you. I looked at her and loved her so much right at that moment. I wanted to kiss her more than I wanted to breathe. Hawkey started pulling on my shirt and indicated by nodding that we should get out of here. I didn't want to leave her but he kept pulling at me. So Hawkey and I left her there. We snuck around the side of the house and as we did I heard the back door slam. We didn't stop but ran harder out the front yard and down the street. I didn't care about the wet patch in my pants. I was just so exhausted I wanted to go home and sleep. Oh and by the way, it is possible to run flat out with an erection.

'I didn't go to her birthday party later that day and I didn't see Ruby again until a week later. We sort of stopped near each other at lunchtime in the quadrangle. We only spoke for a second. She told me she was all right and about how it stung like the Dettol. Todd had his car accident the day of her birthday. I noticed her eyes were empty and after that day in the school-yard, I never saw her again.

'I have never stopped loving Ruby and I know I never will. When I'm ninety years old and dying and someone asks me what my last wish would be, I won't say, but I'll know in my heart it would be, for just a moment, to be transported back to that day behind the chook shed, looking down on Ruby turned over on her side in the flattened grass. I would lean over and kiss her on the lips. I just wished I'd kissed her, that's all, I really did. Whenever I think about this I feel the tears well up and I never feel much like a hero like my father had said. People would probably say, look at that stupid old bastard, he doesn't answer, he just sits there and cries.'

Peter looked up at his grandpa and a single tear issued from his left eye and rolled down his cheek. He wondered what regrets his grandpa had had in his life.

'Don't cry, grandpa. Ruby is probably married with children and living a happy life somewhere in Paradise with a husband who kisses her every day.' Peter felt a thickness in his throat as his voice faded. His grandpa heaved a big sigh, then fell silent and still. Peter wiped the tears away from his own eyes again.

Peter stood next to his grandpa's bed and made an awkward attempt to plump up his grandpa's pillow before leaving. He leant forward and kissed his grandpa's cheek and whispered the words, 'Sorry, Ruby.' Peter realised he was watching his grandpa die. He knew his grandpa was taking some of Peter with him. He visualised the girl's body on the road. Peter knew death. He thought over the story he had just told his grandpa, a story that he had never before told and one that had been trapped inside him all this time. He felt like a teenager again telling it to his grandpa. He had lost Ruby; well he was too young to do anything about it, or to understand how powerful that day with her would eventually be. He had lost Belinda. He wondered if this was his lot in life, to lose precious people. His grandpa was on the verge of death. This story had unleashed itself upon him. He felt a little calmer in some way as though something had changed for him, although he couldn't say exactly what might be different.

Peter recalled how Ruby had touched his hair and smiled at him in the school-yard the day she had asked him to break her hymen. He had felt so privileged to be the beneficiary of her smile. When she said he could bring someone else along to help, it never occurred to him how ridiculous it all was. Those were very innocent times when, for all he knew about life and girls, perhaps it would take the combined might of two schoolboys to break through that little defiant body tissue. He had this ridiculous thought of two school boys pushing with all their strength against a brand new hymen, and the thing being so strong that it springs back and sends the both of them catapulting out over the chook shed, clearing the hills hoist and landing on the back step of Ruby's house in front of her mother who then holds out a plate of her fantastic teacakes.

Ruby's suggestion that Peter bring Hawkey was easier than it sounded, for a start it would likely require a conversation with him. Ruby had seen him around the school, although she had never spoken to him herself; there had never seemed any reason to. Needless to say, no one ever met Hawkey by joining the debating team. Hawkey had lost his sister in the road accident on the Great Southern Road. She was Hawkey's triplet sister and while no one could recall if Hawkey was much of a talker before the accident, after, it was universally acknowledged that he had withdrawn, he no longer spoke unless it was absolutely necessary and only if anything he might want to say couldn't be conveyed in a nod or a shrug. People left him alone, even the teachers didn't require him to speak; everyone thought he would speak when he was ready – that never happened. Ruby then said something that amazed Peter. She said he might be a good choice because Peter was his only friend at school. This was weird, given that Peter and Hawkey had yet to speak a word to each other. They played the doubles match for the school tennis team, but that's it. Even so, she was right, although it wasn't until that moment that Peter had even realised he and Hawkey had become friends. She was also right that Hawkey was the right choice to assist Peter in this hymen-breaking mission. Hawkey was someone you could trust. Peter agreed to help her and recruit Hawkey, how could he not; she had touched his hair and smiled at him like no girl had ever done before. She seemed to really want this and Peter realised at that moment he could never let her down, however scared he was at the prospect of doing what she was asking.

Peter saw Hawkey at school at lunchtime the next day. He went and sort of stood nearby where Hawkey was sitting in the shade on a bench alone, eating his sandwiches from which Peter could smell the strong aroma of warm cucumber. The afternoon heat was heavy. It was the first time Peter had anything to do with Hawkey, since the tennis tournament, and in reality this would be the first conversation Peter had ever had with him apart from Peter telling Hawkey he had a good shot during their tennis games but you wouldn't call that conversation. Peter had felt nervous while both of them watched the younger kids playing their All Over Red Rover game. Peter saw the familiar sweat tracing lines down their ruddy faces in the heat. Their shirts were hanging out and flapping listlessly as a result of being tackled and caught during the game. The school-yard noise from the shouts and cheers as the game progressed competed with white noise of a zillion cicadas. He recalled the excitement of the mob waiting to catch the last few stragglers. The last remaining were always the fat kids who were big enough to crash through any resistance in the early stages of the game and repulsive enough that no one was too keen to want to touch them. Finally, they were all that was left and the mob turned on them with pent-up violence encased in mob anonymity and brought them to ground with ferocious brutality. When this moment in the game occurred, the dynamic changed and the centre mob galvanised into a single *Lord of the Flies* menacing unit where individuality no longer existed and civilised behaviour was crushed.

Peter introduced himself to Hawkey. He reminded him they had played tennis together once. Peter remembered how stiff this seemed, as if Hawkey didn't know him or wouldn't remember the tennis. But Peter didn't know how to get started. Hawkey never answered or spoke, he just sat there and rocked on the seat and kept eating his cucumber and tomato sandwiches from his Tupperware tub. He had one of those blue freezer packs to keep his sandwiches cool, but it had melted in the heat and the sandwiches looked pretty warm. He pulled a slice of tomato from the centre of his sandwich; it was the core end. He flicked it a few metres to the rubbish bin nearby. It was like his volley shot, Peter remembered, effortless and no more power than was needed, and deadly accurate. He took the occasional guzzle of lime cordial from a plastic bottle, which had been frozen and still had some bits of ice in it, which he tried to get out with his tongue. Peter remembered the sound the ice made as it flopped back and forth in the bottle. Hawkey wiggled the bottle around trying to help some more of the ice melt between holding it vertical in his mouth. Between all this, Hawkey read from a book resting on his lap. Peter could only make out the author's name from the spine when Hawkey closed it to attend to his lunch. The author was someone called Reynolds, a doctor of some sort. Peter had noticed Hawkey read books no one else read at school. Hawkey's reputation was that he was known to be very bright. Peter thought he could ask Hawkey about it, but then he figured Hawkey might have a limit on the words he spoke and to the words he could take in. In spite of Hawkey's silence, Peter felt they were, nonetheless, having a conversation, even though Hawkey wasn't speaking, or looking at Peter, or doing anything people usually do when they are engaged in conversation. But there was some indefinable connection between the two of them. Peter sensed that the awkwardness was probably what they had in common, in as much as you can have anything remotely in common with someone who has lost a nine-year-old triplet sister. You could never match something like that. Peter, having witnessed the accident, felt he had at least some connection with Hawkey.

Peter cleared his throat and, ready or not, launched into the whole story about the hymen and who the girl was and everything, as well as his butterflies. He didn't hold anything back, the more Hawkey said nothing, the more dead air had to be filled and Peter just kept talking. When Peter had finished, Hawkey just got busy screwing up the wrapping left over from his sandwiches and put it in his tub and then worked the lid back on, sealed it and then just held it lightly in his hands along with the book, looking out at nothing in particular, and nodded. And that was that. His nod didn't give any hints about whether he wanted to do it, or he didn't want to do it, it just indicated he would. Peter had the impression from Hawkey's nod that he was agreeing to do this to help Peter out, like it was something he was doing for Peter. This was when Peter learnt how much communicating Hawkey could muster out of a single nod. Peter felt that he did indeed have a friend in Hawkey, and Ruby was right about that fact. It didn't do much for Peter's butterflies but at least it wasn't all on his shoulders now to break Ruby's hymen and the fact that his friend Hawkey, a person he had never before had a conversation with, was willing to do something of this order to help Peter out gave Peter a confident feeling, a new feeling for Peter. He thought that he didn't feel quite so alone any more, that there was someone in the world with whom he had a relationship of sorts, however tenuous or undefined it might be. If he was still alone, at least he was alone near someone else who also appeared to be alone. Peter and Hawkey were friends.

33

TOMMY

Tommy was still all skin and bones, and looked barely alive, but over the past few months, with the constant attention from Flat 5 Lady, he had begun to improve. She did two things for him. She tended him with Ruby's teacakes to help with his convalescence and she told him a story about her son. Her son was the good Doctor Robert Reynolds, psychologist, in fact the very psychologist Tommy had been seeing. Doctor Reynolds, according to Flat 5 Lady, was the author of a book on trauma and its effects and the importance of 'personal story' as a therapeutic strategy. He was currently working on his second book incorporating case studies to extend his thesis. Tommy knew Doctor Reynolds all too well.

Tommy had hated Doctor Reynolds more than he could say, more than he had ever hated anyone or anything, even Lemon Guy, whom he hated a lot. But as Flat 5 Lady had started to tell Tommy the story about her son, Tommy began to see the truth. The fog in his head began to clear. This story about Doctor Reynolds was the real story the doctor had refused to tell, or perhaps it was that he was unable to tell it. Tommy knew all about that dilemma. Tommy listened to Flat 5 Lady as she spoke of her son's experience and Tommy, as he grew stronger with the telling of this story and Ruby's teacakes, began to write down Doctor Reynolds's story in his exercise book. Slowly his energy returned. Bit by bit, he discovered the truth in his work, from discovering the truth in another's life. This gradually led to Tommy finding the truth in his own life. He stopped vomiting; the blood stopped dripping. He had been dying at his own hand. He realised he had started dying the day of the car accident, the day he took a young girl's life. He had a lot in common with Doctor Reynolds's dead wife. Tommy knew what it was like to be a killer, even if like the doctor's wife, you were a killer by accident.

Tommy wrote in his book the following well known adage: 'truth is stranger than fiction'. But this was not quite the case, in his view. It is more that truth is a zillion times more incredible than fiction – fiction to be believed has to be based on truth, while truth never need worry itself about how it appears or how much coincidence might occur. It is just what it is, it doesn't ever have to apologise for coincidence, or how improbable it is, or its style or whether it is inconsistent or not, or that it is just unbelievable. When it is the truth, nothing else needs to be explained, you just go phew! You're incredulous, but you have to accept it, that's all there is to it, with the truth there is no arguing.

Life, when it comes down to it, Tommy thought, appeared both incredible and credible in the same breath – that is, unbelievable enough to be true and just believable enough not to be. Such is truth's paradox. Tommy thought about all this and wrote it down; he felt that he needed to remind himself of how his own truth seemed incredible.

Tommy began to write Doctor Reynolds's story as told to him by Flat 5 Lady. He thought it would be good for him in a way he couldn't explain. So this is the doctor's story as interpreted through the prism of Tommy's life. Tommy began the discovery of truth in his own work as a writer. It covers the time in Doctor Reynolds's life when he was living in Melbourne, after he had lost his wife, Mary. It explains the doctor's obsession with trauma and story. Tommy felt that this was perhaps the finest writing he had produced. It contained truth, both personal and universal. It was bigger than him; it liberated itself from its author. To plagiarise his own work and perhaps over-extend the metaphor, or his literary 'folly', it was fiction revealing truth, like the tea bag releasing, not the tampon absorbing.

Le Petit Mort

Robert sat under Kate's window on the cold concrete, staring at the ants running over his shoe. It had been nine months after Mary's death before he had masturbated.

'I'm sorry to tell you your wife died at three o'clock this morning. Mary woke and screamed in intense pain for several hours, eventually biting the steel frame at the foot of the bed, broke a couple of teeth, then passed away peacefully. Can I leave you with an invoice for the repair of the bed? – there's no rush.'

'What do you mean she died? She only came in to visit someone.'

'Sorry... I kept Mary's broken teeth for you, as a memento.'

Robert relentlessly played these silent conversations – he thought of them as dialogue chiselled from life. Black thoughts, bordering on disgusting, certainly macabre, but he was unmoved by them. He saw their bad taste but he didn't feel their bad taste. He wondered if it meant he was over it now, or over it as much as he will ever be. On the other hand, did it mean he has developed an unhealthy obsession, a fixation? Or perhaps it's just that he was disillusioned with language, particularly the language of his profession. He didn't know the answer; it didn't seem to matter. The feelings of exhilaration didn't seem to matter. Mary was gone.

Nine months before he masturbated. He had to wonder how significant the period of nine months was; you can't trust your psyche. As a psychologist, he had often argued that there is no such thing as free will.

'Mary, that bump you just felt while backing up was my baby, would you mind driving forward a bit?'

'Well sure, Kate, but I'm in a bit of a hurry and I hope it hasn't made a mess on the paintwork.'

Mary never recovered from crushing the baby, which Robert considered ironic for a grief counsellor. Later, he saw the baby's crawl marks through the daisy bed separating their two front yards – he made plaster casts of them. The baby arrived on their driveway behind Mary's car. Robert caught his eye. For an instant, time froze for an eternity. When truly shocking things happen, your precise location at the time of the event is seared into your cortex. This event of Mary backing over the baby is one of those speed bump moments.

Mary killed herself with a cerebral haemorrhage.

The doctor called it a CVA. A cerebral (vascular) accident. Doctors feel confident with an abbreviation – Robert had used many himself. There can be no argument, no dissatisfaction, not when something can be reduced to an abbreviation or even better, an acronym. The doctor was sanguine when he said the letters 'CVA'. He told Robert it was the lottery, it happens. But Robert knew that Mary did it to herself. Mary was always the stronger of the two of them; she could do anything she wanted. He admired this quality in her and she despised the lack of it in him. She collapsed out of the car. He remembered she was a bag of bones, no connecting tissue, her connections had been severed. He felt her bones rattle. Mary remained sedated for weeks; eventually she stopped taking the pills, but this had no effect. She was a zombie. She started sniffing, not all the time, but spasmodically, like a sigh but it was a sniff; a foreboding sniff. He thought of it as the sound of her impending destruction, like a straining creak from a bridge or building ready to give way and collapse. He could sense it happening. He could see it happening; he could do nothing to stop it. He did nothing to stop it. The confusion immediately after the accident didn't help her. No one knew who to attend to. Robert didn't know. The baby? The baby was dead. Its mother, Kate? His wife, Mary? Robert didn't know.

Kate was a single mother. Now she was just single. Robert had an obsession with Kate. It took hold almost from the day she moved in next door. She fascinated him. He should have known better, but he was powerless. He couldn't walk out the back or the front without glancing over to her house. He was desperate to look at her, and thus he couldn't stop from walking out the back and out the front. This he did with autistic compulsion. He saw her pass her windows and he loved her. He'd wave in time, in parallel, when her thick auburn hair waved as she walked. He'd look at her curves and feel desperate. He couldn't eat without seeing her face in his dish; he ate from her lips, her eyes, her nostrils, even the dimples in her cheeks when she smiled up at him. He pushed his food around his plate and positioned mouthfuls in her open cunt and then scooped it up with his tongue and lips. He couldn't sleep without feeling her. He'd look for her everywhere. She'd flick her hair the way she does and he'd look up. Once he saw her hanging out the washing; it was the most carnal vision he could ever remember of any woman in his life. He didn't tell Mary. They never spoke to Kate. The first time Robert and Mary had any contact with her was when he introduced himself to her on the day of the accident. 'Hi, I'm Robert, your next door neighbour. Sorry about my wife running over your baby like that. You don't happen to know when you might be hanging out the washing this week, do you?'

Sometime after the death of her baby, Kate began 'entertaining' male visitors. Robert watched them come and then go. There were her regulars; her slinking regulars. She didn't do it often, maybe twice a week. It was after he figured it out that he masturbated for the first time since Mary's funeral. Robert once or twice, perhaps more often, sat on the cold concrete below Kate's bedroom window when she was with a client. He listened to her. She opened her window, and then closed it after she'd finished. Lubrication was needed, she struggled, force was necessary. It was remarkable, he thought, how the sounds she made in her bedroom were identical to the sounds she made the day Mary killed her baby – sounds that erupted out of her like hot air farting out of mud. It was like nature had said, 'I like that sound, what else can I use it for?' Nature was like that; there were economies if you looked for them. Dualism. Symbiosis. And balance. Nature was partial to balance, which, of course, was how it achieved renewal and it mercilessly used synchronicity to achieve its ends.

'Misty, a lonely abandoned young body, numb, needs awakening from its deep silence. Private matters. Please help me.' Robert spent hours writing ads for Kate. The kind she might have placed in the classified sections, to attract her customers. He searched the papers for an ad that might be hers. He was sure she wouldn't use her real name but none sounded like her. None of them had any sub-text, no psychological agenda. He didn't know how she got her clients; maybe she casually met them somewhere. He imagined her in the supermarket, dropping something so a man could bend down to help her; a smile, *then a hesitation, so he could glimpse her and take in her humid bouquet. Robert followed her. He followed her scent. She didn't seem to go anywhere; she didn't seem to meet anyone. She just pulled him along after her. He kept the lights on in his house. It excited him to feel his light flowing to her bedroom, splashing and licking its way towards her in her darkened room, like a wave surging through rocks, finding a crevice and leaving some of itself behind then retreating and coming again over and over in the act that renews. He had taken to expressing everything in obvious metaphor and simile – the more obvious the better, he was sick of subtleties, of nuances, of sophisticated euphemisms and ethereal esoteric bullshit rife in his profession. He wanted crude, blunt, hungry, vulgar, a vulgar vulva, a crude cunt, spitting penis, cleaving cock. Except for the lack of alliteration, he wanted to bite through a fork.*

Mary and Robert were arguing again the day of the accident. Same argument, only the subject matter changed – he would stay home and keep vigil. Mary never accused him of this outright.

A late summer's afternoon; the hot black sky threatened to crack open. Kate sat in her front garden, spraying her baby and herself with the garden hose, trying to cool off. She wore a pair of shorts and a sloppy white cotton T-shirt, nothing else. Robert had earlier watched her dress; she left the curtains apart, like two big lips. The baby sat in a small plastic swimming pool surrounded by his floating toys. The phone rang. Kate turned off the tap, took the baby out of the water and put him on the lawn, simultaneously admonishing him about staying out of the water while she was gone. She paused and darted a look at Robert's feet; it was for Robert, to silently commission him as the responsible adult since he was in the front yard. No eye contact, no physical gesture to engage with him in some way, just the deliberate pause to set the matter in place. She ran inside to take the call. A blissful domestic scene, to be converted to a bloody event that will always seem as though it could just so easily have been undone, just stop the clock, just don't believe it happened, just act, just turn back time, not much just a few seconds, who would know or care? Just act, do something. You can only believe something like this has happened to a certain level, you can't dispense with the disbelief, not entirely, or not for a long time. This is after the event, during the event you can't believe it is happening at all. You just float with a buzz in your head. Robert saw what was going to happen, he saw it happen, and then after, he could believe it happened because the facts were irrefutable. But now he was not sure if he didn't imagine it all.

Mary, sick of the whole argument and the arguing – especially with someone who was always out the front or back door and never still – slung herself in the car. She slammed the car in reverse and screeched out of the driveway and over Kate's baby. Thud... squish, that's all it was, thud... squish. Nothing to it really, anyone could do it, it took no effort. Easy peasy – just a little death. Robert couldn't remember who, if anyone, cleaned the baby out of the tyre tread.

Three months later Mary died. By the time she died she weighed less than her clothes. Death is lighter.

Robert wanted to fuck Kate. He was a disillusioned man; he was a disillusioned psychologist and a disillusioned human. All he wanted was to fuck Kate just one time. It didn't make any sense but it was the only sense left, it had so obviously become his life's work. He was willing to pay her, but he wanted her to want him, or minimum, not be disgusted by him and to be ripe for him. He wanted this ever since the day of the accident. He held Kate in his arms consoling the inconsolable, and he caught himself looking down her T-shirt at her naked breasts. He saw himself slip his hand in and cup her breast and rub his fingers over her heavy nipples. That moment when she fell into his arms, he wanted to fuck her right then and there. He wanted to stop her sobbing by filling her. Stifle the heaving. Convert the heaving. He thought he could.

She asked him if he wanted to. The day of Mary's funeral, she appeared in his kitchen after everyone had left. She just came out with it, while she was emptying the last of the sausage rolls into the pedal-bin. 'Do you want to fuck me?' she asked. It was the first and last time she spoke. It was the only thing she ever said to him. And he managed never to utter a single word to her. He could not risk talking; she knew what he had to say.

Robert had sperm counts. He had them monthly. He donated but the donation was not his motivation, it was the count he wanted. He was fertile. He had good mobility. His viscosity was excellent and he averaged 140 million sperm per millilitre, 320 million per ejaculation, with perfect pH and only plus or minus .05% abnormal sperm. He had been graphing his count. He found that levels increased if he stopped masturbating during the month but proportionately 'abnormals' increased. Masturbation and wet dreams were like a forest fire, they purged the weak, increased purity but you lost some trees – it was only renewal that made any sense.

Robert sat in a small room with a jar. The nurses knew him. They seemed happy to see him. They provided magazines of naked women but this was unnecessary. They highlighted with a marker particularly good letters to the editor they thought he should read to get himself going. They opened the centrefolds up and showed him what he was missing. He smiled and said no thanks. They closed the door to leave him in the small room. But one or other of them always returned to sit with him. They seemed scared to leave him alone. He left the pulsing fluoro on. He sat with his eyes closed and thought about the opening and closing of Kate's window – no force was necessary; it opened easily for him. He saw the baby crawl through the daisies. He saw it stop behind the car. Frame by frame, he saw the car reverse and stop with a shudder. He squeezed his eyes closed but the tears still got out. There he was, in the front yard no more than a few metres from the baby. He looked away. He looked for Kate. She stood at her window on the phone. He watched her breasts bob when she laughed. He saw her hand flick her hair – his obsession. He heard the screeching brakes. He saw Kate's milky breasts, heavily floating – innocently primed. He saw his hand reach down and release the flow. His body jolted. He envied Mary. His eyes swelled then shut for the coming of the little death.

That was Robert's story, but one he never related to anyone. Tommy filled an exercise book with it; he re-wrote it and chiselled it over and over. As he peeled back more and more truth, he grew stronger and stronger, and his 'voice' emerged from his catastrophic darkness – Tommy declared the story a celebration of both form and function.

Belinda arrived in Melbourne and introduced herself to Robert as Kate's sister. She came to his home, knocked on the front door and asked if she might come in. Kate had deteriorated. She was now incapable of looking after herself any more. She had tried to kill herself and Belinda had no choice but to abandon her life in Adelaide, to save her sister. It broke Belinda's heart to leave Peter but she felt she had no choice. Belinda moved in with Kate and watched over her for nine months but it was no good. Kate was dying and needed constant professional care. One day, Belinda took Kate to a home, where Kate spent her time sitting in a chair. She rocked with dry eyes and tireless fists. Belinda had to see to this herself, her parents were incapable, they couldn't help either of their two daughters or themselves; insanity lurked in their family like a spider ready to pounce. She knew this and she knew she couldn't inflict this on Peter. She couldn't be sure of her own mental health's future, nor could she risk passing it on to the children she and Peter might have had one day. So she left. She tried to console herself with the thought that it was because of her love for him and this was her duty to him. She hoped he would find someone else with whom he could have a family. She often imagined his gentle kiss just as she went to sleep. This was something Peter always did. He kissed her every time he saw her, when she was about to go to sleep and the moment she woke. She found it so reassuring. Belinda considered for a time whether or not to have sex with Robert, but then decided against it, but not for any particular reason. She thought to do it as a way for her and Robert to forget the things that lurk and hurt, if only for a few minutes. But even that seemed like it would take more energy than either of them could muster.

She continued to live in Kate's house for a while, leaving only to visit her sister daily at the home. She wrote to some friends in Adelaide. She told them she had met someone else. She described him as an Australian writer who lived in New York. She added the detail that he taught creative writing at Columbia University and he was writing screenplays. She explained she had moved to New York to live with him. She invented her story; she even came up with the detail that they lived on W57th. Street between Sixth and Seventh Avenues and that they ordered loose meat sandwiches with a pickle each or bagels and cream cheese from the Carnegie deli and took tea in the Russian Tea Room where he made notes for his screenplays and his classes. She thought the detail would lend credibility to her story, she hoped that it would feel true but it never did, it wasn't her story. But she did this in the hope that it would get back to Peter and that he would resolve his life without her and that he wouldn't harbour any hope of their reconciliation. It was for this reason she removed every trace of her existence from their flat; she wanted to force him to start anew, without her, without anything to remind him she ever existed in his life – she thought it might be his only chance.

Robert eventually took up his practice again by moving to Adelaide, or Paradise as it was then known. He concentrated on victims of trauma. He thought to help them compartmentalise their life's story. He helped them with their story and the search for their truth. It became his obsession. He started working on his long overdue second book on the subject. He met Wendy, a grief counsellor, and it never occurred to him to question why the only two women in his life were both grief counsellors, first Mary and now Wendy. He dedicated himself to his work and even though it failed to satisfy him, he persisted as though the truth in his work could be forced out by effort alone. He interviewed many people and catalogued their stories but none of it amounted to any therapeutic breakthrough. All he achieved was to confirm Mary's criticism that it was all superficial 'pop' psychology and as such, a tragic under-utilisation of his intellect and talent – he wasn't convinced about either. He needed a story himself and rather than confronting his own, he borrowed one from a cab driver he once met. It was short and to the point and did the job he needed it to do.

34

PETER

Madeline got in the car. Peter inspected the paint job on the car before climbing into the passenger side. He felt lighter somehow after telling his grandpa his story. In the car, he smelt Madeline's familiar perfume. She was a good person and had been a very good mother to him. He resolved to try to be more relaxed with her and try to make an effort over coffee to talk to her, find out what was going on in her life at the moment. It saddened him knowing that he didn't have much of an idea of her life. She never complained to him about anything. Grandpa was probably not going to see the week out; she would need his support during this time. It dawned on him that when his grandpa goes, Madeline would be all the family he would have left. What if something should happen to Madeline? It was not something he had ever considered before now, but things happen in this world, as well he knew – his father was already dead.

'Did you have a nice visit with Pa?' Madeline asked Peter while she slid the keys into the ignition.

'Yeah, I did.'

'Did you talk to him?'

'We chatted.'

Madeline started up the car and looked across at her son.

'So you said you had some news?' Peter asked by way of changing the subject.

'I do but I think you need to be sitting down for this.'

'I am sitting down.'

'Can we go to a wine bar instead of a cafe?'

'Well, I guess,' Peter responded, a little surprised; he had rarely seen his mother drink.

'You may need a stiff drink.'

'Really, what have you been up to then? There is nothing wrong I hope, with you...'

'Oh no, nothing like that, quite the contrary actually.'

'Good news then?'

'For me, yes, I hope it is… at least I think so.' Her voice trailed off as another thought took over her mind and she lost track of what she was saying. She checked her mobile again. Still no message from Steve. She sighed and contented herself with her driving. Now she wasn't so sure she should say anything to Peter. For all she knew, there might not be anything to tell him. She didn't know what she would do if she lost Steve. Maybe her worst and constant fear has occurred and the age gap has caught up with him. He had been the saving of her; he had given her her life back. It was more than that though. Up until Steve, she was more or less just thinking her way through her life. Now, she was living her life; it was a completely different story. Like the cliché, it was a new and fantastic chapter in her story.

'You okay?'

'Sure, terrific.' She didn't turn to Peter, but kept looking out the window. She rummaged in her purse, retrieved a tissue and blew her nose.

'You sure you are okay?'

'Have you ever heard from Belinda? I haven't asked you for a long time now.'

Peter didn't answer.

'I'm so sorry you had to go through that.' She blew her nose again.

Peter thought about Belinda. He winced, reminding himself of how stupidly naive he must have been. Madeline seemed content to be lost in her own thoughts and concentrate on her driving. Peter's thoughts turned to the day Belinda disappeared.

Of course he should have known. There was no question about it, he should have. He had intelligence; he had wit, even common sense. There was just no excuse. He felt like an idiot for not knowing. And humiliated. A humiliated idiot. Even Ryan said Peter should have known. But Ryan said *he* hadn't seen it coming himself, although he wasn't surprised, he said. Whatever that meant. The fact is, Peter hadn't known. He had no idea. None. That day he stood in the fading light of the empty flat and wondered if he had ruined his life by not knowing, because if he had known, maybe he could have done something to stop Belinda disappearing. He couldn't forgive himself for not knowing. He could still smell traces of her faint but lingering perfume scent. She left something behind.

'Everything but the kitchen sink,' Peter told Ryan when he finally managed the courage to phone Ryan, two days after he had discovered his empty flat. He had to call Ryan from the public phone down the road, as his mobile phone battery died without its charger, which also had gone. He stood in the phone box watching some kids playing footy across the road in the park.

'Everything?'

'Yes. Everything,' he repeated, but he wasn't sure Ryan could hear him over the noise of the traffic, which at that moment seemed louder than usual.

'Except the sink. She left you the sink?' Ryan's voice crackled over the phone.

'Yes,' Peter reiterated, getting annoyed with the banality of the conversation. He flinched as the kids' football sailed over the road and straight into the phone box hitting him on the head.

'Imagine that,' Ryan added. But it was hard to tell just how Ryan had meant it over the bad connection. With the kids yelling at him to kick their ball back, the escalating traffic noise, and the pain in the side of this head, and the emptiness in his life, Peter hung up. The graze on the side of his head began to sting, one eye was starting to water and the other eye was full of tears. He stumbled home without much sight or focus. He had wanted to call his mother, but then he was a grown man and he didn't want her rushing over to console him with her inevitable 'there's plenty of fish in the sea' lecture. He'd heard this before and he wasn't in the mood for it now. He wanted to sit in the dark and not think.

It hadn't been the clearing of everything out of their flat he cared about. Most of the contents were Belinda's; it was originally her flat. All Peter had there was his stereo (including his much maligned Abba collection, which to be fair he hadn't played more than once, and only then when there had been a revival, and in the spirit of self-deprecation – it was a running joke between them, Belinda never missed an opportunity to send him up over his Abba obsession – anyway, surely people don't leave people because they have a six-set *Best of Abba* collection, do they?) He had started talking to himself about Belinda's disappearance. This couldn't in fact be the case, he assured himself, because she had taken Abba as well. She took it all. Everything. 'But does this matter?' He hadn't cared less about the things.

It was what it meant, how it looked, how he was to interpret it, even how he might explain it to others, and then how he was to survive it – if survival was to be an option. It left him totally bewildered, not to mention devastated. On that day, his birthday, the day he was planning to propose marriage, in the empty flat, tears squeezed out of his eyes and he collapsed against the entrance hall wall and came to rest on the floor. 'She left me the floor at least.'

She had left him one more *thing*: a note under his toothbrush on top of his clothes which said, 'Happy Birthday. Sorry Peter. I have bought you new socks and underwear, so you should be fine for now.' It took several months before he could even think about it without suffering a draining feeling in his gut and without setting off the heat and buzz in his head.

There was so much he couldn't understand. Little things. Like why she so neatly folded his clothes before she left. She could have left them hanging in his side of the built-in robe, except she took all the coat hangers as well. If she hated him that much, wouldn't you think she would have just thrown his clothes on the floor, or out in the stairwell, like a normal human being? He kept clinging to the hope there must have been something between them, something bordering on affection, after all, who folds clothes (including inserting tissue paper in his shirts and slacks to prevent creasing) for the person they are intending to abandon? Except Belinda was a neat girl, impeccably so, so the tissue thing was consistent with her personality – she wouldn't be able to stand the thought of creases. Peter asked, 'Wasn't it a bit extreme to decide your only option was to clear out of your own flat, in order to break off a relationship when a simple "piss off Mr Serious" (Ryan's words) would have been sufficient?' No one answered. Even Ryan had started not answering, not that Peter could blame him. On the other hand (Peter asked Ryan anyway), if there had been any affection, why leave? "Only you can know," Ryan answered, which was more *all-knowing* and sage-like than Ryan had any ambition to be. But the reality was that Peter didn't know, and that was killing him.

'At least you're right for socks and underwear, unlike me,' Ryan mused.

Later that night, or it might have been the next day, after Belinda's departure, Peter found himself staring into his dishwasher. She had obviously turned Mr Dishwasher (as Belinda called it) on before she left – there was one plate, one cup, a knife, spoon and fork, all squeaky clean. So he could have a banquet anytime soon, if the occasion warranted. The fact that her last act was an act of cleansing wasn't without its symbolism, Peter noted to Ryan. Ryan suggested Peter might be over-analysing things. But analysing was all that was left for Peter to do. He analysed everything, over and over, in minute detail. He thought the meaning might be found in the detail; a principle he inherently believed in. But he could find no meaning; there was barely any detail. They had never argued the whole time they had been together. It was *so* bloody unfathomable.

'Not even an argument,' Peter told Ryan.

'Not one?' Ryan asked in his mocking tone, weeks after the event.

'Not even one,' Peter repeated automatically.

'That many?' Ryan made a whistling noise through his teeth. Peter ignored it. 'She did wish you happy birthday though. She was a thoughtful lass.'

A year on from this and on the occasion of Peter's last birthday, he decided to leave work early. The staff had given him an elegant engraved silver letter opener, and Maria had stopped by his office to wish him happy birthday before he left. She kissed him on the cheek. Actual physical contact with any female, apart from his mother, which didn't count, had been scarce since Belinda. It shocked him and he hoped she hadn't seen the blush. He left the building feeling lighter, as though some positive mystery had entered his life. After a year of introspection and healing, this felt good. For many months, he never expected to feel good again. He thought he'd go home and change and give Ryan a call, to see if he wanted to stop work and have a quick bite somewhere. Although Peter knew that he was unlikely to call Ryan and interrupt his shift. It will probably be pizza-for-one. However, having a bit of a plan, even one he had no intention of executing, gave him an almost jaunty feeling.

When he got home, he stood in front of the door exactly twelve months from the day he did this and found the flat empty. He ran his fingers through his hair, turned the key and stepped inside with more expectation in his heart than was good for him. It was shadowy, with a slight smell of paint. Belinda had worried that the floor was dirty, or *dirtyish* to use her word, and the only way to be sure it was clean was to paint it, but they never got around to it. He painted the floor himself a few months back (Ryan helped, if you call splashing paint on everything but the floor a help). Peter had found the job surprisingly exhilarating. Ryan never said a word about why they were spending the better part of a good weekend painting Peter's floor exactly the same colour it already was. A fair question, to which there was no answer.

Here he was, another birthday, in the flat, lingering in the dark, letting the silence and the familiar smell come to him. After a few minutes he couldn't detect the paint any more, his nose had no staying power, which is pretty much the case for all noses – after a while, your brain can block everything out. For a few months after she left, he would stand inside his flat, still life-like, he thought of it as, trying to detect her scent. This was how he described it to Ryan. Still life-like. 'Get it?' he asked Ryan, but there was no sense Ryan got it, there was no sense that Ryan was even listening to him at the time. Belinda was never there. No matter how quietly he listened for her, or how desperately he hoped to hear her moving in one of the rooms, she was never there. He achieved a serene level of quiet and an obscene level of desperation, but none of it helped. She wasn't there. And she wasn't there now on this birthday either. It was a slim and ridiculous hope that she might be, that she might come back on the occasion of a birthday, after disappearing on one. He had clung to the flimsy notion that since her disappearance had been inexplicable, maybe an equally inexplicable reappearance was possible. Over the first few months after she left, flimsy notions were his *modus operandi*, his *raison d'etre*, his *excuse* – they were, in fact, all he had.

At least he had stopped crying. He often dreamed he was crying and woke to a wet pillow. In his bed at night was the hardest. It was when he longed for her the most. He missed drifting off to sleep with the smell of her skin in his face. That smell, that feeling, that was bliss, that was comfort, that was life itself – that was *his* life. He had kissed her every night and every morning, it was his good luck ritual, but now he wondered if it wasn't the trigger that made her leave. He marvelled at how in life, positive things could just as easily be negative things – binary opposites changed places without even extending you the courtesy of letting you know.

He tried to explain the thing about the paint smell to Ryan. That he only ever registered its presence just as he entered, as though it was there to greet him, as though it had some higher purpose other than just being a paint smell. But none of it made any sense to Ryan. It made no sense to Peter. In some ways, it would have been much better if Belinda had died instead of just disappearing. Not that he wished her dead, well not any more, but if it had been that she died, at least then it wouldn't have been something he had to take personally, it wouldn't have said 'hideous terrible flaw in personality, I'm out of here'. Her death would have been painful but he could accept that, it would have been something to understand. He wouldn't have spent endless months of his life hoping to find her every time he came home. It would have saved him from constantly walking through their flat to assure himself she wasn't sitting somewhere reading a book, or having a cup of tea and flipping through her fashion magazines, or cleaning out Mr Dishwasher with the latest cleaning chemical she had bought.

As summer decayed through autumn into a light winter, Peter had wilted under the weight and exhaustion of the grey skies that seemed to be stuck on the tops of the city buildings. He forced himself to keep up appearances at work. He was determined to keep his misery to himself. For the most part he was sure he pulled it off. No one knew. The partners knew that his relationship had ended, but they didn't know the details and no one asked. The office staff gave him a wide berth on anything personal or social. He was grateful for that. Even though the defeating lack of sense to it had derailed him so completely, he pushed on and eventually saw off the winter months. So long as you are still taking in a breath, there is little else you can do. He kept up with his football during the winter and lost himself in the concentration and physicality of the games. The suddenness of spring seemed to make a difference; maybe there was something to all that re-birth and renewal business that had the effect of lifting spirits, but he did slowly feel better and then finally some clarity came, something solid for him to hang on to. It came to him while hanging out with Ryan in the flat one Saturday morning.

'The reality is I'm only a passing guardian of this flat,' Peter said, without knowing where this statement came from or where it was leading. It just popped out. A rogue sentence, as though it had broken away and made a clear run for it before he could stop the damn thing escaping. And the moment he said it, he wished he hadn't, because while it made *sense* to him – it had a slight feel of 'everything's okay' about it. He looked over at Ryan to see what impact his sentence might have had, but Ryan wasn't exactly riveted by Peter's relationship with his flat. Or the minor break-through it represented to Peter. Ryan's lack of attention at this point was hardly surprising, given his immediate preoccupation.

'Ah huh,' Ryan answered, rotating his *Playboy* magazine, as though the anatomy of the centrefold would make more sense if he held the picture upside down. Peter preferred not to dwell on this image, but decided to be bold and continue his thoughts. It wasn't like the floodgates had just opened, but he had started now, he might as well go on, see where it took him. He felt braver these days for such thoughts – albeit a fragile bravery that had crept up on him and taken up residence on his shoulder.

'Rather like the human race is a passing guardian of the planet, you know?' Peter pushed on.

'Ah huh.'

'This is the conundrum, in the vast enormity of the universe, I feel insignificant while still somehow relevant. But mostly insignificant.' Peter paused to see if Ryan would take the opportunity to disagree, or agree, or do anything that indicated his mind was operating above its base level to appreciate what Peter was saying.

'That's you, Mr Insignificant.' Ryan demonstrated he could concentrate on what Peter was saying if he had to, while simultaneously catching up on his gynaecological studies.

Peter continued his 'passing guardian of the planet/flat/Paradise' thought in silence. It was a big thought and needed his full attention. It felt comforting in a way he couldn't explain. He thought being a guardian, albeit passing, at least made him feel he was a participant in its history, so that was good, that was a positive thought, some progress. But he could only safely feel this in relation to his flat's history, he couldn't be sure he was participating much in the history of the planet, perhaps a little in Paradise's history with the design and erection of the buildings he was involved with, but ultimately he knew his impact was virtually zero. This was one of those disappointing realisations, that come as you get older, that you are not going to make a major impact on the world or humanity after all; with age comes the realisation of irrelevance. That had been something his grandpa had said to him long ago, and only now made sense to Peter. He found it all a bit sad and disappointing, and while he felt the disappointment in himself, it was also in its own way a relief. He wondered if it might have contributed to Belinda's disappointment in him, assuming of course that disappointment in him was one of her, well, disappointments in him.

'We are all just one of the inexhaustible links in the human chain of tenants,' Ryan chimed in as though he had been listening in to Peter's thoughts. Ryan looked up from his magazine to emphasise his multi-task-ing abilities. He could concentrate on air-brushed 36C breasts while con-templating his place in the universe. Ryan had bought the magazine at the newsagent before arriving at Peter's flat for their usual Saturday morning run. He also bought a Flake and a Cherry Ripe, a Diet Coke and a roll of Quickeze and some gaffer tape. Their Saturday run took them down Anzac Highway, across the Great Southern Road down to Glenelg, where ritual required each to touch a shoe on the final plank on the jetty before turning and running back. Their run, like life, was cast, pre-ordained and they couldn't change it no matter how much they might have wanted to, or thought they wanted to. Even when Peter's interest in life was so low that all he could manage was to sit in his apartment and stare, Ryan never let him off; in particular in the months after Belinda vanished, Ryan told Peter, 'I'm draggin' you around the circuit if I have to, and if that doesn't work, I'll carry you on my back, but whatever it takes, we are doin' this run, you've got all week to be a tragic figure, and years to become historical. Saturday mornings we run.'

'Historical? I was more aiming for hysterical.'

'Yeah well you're well past hysterical, I can tell you, but at least when you were hysterical, you were interesting.'

'So what are you saying, I'm boring?'

'Boring would be interesting, not as interesting as hysterical, but I'd take boring right now and rejoice.' Ryan threw his *Playboy* magazine on the coffee table. 'None of these angels ever have cellulite on their buttocks. Cellulite is super sexy.'

Peter looked at Ryan and smiled, if slightly incredulously, but then, not really. Nothing Ryan ever said could come as a surprise, no matter how surprising it might inherently be. Ryan was inscrutable. He was inscrutable without knowing he was, which made him all the more inscrutable.

Peter had been developing a thought, which he might relate to Ryan one day, maybe after a long night at Romeo's. It might at least offer an expla-nation for the 'passing guardian' illumination, in the unlikely event Ryan was pondering its meaning. For some strange and bizarre reason he found himself sitting on the kitchen floor in front of Mr Dishwasher one night. He started talking to it. It went like this…

'Dear Mr Dishwasher, getting home from work during the winter months, I find the flat chilly, and in the fading light, it's a moment of heightened consciousness – a punctuation mark. I'm profoundly aware that I won't always live in this flat, this cubicle if you like, and that it'll be nothing more than a faded memory one day; a place in which others will live, and have lived, people I don't even know, but who are somewhere in the world at this moment, or even long gone, and whose lives might have affected mine in ways I can't know or even explain. And then there are the people still to come, whose lives will be affected by me in some inexplicable way, even if only minutely by way of the faint lingering paint smell, without them knowing all that it meant.' He felt connected in this 'chain of tenants', but he also saw through this and in particular, like the death of a schoolmate, how temporary – even perishable – this made him. It was like a single ant in the column, the column being the living entity, the individual ants were irrelevant – destroy an ant, even thousands of ants, the column still lives on, it still performs its basic functions. To ants it's the column that holds the meaning of life, not the life of an individual ant. And so, his flat would go on, even in its less than grand way, quite probably for decades, even longer, certainly longer than him, but he would not. This somehow made the highs and lows of his own life seem less significant, less high and low, thankfully, more manageable. This revelation unwrapped itself to him like a new butterfly, 'I wonder Mr Dishwasher, perhaps too often I'll admit, how my own life has and will be affected by the history of this flat, and how it will all turn out, and what influences of others are bearing on me, shaping my destiny, that I don't know about.' Peter sighed with a kind of resignation talking to his dishwasher, as Belinda had often done. When she did it, it seemed normal somehow.

He would tell this to Ryan. If it was good enough for Mr Dishwasher, it was surely good enough for Ryan. It was profound in a kind of simplistic way. However, it might be prudent to wait until Ryan's *Playboy* obsession passed, or the cellulite obsession. Peter had a suspicion the cellulite obsession might be a little more deep-seated but it seemed harmless enough.

Ryan had been a good friend to Peter. Peter's friendship with Ryan was critical, especially during the months after Belinda had left. It might have been the key to Peter's sanity, or if not the key, at least a crutch to lean on during the times when leaning seemed imperative. Ryan was the kind of friend you are blessed to have in your life, even one of the blessings Madeline often spoke about and in her view the kind of blessing that should be counted. Peter thought that if you started counting your blessings and you started with your best friend, and your best friend happened to be Ryan and he was the only blessing you came up with, you would still be very well off in the blessings stakes.

Peter's life rotated between only a few geographical locations, but mainly work and his flat. The exceptions were his Saturday morning runs, and Sunday nights at Romeo's with Ryan in search of romance (as Ryan like to call it) and playing football every Saturday afternoon. Of course when they were at Romeo's, all they did was drink too much and talk all night about women. Actually Ryan talked about women; Peter talked about Belinda, which he acknowledged must stop.

'You need to stop thinking sad,' Ryan said. 'The "Master of Sad", "Mr Gloomy",' Ryan said.

'I thought I was Mr Insignificant?'

'You are. You are ambidextrous.'

'Mr Gloomy and Mr Insignificant. I could be a couple of children's television characters.'

'Yeah, it explains why the fillies aren't lining up for you.' Ryan repeated this sentiment frequently as they sat in the busy Romeo's, as though it was somehow Peter's fault they were both single, like there might be some kind of funk surrounding him that repelled women, told them to stay away. Peter assumed this accusation was Ryan's way of trying to jolt him out of his melancholy. But was Ryan right? Now that he thought about it, the only girl apart from Belinda who looked at him with anything like a connection was Ruby. He remembered that had occurred the day he witnessed the accident. Ruby was standing next to him hanging on to the bus shelter. Madeline had covered his eyes and this made him cross; he wanted to look into Ruby's eyes. It was the most compelling experience he remembered from his childhood; the worst aspect of this was that when he had the opportunity to look into her eyes on that day behind the chook shed, he ran away.

Peter felt silly standing in the dark in his flat on his birthday. He flicked on the lights and went into his bedroom. He took off his cufflinks and dropped them on his bedside table, next to the framed photograph of Belinda and himself taken at Victor Harbor. He felt cold in the still silence. He hit the speed dial for Ryan.

'You got any plans, birthday boy?' Ryan had obviously seen Peter was the caller on his mobile and got in first.

'Yeah, Elle McPherson is coming over to discuss how the French Revolution might well have been the catalyst for the birth of the bakery industry.'

'Sounds good, but personally I'd just ask her to show you her personalities, you know. Keep it simple, or in my case I'd ask to see her cellulite.'

'Didn't think of that, but I am not sure she has any cellulite.'

'"A life without a cause is a life without an effect".'

'And you got that off of what cereal box?'

'*Barbarella*, you should get out more.'

'No doubt.'

'So we goin' out?' Ryan asked.

'No plans.'

'Okay what say I cruise by in an hour, pick you up and we go for pizza at Bella's? It is dead quiet, and one more empty cab out here is about as useful as a screen door on a chocolate submarine.'

'Okay, see you soon then. I'll have a cold one waiting for you.'

'Not for me. I'll have to get back out on the road, got to keep chasing the dollars.'

'Understood.'

'By the way, a year or so ago, I had a guy in my cab who's a psychologist.'

'Did you run your cellulite fetish by him?'

'Amongst other things.'

'What things?'

'Things.'

'Sounds riveting.'

'He thought so.'

'You had a free consultation with a psychologist in your cab?'

'It wasn't free. In exchange I gave him something he reckoned he could use.'

'What?'

'A story, but that isn't the point.'

'There is a point?'

'I thought you could make an appointment and see him, you know, it could help to talk about things. He seemed a reasonable guy; I found his business card under the passenger seat the other day.'

'And you can tell his degree of reasonableness after a ten minute conversation you had in your cab some time ago which included, among other things, your cellulite fetish?'

'I don't happen to think it's a fetish. Anyhow back to you. I'm just saying, you have issues, why not give it a go; it can't hurt. When you look at a bridge, you see the bridge not the rivets, but without the rivets, no bridge. Maybe you need someone who can check the rivets, you know, just in case? His name is Reynolds. Do you want his card? It's a bit tatty but you can still read the phone number.'

'Doctor Reynolds? Is it Doctor Robert Reynolds at the Paradise Mental Health Hospital?'

'Yes, do you know him?'

'If you could stop thinking about cellulite for a bit, you would have known I'm working on the new wing at that hospital.'

'Hold on, let me think. Gorgeous women's buttocks with a light covering of cellulite dimples filled with delicious dripping chocolate syrup and just begging to be licked, or your current architectural job. Don't know how I missed it.'

'I think I need a beer. See you in ten.'

Peter replaced the phone in its cradle and wondered if he should take Ryan's advice, but then he thought, the day he started taking Ryan's advice was the day he *would* need a psychologist. A memory flashed through his mind and he remembered that the author of the book Steve had been reading in the school-yard that day was by someone called Reynolds, a doctor. He wondered if they were same guy, but then he dismissed it as being too much of a coincidence.

Peter remembered Maria's kiss and her softness and how her perfume smelt. He smiled to himself. Hey! He smiled, right there in the flat, was it the first time for what seemed like a lifetime? Surely not, but you know, maybe it was. It felt good, then he realised he hadn't had sex for a year either, no wonder he wasn't smiling much. Maria's kiss was thrilling. He felt thrilled remembering it. 'Thrilled,' he tried saying out loud. It felt pretty stupid saying it out loud and listening to it echo around his single-person-barely-furnished flat – even Mr Dishwasher ignored it, given that Mr Dishwasher held the opinion that the domain of noise in the flat was his, and his alone.

'Do you still miss her? Belinda I mean.' Madeline had composed herself while they had driven up to North Adelaide and parked the car in front of Romeo's.

'I am okay with it now.'

'That shouldn't happen to any of us. It is so hard to understand why she didn't tell you why.'

'We all have our peculiarities.'

'Yeah, I guess,' Madeline pondered without much conviction.

Peter ordered a bottle of Shiraz. Madeline sat opposite in the darkened wine bar, where each night so many hopes of so many people were paraded out as the search for the perfect mate continued. Even the fact that the success rate of finding your lifetime partner was appallingly low, this didn't stop the bar from filling every night with hundreds of hopeful Juliets and Romeos.

Peter looked across at his mother for a moment and realised he had spent most of his life losing things: his innocence when he saw the girl die on the road, his teenage heart to Ruby, the opportunity to kiss Ruby and love her. He had lost his relationship with Steve. He lost Belinda, of course. He had lost his father, who died in the saddle, as he would have described it − although this loss had much less impact on him than he might have expected. Maybe he had lost his relationship with his mother, or failed to put in any effort needed to maintain it. In total, this seemed like a lot for one person to lose. What was it that he was doing that brought all this on, how could he change things for the better? Even some of his mother's homegrown and often trite philosophy was beginning to make sense to him. Even Ryan's clichés made some sense. He wondered if all these trite and often twee homilies of life weren't more important than he had supposed. People seem to rely on them far more than he had realised. Maybe they were the way people tried to make sense out of their lives, or maybe it was just a way of keeping the absurdity at bay.

He wasn't making the best of his life, he had not done so since, well, perhaps since he saw the young girl die and had subsequently come to realise how fragile his own life was. This realisation dawned on him with its full impact. If the realisation had happened more profoundly and more quickly, maybe he might not have lost Ruby, and then later Belinda. But how hard could he be on himself? He was only nine years old at the time when the girl died in front of him, and then just an awkward teenager when he had failed and lost Ruby. And maybe Belinda leaving had nothing to do with him and wasn't his fault after all. He resolved to address his life as it was, not as it might have been. It was time to eliminate the 'if only's and the 'what if's and, well, as they say, 'accentuate the positives'. Right then it occurred to him that he still owed Ruby a kiss. He smiled at the thought and wondered if he should track her down and see if it was possible to redress the debt.

This started as a silly notion but the idea of playing detective and tracking down Ruby, and Steve while he was at it, had a sense of satisfaction to it. He wouldn't interfere with their lives, just see them perhaps; that is all he wanted, just to know they had survived. It would be something concrete to do which could mark the point of the beginning of his new 'get on with it' life. He decided not to confide this to Ryan. It would end up with both of them drunk and solving the world's worries only to find that the next morning, they had solved nothing but now they had terrible hangovers. Having made this resolve, he knew that within an hour of a drinking session at Romeo's, he would tell Ryan everything as usual.

Peter made some decisions sitting quietly opposite Madeline in the near empty bar. He was going to start counting his blessings, he had some and they should be counted, he decided. He had his career. He had a good friend in Ryan. He loved playing football. He had a good mother whom he had not spent enough time appreciating. He also decided to track down Steve and find out how he was getting on. He felt guilty that he hadn't kept in touch with Steve, especially given the trouble Steve had gotten himself into. He knew Steve, he thought, better than anyone, he knew he was not a bad person. Steve was very intelligent and did very well at school but he had just never recovered from the loss of his triplet sister in that accident which seemed to have affected a lot of people in many different ways. He expected Ruby, if he was lucky enough to track her down, would be happily married with a family somewhere; she was bound to have met some fabulous Prince Charming. He didn't know what might be achieved by this, but he felt even if he didn't actually speak to her, he would be contented to know she was all right. He could just find out where she was and watch her without her knowing. On the other hand, he had not the slightest notion as to where he might find her, or Steve, for that matter. Perhaps Steve would not want to revisit his past and not welcome Peter making contact.

He thought also that he could have this conversation with his mother. She would understand. He felt now he owed her something of himself. She seemed quite upset in the car, like she was regretting something in her own life, which was very unlike her, he thought. But of course, regrets are the doppelgangers of hopes and everyone harbours hope. It would be alien to the human condition not to hope. In fact, Peter thought the human species might not survive if it weren't for the great universal emotion of hope but equally, in a mirror reverse, hope was also the genesis for all despair and disappointment. He looked across at his mother and wondered what hopes she had started out with, what hopes she had generated through her life, and how many of them had failed her, or how many she had realised. He watched his mother and felt a mixture of sorrow and affection for her. It was time for him to be as good a son to her as she had been a good mother to him. She sat silently, lost in her thoughts, holding her mobile and sipping at her wine. She didn't seem to want to talk. He took her cue and let her be but he was prepared to stay with her in the event she wanted to talk. He decided not to press her about her news. He would wait until she was ready.

Peter remembered Ruby when she was lying on her side in the grass behind the chook shed. She was so innocent and trusting and vulnerable. Sitting opposite his mother, this was the first time he had ever seen Madeline as someone who was vulnerable, even at risk in some way. He put his arm around his mother and reassured her. He felt older than her for the first time in his life. She broke from her thoughts and smiled at him but didn't speak. She seemed happy to sit with Peter without talking. He had the feeling that she was fighting the urge to cry.

Peter made one other firm decision in the bar that day. He always thought hoping for too much in life was as bad as having no hope at all. He believed in himself, he had faith in himself but faith, hope and belief were not the same thing. Anyway, he decided that he shouldn't give up on any of these three tenets but keep them in perspective and measured. He owed it to the young girl who died on the Great Southern Road that day to make the most of his life. Her life and her hopes ended so tragically and suddenly. His did not, and it would be an even greater tragedy for him not to fulfil as much of his hopes and dreams as he possibly could, in her name, and for her sake, if for no other reason. Madeline had been telling him this for years. Even Ryan in his own wise way had been urging him to get on with his life. Madeline stood up ready to go. Peter followed her out of the bar. When she stopped the car in front of his front door, she turned to him and said sorry. He opened the door and got out. He looked in and said to her. 'No Mum, I am the one who is sorry.' She smiled and he closed the door and watched her drive off.

Peter was a little excited at the prospect of seeing Ruby again, no matter what her circumstances might now be. He just thought if he could see her, he would somehow fill in a gap in his life, it would help him to take stock of things, even perhaps close off something outstanding. He didn't know why, he just knew that was what he should do. And of course, though he dared to hope, who knows how it might turn out?

It was April 2nd, a chilly clear-skied day. With hope in his heart, faith in himself and a belief in life, he thought it was as good a day as any to start the rest of his life. Ryan would love the cliché filled sentiment, as would Madeline. Actually, he didn't mind it himself.

35

RUBY

It was April 2nd, a chilly clear-skied day, at the back of the big water slide at Glenelg, opposite the Stamford Hotel, on the edge of the popular beach, with seagulls squawking above, when Ruby's life ebbed. She had a needle stuck between her perfectly pedicured toes.

She was found mid-morning; her eyes shut, her face calm, her mouth frozen in open rictus. She had scratches over her legs. A large spider was crawling away from her. In an instant, it disappeared under the crush of a grinding boot. The boot left nothing to chance; it ground the spider into the concrete with malice. The spider's long legs twisted and lashed against the outer edge of the boot in a wretched attempt to save itself. Slowly the legs collapsed and quivered no more. A white emulsion issued from under the boot.

It was a cold but bright sunny Paradise morning and death was in the air.

Tommy lifted his boot tentatively; he watched the spider's crushed body to see if it moved. It didn't. He kicked it away. It rolled in a twisted carcass of limbs and body over the gutter and landed in the middle of an upturned hubcap. The spider was dead. Tommy knelt down at Ruby's side. He pulled the needle from between her toes. He cupped her chin in his hand and gently closed her gaping mouth. He leant down close to her face and caressed her hair and cheek. He kissed her cheek and whispered, 'Sorry, Ruby, I'm so sorry.' He wept uncontrollably. He wept for her, for himself and for the nine-year-old girl he had killed many years ago when the car he was driving accidentally ran into her on the Great Southern Road. He had passed his driver's licence two days before. It only took two days for him to become a killer, an accidental killer, but a killer nonetheless.

Tommy pushed his arms under Ruby's limp body and, struggling to his knees, he lifted her and cradled her to him. Her head fell back. He cried out loud in front of a pastry shop. He had failed her, and it had been his job to save her. Tommy had followed Ruby that morning, but he had become distracted and lost sight of Ruby for a moment. Then he saw her lying on the ground. He ran to her.

He had only one job, one person to look after. He didn't have the strength when she needed him most, yet in an ironic cruel twist, it had been her kindness and her delicious teacakes that had helped save him. It was the wrong way around. Nothing in life ever worked for Tommy.

She found him hanging in silence from a rope tied to the staircase railing. She found him circling and warm. She collapsed on the cold marble, like her skeleton had failed her. He was pronounced dead at the scene. The knot had fractured his larynx, broke his neck, then asphyxiated him. He would have enjoyed the mini narrative of it all. It was his story in three acts.

PART FOUR

36

Life is not about who's the cleverest, or who's the prettiest or even who's the most talented. It's about who's left. Only survivors, however beaten and battered, have any chance of claiming the prizes of life, or such prizes that may be offered in Paradise.

I am yet to reveal my identity, although I trust that many of you will have deduced this before now and only require me to confirm your suspicion, but before that, there are some loose ends that need attending to. I trust you will allow the indulgence.

Doctor Reynolds was working late one evening putting the finishing touches to his manuscript, which, in broad terms, presented the case studies of the stories of the people described in this work, all of whom had suffered from, or witnessed a trauma (in this case the same one, a fatal car accident). Apart from some interesting, if not necessarily original insights of the effect of re-naming Adelaide as Paradise (more on this later), his conclusions were not startling and he felt the entire effort did not represent a win for insight, or indeed, any advancement of importance on the ground broken by his first book, such as it was. He concluded that many people, after experiencing a life-altering trauma, tend to build a narrative around the event and materially benefit from talking it through. Indeed, therapy and social counselling to help people position the event in their personal life's history, or 'story' as he preferred to call it, appeared critical to their mental health and formed a foundation underpinning progress through their respective lives. He contended that discovery of your own story, and through this your identity, helped to isolate trauma into a psychological cubicle so to speak, and this helped to prevent it from infecting your life, and often appeared to relieve the negative aspects. He also contended that it is better to try to find meaning in your own life rather than the fruitless quest of relentlessly hoping to try to find meaning in life in general, or indeed, events outside your control as it seemed many traumatised people tended to do. He concluded that once this was done as a distinct therapeutic strategy, many people went on to fulfil their various hopes and dreams, although some did not, but it was not conclusive to say that this was as a direct result of the trauma or merely the statistical sociopathic nature of people across a population. In other words, some make it, some don't, and time and determination will work to fix most problems for most people. The critical element is survival. Doctor Reynolds had to acknowledge the world did not need his case studies and manuscript to deduce this outcome of life and that the people of Paradise probably already knew this without any help from a psychologist. He conceded that his deceased wife's criticism of his 'pop' psychology as being redundant and a disappointing use of his so-called 'precocious' talents was probably true enough. The effect of all this for him was to call into question the very existence of these 'talents'.

Unfortunately, Doctor Reynolds himself was one of the statistics that didn't make it. Wendy found him hanging in silence from a rope tied to the staircase railing. She found him circling and warm. She collapsed on the cold marble, like her skeleton had failed her. He was pronounced dead at the scene. The knot had fractured his larynx, broke his neck, then asphyxiated him. He would have enjoyed the mini narrative of it all. It was his story – first act, a fractured larynx – cessation of speech. Second act, a broken neck – cessation of movement. Third and final act, asphyxiation – cessation of life. The dénouement. Being talented doesn't guarantee your survival.

His manuscript was subsequently published, given that his own inability to address the trauma of his deceased wife and her incident of running over the baby tended to be seen to give the findings some gravitas. This might not have been the case if he hadn't committed suicide upon its completion. Q.E.D., as some might say. It turned out that Doctor Reynolds had eschewed an academic style in his book. Instead, he told the stories about his case studies in a more lay style, utilising a narrative structure from the perspective of the individuals studied. He did this in order to humanise it more than would have been the case had he adopted an academic, and thus clinical, approach. Much was made of the book's title, *Sisyphean Escape*. It garnered some good reviews from both the academic and the popular press. Such reviews tended to concentrate on style rather than content, or form over function, as it were, and were evenly divided on whether this was a good or bad element. The academic world treated it, for the most part, warmly – they liked the title and the fact that the author was now dead and represented no threat to egos or tenures and left the field open for follow up exegetical examination and critical reviewing. The popular press liked it because it wasn't academic and as such they could understand it. The work, if predictably, was actively and aggressively condemned by orthodox religious groups, which created notoriety and, not unexpectedly, helped to further promote the book.

Wendy, the grief counsellor, was guilty of not recognising that Doctor Reynolds was indeed suffering from grief. That aside, she had been in the best position to rationalise herself through the agonies of her own grief. She made it her mission to promote Doctor Reynolds's book, which gave her a purpose and kept the connection between herself and her lover in a way that she found efficacious. Out of this, she managed to forge a new career as a radio and television media personality and commentator, which enabled her to leave grief counselling behind (not a bad thing, one would have to say). Her new career included negotiating the film rights for Doctor Reynolds's book with an independent English film studio. There had been talk of Mike Newell directing, and a rumour that the New York-based Australian scriptwriter Gary Lines, who taught creative writing at Columbia University and who, it was said, frequented the Russian Tea Rooms on W57th Street, had already been commissioned to write a script. Why a scriptwriter who lived in New York should be commissioned to write a script of an Australian manuscript for an English production company, which intended to use an English director, was anyone's guess. A rotation of English and American stars had been connected with the project, although at the time of publishing, nothing concrete had eventuated beyond the commissioning of the script. It was said a first draft had been completed and rejected.

We know and we don't know what became of Belinda and her dedication to her mentally disturbed sister, Kate. It is of little import given that Peter had come to terms with it himself, more or less. All we know is that Belinda felt it was necessary to leave Peter the way she did. She dedicated herself to her sister who had been clinically depressed all her life and suffered from a number of debilitating mental conditions. Losing her baby in the tragic accident sent her over the edge. Belinda determined it was best for Peter that the two of them did not end up having a family together, given Belinda's family history of mental illness. Belinda's privacy and motives should be respected and philosophised by saying that we all have to live our life the best way we can, make the decisions which are necessary, and live with the outcome, again this is called survival. We trust and hope that Belinda has found some peace and happiness, which is her due, as it is for us all.

Ryan: well, there's nothing much to tell. Ryan is probably the best adjusted individual of the group. He seems to live uncomplicatedly and sees life as it is. I am reminded of Einstein's quote, 'life should be kept simple, but not simpler'. Ryan's priorities are those that he finds essential for his own level of happiness and expectations. He is Peter's best friend and has proven himself to be a very good supportive friend. He is in search of love; he drives his own cab, and makes an honest living. He will be Peter's best friend for as long as Peter wants him to be. Loyalty is chief among his attributes. It is not entirely true that Ryan had never witnessed a life-altering trauma, however, it would appear he has managed not to have suffered particularly from it. Apart from his affectionate interest for cellulite-laden female buttocks, sadly lacking in *Playboy* magazines (as he points out), and an unaccountable dislike for knapsacks (he refuses anyone entry to his cab who might have one), he remains even tempered and never surprised at what life throws his way. He counts among his best times as a child the simple pleasures found in sitting in bulrushes, catching tadpoles, and the times his mother took him to the circus on his school holidays. Perhaps these convenient compartmentalised memories are the reason for his sunny positive outlook. He has his story organised. However, it is likely that even if he had witnessed the same trauma as the others in our story (the death of the young girl), he might have been better equipped than most to recover from it and survive. The Ryans of this world are too easily dismissed as one-dimensional (a stock character in a screenplay or novel), perhaps lacking the depth to truly understand the pain of life, but to underestimate Ryan would be a tragic miscalculation. Peter understood and appreciated this about his friend. Peter conceded willingly that he might not have survived Belinda leaving him, nor come to grips with his left-over legacy of seeing a young girl lose her life, without Ryan's support.

And by the way, Ryan has a second date lined up with the barmaid from Romeo's. He's taking her to the circus.

Steve and Madeline? In the interests of protecting their privacy, all I will say is that Ryan summed it up when he identified that they had found a way out. Nothing is guaranteed and both of them would be the first to make that observation. Both would hold to the notion that every day is a new life and a chance to start again, with hope only for the day at hand. They both might agree with Albert Camus when he observed, 'He who despairs of the human condition is a coward, but he who has hope for it is a fool.'

The Minister of the Interior suffered politically over the collapse of PERP and when statistics revealed that tourism numbers had dropped after he had orchestrated the re-naming of Adelaide to Paradise, he resigned, no doubt feeling unappreciated. He returned to his original job – a job for which he already had the perfect smile. He took over Easy Motors, renamed it Easy Paradise Motors, concreted over the weeds, demolished the toilet out the back and added an extension to the showroom which included a meeting area and installed male and female facilities.

The Sales Manager of Easy Motors was discovered eviscerated on his desk; the instrument that had been used to perform the surgical opening had been a bloodied trophy found next to a rusting Christmas tree on the floor of his office. The killing showed a similar, but not identical, *modus operandi* to the ritual killings that had plagued Paradise from the time the city had changed its name – however, no trophies had featured in any pre-vious slayings. The detectives on the case determined that it was either the same killer who had become bored with his ritual and made some minor changes for the sake of keeping his work interesting, or he wanted to avoid the trap of repeating the same action over and over again and then finding himself trapped in one of life's ruts – his Sisyphean trap if you like. Or it was a copycat, who knew some of the MO of the 'Paradise Slayer', as the press had dubbed him, but not all of his method. Of course the 'Par-adise Slayer' had concentrated on the sacrificial ritual of young Paradise women of loose moral behaviour, and so the slaying of the Sales Man-ager represented a considerable departure, and as such brought into question whether this was a departure or a copycat. Either way, there were no clues or forensics and the detectives, apart from the routine of asking the public to assist with any pertinent information, declared the case remained open and unsolved. The police announced that the Sales Manager had been known to them as a heroin trafficker and that he was suspected to be involved in prostitution and the like, and it was considered that the most likely scenario was an underworld payback. After this, no one, the police included, seemed to have much interest or energy in solving the case. Coincidently, and strangely (or perhaps it isn't so strange), the killings of young women and sleazy car Sales Managers ceased when the city changed its name back to Adelaide, or at least such ad hoc events as kidnap, murder and dissection, and disappearances returned to normal statistical levels for Adelaide, and rituals per se no longer featured among them.

As it turned out, it was Peter who discovered the Sales Manager's body. Peter had tracked Ruby down to her flat in Clovelly Park by doing nothing more than looking her name up in the phone directory – Ryan's suggestion (Ryan being an advocate of the application of the Occam's Razor theory as a first step to solving life's quandaries, first and last). Peter kept a vigil for several days outside her building in hope of catching a glimpse of her coming or going, but she never appeared. Ryan cruised past in his cab late at night to bring Peter coffee and check any activity. Ruby's flat remained dark. Peter thought she may be away, or had left her flat. He had managed to clamber up on a rubbish bin to get a look through one of her windows. He observed a very neat flat, with a tiny white kitchen, a sofa with a single indentation. He could see through the open bedroom door to a bedside table. He noticed a small book, but wasn't able to make out the title. It sat on top of the bedside table and had a book mark lodged about three quarters of the way into the book. He saw two teddies waiting on the bed. A collection of little toys lined up around the living room covering every available flat surface. He saw a rooster tea cosy sitting on a teapot. He saw what could only be described as a small home, loved and well looked after, waiting for its owner to return. He also noticed the ceiling had been recently painted, although his architectural eye saw the suspicious looking dark patches in the corners that had resisted the fresh paint. He did not see Ruby.

During Peter's daytime vigil, he observed a woman several times entering and leaving the building. She wore a black ornate dress and a rather alarming black hat and veil. He saw her check the number 5 letter box. He climbed the stairs which had a rather sickly lemon smell to them and he noticed a dark patch on one of the landings. He was aware this building was targeted for refurbishment, under the PERP scheme, but as this scheme had stalled and had been cancelled, the stain and the smell would remain.

He knocked on the door of flat 5. The lady spoke to him at length and he discovered she was in mourning for her recently deceased son. Peter soon realised that she was the mother of Doctor Reynolds, from the Mental Health Hospital.

The lady confirmed that Ruby did live in flat 3, but she hadn't seen Ruby for some time and she was getting concerned. She said she liked Ruby and missed her. She was aware that Ruby worked as a car salesperson at Easy Motors next to the crash repairer on the Great Southern Road, and suggested Peter might check there. The lady seemed lonely and in need of company and went on to tell Peter a bit about her son, how he had been a brilliant psychologist but had ended his own life. Peter listened attentively and did not reveal he had worked with her son on the new hospital, as it seemed unnecessary and would only act as an unhelpful distraction to her narrative. She told Peter of another resident of the building who was also missing; a young man named Tommy, who had been very ill for a long time, but hadn't been seen since Ruby had gone missing. She said she thought the building was bad luck, and one of the residents' cats had been killed; she was pretty sure that that was an accident, still it all felt odd.

Peter extracted himself from her company and headed to Easy Motors, which was next to the crash repairer just as the lady had said. It was there that he made the grisly discovery of the Sales Manager. Peter found himself mesmerised by the Sales Manager's tie. He noticed the tie had patches of blood on it but this seemed in a peculiar way to enhance the mix between other existing stains of unknown origin and the actual design pattern of the tie, featuring stains as the motif. Focusing on the tie saved Peter from looking into the dead eyes and the ridiculous grin on the Sales Manager's face.

Peter broke his stare and thought to run next door to the crash repairer's for help when a salesman came back into the showroom, having finished a test drive with a 'punter'. Peter told him what he had discovered. The salesman seemed distressed at hearing the news, but not as you might suppose for his now disembowelled boss, but for the fact that he was about to close a deal with his punter and now unable to go through the usual ritual of saying he would have to 'see if I can get this deal by my Sales Manager'. Usually, this meant he would sit in the Sales Manager's office for five minutes, leafing through the permanent *Playboy* collection before coming out, feigning an 'I've just been through hell for you' look, and telling his punter that he had to call in all his favours to get the deal through, but the deal had to be done now or the Sales Manager would withdraw the price and so forth and so on. Now the salesman had no way or idea of what to do to close his sale, as he couldn't sit in the office next to his boss's corpse with blood everywhere, and it was this that was causing him the most distress. Peter managed to establish that Ruby worked there but hadn't turned up for work in over a week. The salesman had no idea or apparent interest as to where she might be.

Peter couldn't help but notice the shiny smear across the salesman's chin and wondered whatever might have happened in Ruby's life for her to have ended up working in such a place with these people, given that at school she was always considered one of the brightest students.

The police arrived and interviewed Peter on the spot, then cordoned off the entire lot with police tape. Peter was dismissed by the police. He had now run out of leads to find Ruby, and felt a rising dread in the pit of his stomach. He tried to tell the detective about her disappearance, but the detective was preoccupied with the coffee machine in the Sales Manager's office, and at the same time yelled instructions to her uniformed officers to get more police tape around the crime scene. She took down Ruby's name and address, which was all the information Peter had, and said she would get to it sometime. She asked Peter if he knew anything about coffee machines.

There being no further leads to follow up on Ruby, Peter decided to add the search for Steve to his agenda. When he got home he vaguely recalled that Steve had become a crash repairer. He poured himself a Shiraz and thought how it would have been a funny coincidence if he had gone into the crash repairer next to Easy Motors for help, and found Steve working there, but of course that would be too much of a coincidence. He picked up the phone and called Ruby's number again. There was no answer.

Peter was in for a shock. Steve, as it turned out, was not the least bit difficult to find. Madeline had invited Peter to dinner a few days after their chat at Romeo's, which was the same day he had discovered the murdered Sales Manager at Easy Motors. Peter arrived and knocked on his mother's door. The door was opened by Steve.

Madeline had spent an agonising twenty-four hours waiting to hear from Steve, during which time she had convinced herself that he had decided to end their relationship, and typically for Steve, she figured, he didn't have the words to actually say it to her. She stopped wearing yellow hats just in case the universe had started acting back to front. She resisted calling him. She felt that if it was to end, then there would be little point in talking to him if he had decided not to contact her again. She couldn't help but see the parallel with Peter's refusal to contact Belinda after her departure. Now Madeline, faced with more or less the same situation, could understand her son's behaviour. She would just have to take it on the chin, as painful as that would be.

Her concerns as it turned out were unnecessary. Steve turned up at her front door with a suitcase. He explained he had needed to think about his future. Standing at Madeline's front door, he asked her to marry him. He explained how having lost his triplet sister, he had spent his life avoiding close relationships. This he had thought was the best way to avoid the pain from losses. He didn't want to lose Madeline. He said all this in the first person.

There is no need to go into the ensuing conversation between Steve and Peter, while they both stood in Madeline's front door. Suffice to say that Peter was flabbergasted and as a subsequence, spluttered out all manner of confused nervous chatter while Steve held the door open and said nothing. Peter told Steve that coincidentally, and only in the last day or so, he had decided to track him down. He added he was so pleased to see him, and they had a lot to talk about, to which Steve managed a nod. Peter referred to Steve by his nickname Hawkey, but corrected himself when Steve's face somehow indicated he was not using that nickname any more. All this confusion played out as Peter came to grips with the mysterious business of finding Steve opening his mother's door in the first place. Before he could compose himself, Madeline appeared at Steve's side. She brought Peter into her flat, and poured him a glass of wine, while he sat waiting for the story to unfold.

It didn't take long before he determined that it wasn't all that mysterious. He assumed the obvious that Madeline had tracked Steve down herself, and invited him over to meet Peter as a surprise. It was an amazing coincidence, and one of those timings that no one can explain, but Madeline loved.

Steve and his mother were to be married. By anyone's measure, this week had been packed full of life changing events, he thought, but he felt he had handled them all sanguinely.

It was a bright morning in Adelaide; Peter had slept the best he had for a long time. He still had a nagging feeling about Ruby, but apart from that, he was rather pleased with his reaction to Steve and Madeline's news, as strange as it still seemed. He realised that Steve had lost his habit of speaking in the second person; he wondered if finding Madeline had anything to do with that.

This had been a big week. He had witnessed another death. He had found his schoolboy friend. His mother announced she was to marry his schoolboy friend. He had told his grandpa an important story. He realised how much his mother meant to him. In an odd way, he felt a release from things, perhaps especially from Belinda but also from the weight of carrying around his past when he saw his young schoolmate crushed under a car. His plague was coming to a resolution, if not an end. The accompanying relief made him feel positive about his life now – this was new.

Ryan called first thing that morning and when he heard the news about Madeline and Steve, his response was, 'Good on them, nothing makes sense and you can send yourself mad trying to make sense of anything, you can't beat the odds, at least they found a way out of the box.' Peter thought how right Ryan was. In fact, Ryan, with all his clichés and desk calendar philosophy, was often right in his take on life and its absurdities – like the day he declared he and Peter were in danger of becoming 'numb and number', making it clear who he thought 'number' was out of the two of them. Peter put the coffee cup in Mr Dishwasher. He slipped on his jacket and headed out to visit his grandpa who was defying the odds and remaining alive, while still in a coma. Peter felt that he might in some way be giving his grandpa something to hang on to. He had been to visit his grandpa every day for the past week and had regaled his silent grandfather with much of his life's story. It hadn't escaped Peter that this process might have been more beneficial to him than it necessarily was to his grandpa. Peter didn't want to give up on finding Ruby, but that was proving difficult and he had no further clues as to how to proceed. He had asked his grandpa to give it some thought.

As it turned out, a sequence of events, coincidences and synchronicity worked together to help Peter with his final quest of finding out what became of his teenage sweetheart, Ruby. The day after Madeline and Steve's announcement, he was late visiting his grandfather. Peter had stopped on the way at a florist to arrange for some flowers to be delivered to his mother by way of a congratulations gesture. When he entered his grandfather's room he was a good forty-five minutes late. This was unusual for Peter because in the normal course of events, Peter was nothing if not punctual and a creature of organisation. The moment he entered he found Tippy finishing up a massage on his grandpa. Peter felt embarrassed that he hadn't known that Tippy's full time career was as a physiotherapist and masseuse for the Adelaide Hospital. He just hadn't given any thought as to how she filled up her time between Saturdays at the football club, but now he had found out, it made complete sense that this was her career. On top of her normal duties, she gave massages to coma patients in her own time. Tippy told Peter that she had given Peter's grandfather a massage every day, but today because she had a dental appointment, she was earlier than usual. Peter would never have known about Tippy massaging his grandfather, had his mother and his school friend not met, fallen in love, and then decided to get married, necessitating the side trip to the florist; more of Madeline's coincidences and synchronicities.

Peter and Tippy spoke briefly and in that time Peter found out that Tippy's brother, Tommy, was also in the hospital, but not as a patient – as his health had taken a remarkable turn for the better lately. He was there as a visitor.

Ruby dreamily imagined the erotic caress of a kiss across her full lips. Often she had fantasised about a dark stranger with a dashing black eye-patch kissing her, then sometimes she thought of the boys from high school, one in particular named Peter. He had attended to a special need for her on her sixteenth birthday. As intimate as he had been with her that day, she regretted the fact that he had not kissed her, as much as she had wanted him to and hoped he would, he never did. When she let herself go, she could even conjure up his exquisite and mysterious honey-breath. It was in fact his honey-breath kiss that woke her from her coma. When she opened her eyes and squinted against the light, she imagined for a moment as her eyes struggled with the glare, that she saw a dark stranger leaning over and kissing her on the lips, the light and shade around his face looked familiar to her and for a second she thought he had a dark eye-patch but as his face became clearer in the light, and her fog lifted, she recognised it to be Peter. It seemed so surreal to her that she wasn't sure she was still alive. The tingling on her lips from his kiss convinced her that her Prince Charming had just brought her back to life. She smiled her beautiful disarming smile.

Peter discovered through Tippy that her brother Tommy had saved Ruby. He found her on death's door down at Glenelg. He saved her by removing the needle from between her (perfectly pedicured) toes. He had picked her up and leapt as fast as he could to get her immediate medical attention. She ended up in the Adelaide Hospital where she was kept in an induced coma to give her system time to rid itself of heroin and to get over her withdrawal.

Peter immediately took leave from work and assumed the vigil from Tommy. He stayed by Ruby's side day and night. Tommy was happy to hand Ruby's life over to Peter. Tommy knew that this was the best thing for Ruby now, and Tommy could finally resolve his life in the knowledge that he had done his job of saving Ruby. Peter leant over and kissed his sleeping beauty every morning and every evening. He owed her a kiss and he was repaying his debt with interest.

When the day came for Ruby to be discharged, Peter took her home to her flat in Clovelly Park. He helped her up the stairs and straightened out the sofa cushions, plumping them up and smoothing out the indentation. He settled her on the sofa with a rug around her legs. He made her tea and offered to cook dinner for her, but she said she was feeling fine and that she wanted to make some teacakes for him. During his vigil by her side in hospital, he had time to think. He decided to give her a present. It was a small box. He asked her to wait until he left to open it. She put it on the table and with a smile began making him a batch of teacakes. For the first time ever, she did this clothed, and felt in complete control.

Peter had never tasted anything quite so exquisite in his life. He had never forgotten the fabulous teacakes Ruby's mother had served him on

Ruby's sixteenth birthday, just before he had been intimate with Ruby behind the chook shed. But as fantastic as he remembered them being, they were no match for Ruby's. He gorged himself on Ruby's teacakes. He had no idea how she got such wonderful taste sensations into something as humble as a teacake but he felt in his heart, without necessarily understanding it, that somehow this moment, like the day behind the chook shed, would be life-changing for him, perhaps representing something akin to a metamorphosis – these teacakes looked like teacakes, smelt and tasted like teacakes, but they were not just humble teacakes, not to Peter. These teacakes made Peter a part of Ruby's life. It might seem slightly ridiculous to place so much importance on something so small in the scheme of things as enjoying the pleasure of Ruby's exquisite life-restoring euphoric seductive teacakes, but as Peter knew, it was the little things that counted, the detail, it was where the truth was located. Peter had never felt so calm and reassured about his life as he did with Ruby that evening.

Peter took his leave. He kissed Ruby gently on the cheek and gave her a long hug before he left. She found herself in her flat alone for the first time for what seemed like a lifetime, perhaps it was she thought – her life at the car lot seemed so far away, it might have happened to someone else. She struggled to remember herself as a checkout girl now. She felt happy and contented, even excited.

She cleaned, scrubbed and polished the kitchen and remembered the present Peter had given her earlier. She opened the box to find her little dolphin inside. She lifted it out carefully, examined it and then turned its tail. It began vibrating and she held it in her hand remembering all it represented to her in her life. She turned off the vibration and then made some space amongst the toys, giving it pride of place. She stepped back and looked at it amongst her collection and decided that the collection was now complete; the addition of her dolphin provided meaning and made perfect sense to her and she decided that first thing tomorrow all forty-two toys will be packed away; she didn't need them on display any longer. She noticed that in the box there was another, smaller box. She lifted it out and opened it to find a diamond ring inside. It was so beautiful she had trouble breathing. In fact, she had never seen anything quite so beautiful in her life. She dared to slip it on her wedding finger. It fitted perfectly, as though it might have been destined for her, as though in all the land this ring had searched for the one and only finger it would magically fit. She looked at it sparkling in the winter night. She slipped it off and returned it to its box. She carried it to her bedroom, and placed it on her book of poems on her bedside table. She switched on her lamp and the warm glow hugged the room. She undressed and slipped into her pyjamas. She placed the teddies on a chair in the corner of the room and covered them with their bunny rug and tucked them in and kissed them both goodnight. Just at that moment there was a sudden downpour and she could hear the cleansing rain splashing against the windows. It felt good being back safe in her little home. She climbed into bed. She found the sound of the rain outside comforting as she snuggled under her bedspread. She sensed Peter's voice in the distance of her mind, telling her a story, a story about him and about her, when they were young and still at school and found the world an overwhelming place. She kept her body still and held her breath, but this time it was to savour the moment. It was a moment of clarity when something from deep inside her emerged. She felt the flush of tickling tentacles of optimism flutter across her skin. She came to realise that it was during the coma that her mind had listened to Peter's intimate story, and as a subsequence her subconscious allowed its secret to be released from its trapped dark recess. She knew now what her mind had always known. She had always been in love with Peter and it was Peter whom she had wanted to be her first. As it turned out, in every way that counted, Peter had been her first, the only important element that had been missing was his kiss. She re-opened the box and took the ring out and put it on her wedding finger again. It sparkled in the dark, as though it had a purpose now it was out of its box; it seemed to be saying something to Ruby, something like it was grateful she had released it from the small enclosed cubicle where it had waited to show off its sparkle. The ring seemed contented to remain on her finger, at least for now, and to sparkle just for her. With no tormenting spider, no heroin addiction, the dolphin to complete her collection of little toys and the lingering memory of Peter's awakening honey-breath kiss, she felt happy and free. She felt that the pull from the little girl who died in front of her that day had been finally loosened, and now she might be free to be herself. Ruby knew now it was no longer important to keep up the strain of trying to be 'hopeful' about her life, she just knew everything was going to be fine now, whatever the future held for her. She hoped she would see Peter again, she hoped he meant for the ring to be there, but even if she never saw him again, she knew she was going to survive and that she was no longer waiting for her life to begin; the waiting was over. She decided that she would return to complete her administration studies and then see where life took her. Then she became aware of a curious and surprising thought forming in her mind. She blinked twice and thought about the thought. It was a grand thought. It was an exciting thought for Ruby and now there was no spider to destroy the tickling of optimism she felt still fluttering across her skin. The thought she had, and was now developing, was about becoming an architect as her father had always hoped, and she dared to think this might be the beginning of her new life.

She kissed the ring, took it off and put it on top of her book of poems to let it sparkle and light the room for her while she slept. She closed her eyes, slid back into her warm bed and was immediately aware of two things: her armpits were not damp and her nipples were tingling. She smiled and imagined Peter kissing her again and she dreamt of a life that no longer required the stress of everlasting vigilance in a *happy city*.

PART FIVE

Epilogue

Well that concludes this chronicle, or as much of it as seems pertinent. At this stage, I am reminded of the D. H. Lawrence observation, 'Never trust the teller, trust the tale'. Perhaps I will leave it to you to deconstruct and ponder the veracity and meaning of this observation when you are inspecting this tale for its truth. In the meantime, we might remember the sign in Doctor Reynolds's office – *If you lie to your Psychologist, you are still telling the truth.*

I can report that my own health began a steady improvement, to the degree that I was strong enough to find and help Ruby in time to get her the medical assistance she urgently needed. I owe a debt of gratitude to Flat 5 Lady who looked after me with great care, and passed on Ruby's curative, delicious teacakes. I also am indebted to Flat 5 Lady for telling me the story about her son, Doctor Reynolds. This was seminal, giving me the strength to find my own story and, in so doing, I began to find my voice. It was through this work and my contact with Doctor Reynolds's research that I was able to chronicle the stories (with the generous permission) of Ruby, Steve, Peter and Madeline, all of whose lives I had inadvertently affected and infected.

I have been putting on weight but not in the same way as occurred to me after I drove a car into a nine-year-old school girl and killed her. That day almost destroyed me, sending me to the very brink and the black abyss. I was in the wrong place at the wrong time, and so was the nine-year-old girl, as was Ruby, Madeline and Peter, and of course it was Steve's triplet sister I killed. It is just goddamn synchronicity – *impartial, disinterested and unpredictable.* On that terrible day, I looked away from the ruined body on the road and was drawn into the melancholy in Ruby's eyes as she watched the accident unfold. I looked into those eyes to avoid looking at the dead girl, and I realised that Ruby's life was also in jeopardy from that moment on, as was mine. I knew I had to be her guardian angel, and I had to save her, and thus myself, in order to somehow make up for what I had done. I can never bring that little girl back, I have to live with that, but I hope that in some way having finally saved Ruby's life, well, I think you know what I mean.

I was at one point very scathing in my criticism of Doctor Reynolds, but I now understand that he helped me find my story and thus helped to save me in ways I was incapable of understanding at the time. He had a story himself, which it seems he denied or was unable to resolve. I found the way to my own story by discovering his truth. I am very sorry that he could not find a way to save himself as he has saved others. Each person responds in their own way to the plague of the human condition's need for hope by trying to make sense of their lives: paraphrasing Camus, *some resign themselves to optimistic fate, some seek blame, and a few, like* Dr Reynolds, *resist the terror*. It's one of the ironies of life that a man who had dedicated his life to finding meaning for people found none for himself – suicide is the final human ironic revolt against the absurdity of the search for meaning, and the reliance on hope in the face of there being no resolution to the question of the meaning of our lives.

I am pleased, though, that Doctor Reynolds's book has done well and that it may represent his legacy in the business of helping people like myself, Ruby, Peter, Steve and Madeline to get over the traumas of life by finding the truth in our stories. This is the only place sustainable and valid hope can be found. The good doctor told us this with the Anaïs Nin quote, 'We don't see things as they are, we see them as we are.' And as an aside, and by way of a working example, he continued with this sentiment to make the point that we don't see Paradise the way it is, we see it as we are.

So what of the city's name change? Was it successful or a failure? Some say that on certain levels the answer to this question is both. Adelaide was no Paradise, but then neither was Paradise, except Paradise was isolated, a walled city, a cubicle cut off in a way that Adelaide was not, but simultaneously and impartially offering ecstasy and tragedy. Adelaide was not in effect ever seen as the last hope, but Paradise was. The citizens have seen to it that the name has reverted to Adelaide but the experiment will never be forgotten. This, however, is discussed in Doctor Reynolds's book, and far more elegantly and more eruditely than I can hope to manage. So I will leave it to you to read what he had to say on the subject, or you may wish to draw your own conclusions about the absurdity of life's questions inherent in this experiment.

To quote the indefatigable Ryan, 'Everything in life seems to take an eternity; life itself is over in an instant.' So my advice, as trite as it may seem to some (and it was good enough for Albert Camus), is to 'strive to live every instance free of prejudice, unrealistic hope and blame and accept the bane and enlightenment', as best you can.

As a small note, the new world class Mental Health Hospital retained its 'Paradise' name; a place where you are TRAPPED, HELD, FED, NUR-TURED, ADORED and if you are lucky, RELEASED – like jail, like Paradise, like the 'cubicle'.

It is now a few years on from the times of these events and this, my own manuscript, has finally been completed. I acknowledge the contribution of all the people described herein and thank them for their generosity in allowing me to document their lives to the degree that I have done here and for allowing me access to their case notes. I apologise in advance for any licence I felt was necessary to present their stories but in these post-modern times, facts are redundant, only story counts, it is the only place to locate the truth of our lives.

I leave you with a final thought to consider; I admit to being D. H. Law-rence's 'teller' and I am also a killer, as you know. If I might remind you and quote myself, *Tommy was a killer, that was a proven fact and if he had to, he ought to be able to rely on that trait if necessary.* So I will admit to the following only. I killed a nine-year-old girl, it was a tragic accident and one from which I can never expect to fully recover, and nor should I. I also admit to killing Lemon Guy's cat, also an accident, and of course the spider, which was no accident. I categorically deny killing the Sales Manager of Easy Motors.

Synchronicity and goddamn hope, separately and together, they are equally killers and liberators, depending on your angle of vision.

THE END

About the Author

Adelaide born, Gary N. Lines has lived in Sydney, New York and Los Angeles and finished this novel in Paris. In recent times, he completed a Master of Creative Arts at Flinders University, South Australia.

Acknowledgements

Recognition must go to the Flinders University English Department in South Australia, in particular, Assoc. Prof. Steve Evans, Dr Giselle Bastin and Assoc. Prof. Kate Douglas for their intellectual engagement and academic guidance and support.

I also want to acknowledge my influences. Within the novel, for those literary detectives amongst us, you will note *homage* has been paid to a number of great writers. In particular, Albert Camus (his novel *The Plague* and his essay 'The Myth of Sisyphus'), Leo Tolstoy, Franz Kafka, David Foster Wallace, Joseph Heller, Don DeLillo, Umberto Eco, Erica Jong, Sir Arthur Conan Doyle, Anaïs Nin, Bret Easton Ellis and David E. Kelley's hyper-postmodern treatise *Boston Legal*, and the much missed Douglas Adams – master absurdist.

I need to make a particular point in regard to Albert Camus' novel *The Plague*. If you are familiar with his novel, you will recognise the deliberate paraphrasing of his prose and structure in the Prologue of *Doing Life in Paradise*. This post-modern literary convention is deployed, in this case, to set up the novel's *Absurdism* discussion, a notion Camus interrogated in his fiction and in particular his essay 'The Myth of Sisyphus'.